ANGEL

Also by Carola Dunn

Lavender Lady

ANGEL

═ Carola Dunn ═

WALKER AND COMPANY
NEW YORK

First published in the United States of America
in 1984 by the Walker Publishing Company, Inc.

Published simultaneously in Canada by John Wiley & Sons
Canada, Limited, Rexdale, Ontario.

Library of Congress Cataloging in Publication Data

Dunn, Carola.
  Angel.

  I. Title.
PR6054.U537A83   1984   823'.914   83–19693
ISBN 0–8027–0756–4

Library of Congress Catalog Card Number: 83–19693

Printed in the United States of America

10 9 8 7 6 5 4 3 2 1

=1=

"BUT ANGEL!" EXPOSTULATED the eldest son of the Duke of Medcliff, "you cannot suppose that *I* am after your fortune!"

"Of course not, Damian," responded Lady Evangelina Brenthaven with dignity. "I was merely pointing out that most of my suitors are more interested in my inheritance or my title than anything else."

"Fustian!" The young man studied her golden ringlets, her exquisite heart-shaped face, and her deceptively melting eyes, the blue of the sky at dusk. "With a face and form like yours, you'd be the toast of the town if you hadn't a penny to your name."

"But I would not have received seventeen proposals of marriage, eighteen now. Besides, that is quite as bad. All you gentlemen care about is a pretty face, you don't want to know what is behind it, what I am really like."

"Dash it, Angel, I've known you since you were seven!"

"I expect that is why it has taken you the better part of two Seasons to make up your mind to offer for me," said Angel gloomily.

Remembering some of her more outrageous youthful exploits, Lord Wycherly looked guilty. "That's all over," he assured her hastily and hopefully. "I worship the ground you tread, and your face floats through my dreams like the moon in the night sky."

"Very pretty, but you are just proving my point."

"Then you really won't marry me?"

"Oh, Damian, I like you very well but I want to be in love with the man I marry, and I want him to love me, not to worship the

5

ground I tread on. I am honoured by your offer, sir, but I do not believe we should suit.''

Lord Wycherly sighed. ''Perhaps you are right, though I'm deuced fond of you, you know. I hope you find the right man in the end. Shall I see you at Almack's tomorrow?''

''Yes, but if you dance with me, everyone will be sure you did not come up to scratch. All the old tabbies think I have not married because I am casting out lures for you. Could you not stand in a corner looking gloomy, like Lord Byron, so they will know your hopes are blighted?''

''And have Caro Lamb transfer her allegiance to me? Not on your life! I'll drop a private word in Lady Jersey's ear, if you like. 'Silence' will make sure everyone knows.''

''I daresay they will all think me run mad to whistle such an offer down the wind.''

Modesty forbade any expression of agreement, but Lord Wycherly would not have been surprised to hear Angel's mother's reaction to the news.

''Dearest, how *could* you? He will be duke one day, and such an amiable young man! I quite thought you meant to have him!''

''I did consider it, Mama, then found I could not.'' Angel had run her parents to earth in the library, a spacious, vaulted apartment on the ground floor of Tesborough House. Her mother stood beside the desk at which her father was seated, and both had turned to face her when she entered to make the half-defiant announcement of her rejection of yet another suitor.

''But Angel, you are nearly nineteen!'' cried Lady Tesborough in despair. ''Damian Wycherly is quite the most eligible bachelor on the town and the *only* young and unmarried heir to a dukedom. You will never find another match half as good!''

''Do you dislike him, Angel?'' asked the marquis quietly.

''Oh, no, Papa, but he is like a brother, not at all romantic. I want to be in love with my husband, as Mama is with you—and you with her.''

Lord Tesborough guiltily removed his arm from his wife's comfortably plump waist. "Your mother and I are exceptionally lucky," he pointed out. "Few of our rank marry for love. If you feel affection and esteem for Wycherly, that is a sounder basis for marriage than most are founded on."

"I've told him I'll not wed him. I believe I've met every eligible man in London and I care for none of them. If they are not after my fortune or my title, then they want to set me on a pedestal and simply admire me. Oh, how I wish I were poor and plain!"

"You would not like it at all," her mama assured her anxiously. "Only think how depressing to have to shop at Grafton House, especially if nothing became one!"

"But if a gentleman admired you, you could be sure that it was truly you he wanted."

"Only you would not meet any gentlemen."

Angel dismissed this possibility with a shrug. "Well, perhaps I should not like to be poor, but I begin to think I may never marry."

"There is no reason you should feel obliged to do so," said the marquis, to his wife's horror. "Tesborough Park will go with the title to your cousin Bertram, but you will be a wealthy woman in your own right and may please yourself."

"Frederick, do not say so! Angel, do not heed your father! Indeed, a woman's only happiness is in marriage and I could not *bear* it if you were to turn into an eccentric old maid like that dreadful Matilda Hemford." Lady Tesborough's lower lip was trembling, and tears sparkled in eyes as blue as her daughter's.

"Come, Louisa, do not distress yourself. You cannot mean to compare our Angel to Lady Matilda!"

"I've talked to Lady Matilda and I think she enjoys life very well," said Angel rebelliously. "And look at Cousin Catherine. I know you offered her a third Season and she refused. She is twenty-four now and perfectly content."

"Dear Catherine! But she is a bluestocking, you know. The case is quite different. Maria was always inclined to be bookish, even when we were children. I cannot think why, for I was never in the

7

least clever. Your grandmother was forever taking her to task for it, and none of us was in the least surprised when she only caught a clergyman. Not that I mean to say a word against dear Clement, for they are nearly as happy as I am with your papa, Angel. But they did encourage Catherine to study overmuch and it is *fatal*, I assure you. Gentlemen cannot abide a bluestocking and the poor child never took, though she is quite well looking. A trifle tall, perhaps. So you see!''

"I do not see at all,'' Angel said, "for I am not in the least bookish, as you know well, and no one has ever accused me of being so much as a quarter inch taller than the *beau idéal*. I am not quite at my last prayers, Mama, so do not despair yet. Let's go shopping. That always cheers you up.''

"Oh, yes! I saw the prettiest Paisley shawl in Bond Street. It will go to perfection with your blue mull.'' She bent to kiss her husband's cheek. "We'll leave you in peace to write your speech, dear. It is very shocking that the Prince has chosen Lord Liverpool, I am sure, and poor Mr Perceval scarce in his grave.''

"Perceval was a Tory too, love,'' said the marquis cheerfully. "Don't bother your head about the state of the nation, but go and make yourselves beautiful for those of us who must.''

Angel kissed her father. "Thank you for not reading me a lecture,'' she whispered. "I did not mean to upset Mama.''

"It's your life, child, but your mother must be concerned for your happiness, you know.''

"And she has found hers in marriage. Oh, Papa, I hope I shall too, but where shall I ever find another man like you?''

Fifteen minutes later, as Lady Tesborough settled herself in the comfortable carriage beside her daughter, she echoed this sentiment.

"Your papa is a man in a million,'' she declared with a contented sigh. "Always occupied with his wretched politics but never too busy for his family. There cannot be another such husband in the world.''

"I greatly fear not, and in that case how can you expect me to marry?" teased Angel.

A thoughtful frown marred her ladyship's smooth brow. "I am not at all certain that you would not do better with a gentleman of quite different character, dearest. You are much more independent than I ever was, and much cleverer. I do not think it would suit you always to be taken care of and cossetted. You are so very enterprising, Angel. Only think of all the scrapes you fall into! I was always content to sit with my embroidery, but you must forever be on the go."

"In fact, 'Angel' suits you far batter than it does me."

"That is for your looks, though you were the sweetest-tempered child. Evangelina is a pretty name but too long to be using all the time. Your papa took one look at you in your cradle and shortened it immediately."

Lady Tesborough prattled on about her daughter's infancy. Angel lent half an ear to her talk while she pondered her mother's earlier words. Though it made her feel disloyal to her father, she could see that there was some truth in them. Of all her admirers she was most attracted to those with whom she could argue, those who did not expect her to behave like a demure debutante but stretched her abilities.

There was Sir Derek Amboyne, who had taught her piquet and won two-thirds of her quarterly pin money in the process. She had managed to win most of it back before Papa had suggested it was unwise to be seen so much in the company of a notorious gambler and rakehell. Captain Arthur Spence had challenged her to drive his four-in-hand down Rotten Row at the hour of the fashionable promenade, and had coached her daily in handling the ribbons until she was sure she might have managed it. What a pity he had been sent to Spain before she could try! And then there was Lord Peter Doverhaugh, whose odious conservatism had forced her to recall and employ every Whiggish argument she had ever heard from her father's dinner guests. She had not made a Whig of him but he had been obliged to concede once or twice, and she could still relive the glow of triumph she had felt when he had admitted that the prosecution of the Hunt brothers for sedition was a disgrace.

Perhaps her mother was right: a protective, forbearing, and ever-patient husband would not suit her. With a sudden insight, she realised that Mama had never grown up. She was a darling, but she had never had to accept responsibility for anything more exacting than a dinner menu or the ordering of a new ball dress. There had always been someone to guide her every step, to do her thinking for her, and no need to rebel ever troubled the even tenor of her life.

The carriage stopped before the bow-windowed shop of Bond Street's most fashionable modiste. Angel leant over to hug and kiss her surprised mother, as the step was let down by the footman who would carry her every purchase, large and small, and guard her against the least jostling from the busy crowds.

No, that was not what Angel wanted. She was filled with a vague restlessness—one that was unappeased by the acquisition of a dashing Leghorn bonnet trimmed with a scarlet feather.

The next morning, clad in breeches belonging to her cousin Bertram and accompanied only by that persuadable youth, she rode astride her hack down St James' Street beneath the windows of White's and Watier's. Three things saved her from instant notoriety: she had chosen an hour when few of the dandies usually to be found ogling passersby had yet risen from their beds; it was the end of the Season and the Haut Ton was beginning to disperse to country houses, watering places, or resorts such as Brighton; and last but not least, the previous evening Lady Caroline Lamb had dressed as a page and insinuated herself into an all-male party at Lord Byron's lodging.

Beside such behaviour, Lady Evangelina Brenthaven's exploit paled to insignificance, to her annoyance.

Before she could think up something more outrageous, a letter arrived from her aunt Maria.

Aunt Maria's husband, the Reverend Clement Sutton, held an

excellent living in Banbury, a thriving market town north of Oxford. His own inheritance, together with his wife's dowry and the income from his parish, allowed a life of comfort, if not of elegance. Maria's sister Louisa, the Marchioness of Tesborough, had introduced his daughter Catherine to Society at the marquis's expense, and though no brilliant match had come of it, the rector was deeply grateful. Now he saw his way clear to at least a partial repayment of his brother-in-law's generosity.

He had arranged to exchange, for the months of July and August, his Midland parish against one in the Lake District. Knowing Lord Tesborough's political inclinations, he guessed that he would be tied to London for a great part of the summer by the present uncertainty as to who would form the new government under Lord Liverpool. Louisa rarely left her husband, and while Lady Evangelina would certainly receive many invitations, there would be few she could accept without her parents' chaperonage.

Would Angel, Aunt Maria wondered, like to accompany the Suttons into Westmorland?

"Oh, yes, Mama, I should like it above all things! You know I have wanted to see the lakes this age. I cannot imagine anyone better to be there with than Cousin Catherine, for I am sure she knows all Mr Wordsworth's poems by heart."

"So that you need not be put to the trouble of searching for the relevant stanzas," teased her father. "Your aunt mentions that the parish of Barrows End is under the patronage of the Earl of Grisedale, who lives nearby. I was at school with his brother, Toby Markham, and met him quite often though I do not know him well. I will give you a letter of introduction."

"No, Papa, don't do that," said Angel slowly. "I have an idea."

"Oh, dear!" moaned Lady Tesborough in trepidation. "I always have palpitations when you say that, dearest."

"It is nothing very dreadful," assured her daughter, but the beginnings of a gleeful smile were far from reassuring. "I shall go incognito, call myself plain Miss Smith or something. And yes, I

11

shall make myself plain too, tie back my hair and wear a cap and dark, dowdy dresses, and behave very demurely.''

"But Angel!'' wailed her ladyship, appalled.

"I do not think it such a bad idea,'' interrupted her husband. ''Perhaps it might at least teach you to count your blessings.''

"But Frederick!''

"Maybe I should dye my hair,'' said Angel consideringly.

"Indeed you will not! I never heard such nonsense in my life.''

"Very well, Mama, if you think I ought not. I daresay I can pin it up under a cap, or I can cut it short.''

"No! Angel, how can you suggest such a thing! Frederick, you must not let her. Do not sit there laughing, Frederick. She will be wanting to paint her face next!''

"Oh no, I mean to go as a Puritan, not a Cyp . . . an opera dancer.''

"That is something to be thankful for,'' said his lordship. "Come, Louisa, do not let yourself be thrown into high fidgets. It will do her no harm to see how the other half lives, not that I suppose she means to go without her allowance for the nonce. If Sutton will permit this masquerade, your sister will take good care that it does not get out of hand. Angel is not like to meet any acquaintance in the wilds of the North.''

"Thank you, Papa. I will write to Aunt Maria at once. Will you write a note to my uncle to persuade him? If you do not object, surely he will not.''

Finding herself outvoted, Lady Tesborough summoned up a last feeble protest.

"Angel, pray do not call yourself Miss Smith. Such a common name.''

A fortnight later, early on a sunny Friday morning, the Tesborough travelling carriage departed from Grosvenor Square bearing Lady Evangelina Brenthaven, her maid, and a footman out of town. Descending at the Catherine Wheel in Henley some hours later, the young lady ordered a private parlour, where she consumed a hearty luncheon. Then, with much stretching and yawning, she requested a chamber where she might lay herself down for half an hour, being shockingly fatigued by her journey. She and her abigail retired to the inn's best bedchamber, having paid the reckoning in advance.

Some thirty minutes and a great deal of giggling later, Miss Evelyn Brent, a sober young woman in a grey stuff gown and a plain, concealing poke bonnet, slipped down the back stairs to the stableyard. A grinning footman, sworn to secrecy, handed her into the Tesborough coach, where she huddled back into a corner.

Her maid, meanwhile, sailed openly down the main staircase.

"Her ladyship forgot her comb," she announced with a condescending nod to the innkeeper's wife, waving the misplaced article as evidence of the truth of her words.

A moment later she joined her mistress in the carriage, the footman swung up behind, and the old coachman, shaking his head, drove the fresh team out of the yard and headed north on the Oxford Road.

=2=

THE LONG JUNE evening had scarce begun to wane when Miss Brent, by now genuinely fatigued, arrived at her uncle's rectory. Scarlet geraniums glowed in the window boxes of the long, low house built of mellow Cotswold stone. The front door stood hospitably open, and as the carriage turned into the semicircular drive, Miss Catherine Sutton appeared.

"Mother," she called, "Angel is come."

Hurrying down the steps, she opened the coach door as the vehicle stopped, then paused in confusion, looking from one of the occupants to the other.

Angel laughed. "Do you not know me, Cousin Catherine?" she crowed, untying her bonnet and flinging it to the floor. She shook her head, and a shower of pins let loose her sadly crushed ringlets. "I cannot wait to take off this dreadful dress," she went on. "It is horridly scratchy and far too warm for a summer day."

"We shall have to find you something lighter," proposed her tall cousin practically. "Just because you are in disguise there is no reason to be uncomfortable. Wherever did you come by that hideous bonnet?"

"Is it not odious?" agreed Angel as she stepped from the carriage. "I bought it and the dress, too, from one of the house-maids. I could not shop in London for such dowdy things. How people would have stared! Good evening, Aunt Maria. I am so happy to be with you again!"

Embraces were exchanged and Angel was hurried into the house to greet her uncle, who found it difficult to hide his amusement at the sight of his beautiful and elegant niece in the housemaid's second-best gown, her golden hair sadly tousled.

Catherine bore her off to her chamber.

"We have dined already," she apologised, "as we did not know precisely when you would arrive. Should you like a tray in your room? You must be quite exhausted after travelling eighty miles in a single day."

"I am tired," Angel admitted, struggling out of the grey dress with her cousin's assistance. "Besides, I did not bring anything to change into. I thought I could buy some dresses tomorrow."

"And I daresay you plan to go shopping in your petticoats?"

"I did not know this would be so wretchedly uncomfortable. I suppose I must wear it again."

"I'd willingly lend you something, Angel, only it would take a deal of altering. You brought nothing at all?"

"Only underthings and nightgowns. Even my plainest shawl is too fine."

"You are truly serious about this masquerade then? Do tell me what has driven you to it." Unlike her father, Catherine had no pipe behind which to hide her amusement. Angel was undeterred.

"My eighteenth proposal," she said, candidly if obscurely. "Damian Wycherly is the heir to the Duke of Medcliff so I cannot accuse him of being on the catch for a fortune or a titled wife, but he only offered for me because I am pretty and all the rage. I want to meet people who do not know that I am rich and beautiful and the daughter of a marquis."

"Oh, dear, I very much doubt whether there will be many young gentlemen at Barrows End. It is a tiny hamlet, you know, with a number of outlying farms. Mr Craythorn writes that Lord Grisedale is unwell, and particularly cautioned Papa against mentioning his son in his presence. It seems Lord Dominic ran off to be a soldier and the earl has quite cast him off, so there will be no young people visiting there, I expect, though I believe there is a daughter also.''

"I did not mean only young men,'' said Angel. "Though you must admit that it would be most romantic if a gentleman fell in love with me without knowing who I am. I could be certain that he loved me for myself.''

"Romantic, yes, but he would probably turn out to be quite ineligible himself.''

"You are so prosaic, Catherine! I am looking forward to all sorts of adventures this summer and you shall not persuade me otherwise. Do not you long for romance?''

"I have a melancholy suspicion that I am too old, too plain, and too tall to expect dreams to come true. You must not think I repine. There is a great deal to be said for a life of quiet contentment such as mine. There now, I shall go and fetch your supper.''

Angel leaned back in her easy chair with a sigh and watched her cousin leave the room. Twenty-four *was* rather old, she admitted to herself, but she did not think Catherine plain. She had a vague memory of hearing her mother refer to her cousin despairingly as a gangling beanpole. That must have been six years since, during her London Season, for it was now quite inappropriate. Though certainly rather too tall, she was generously built and her quietly self-confident bearing had nothing to do with gangling. Juno-esque was the word. Her fair-complexioned face and grey eyes with strongly marked brows were pleasant if unremarkable, and her brown hair was abundant and glossy. Too abundant, perhaps. It had never been cut and she wore it in coiled braids which not only added to her height but gave her a somewhat old-fashioned air. Angel wondered if she could be persuaded to have it shortened and curled, then decided it suited her very well as it was.

If no other adventure came her way in Westmorland, it might prove interesting to look about for a husband for Catherine. A dearth of young gentlemen was no obstacle, for at her advanced age quite an old gentleman would do, say thirty, or even thirty-five. That he must be tall went without saying.

Not being in the habit of holding her tongue, Angel unfolded her plan as soon as her cousin returned, with a well-stocked supper tray.

"It will certainly keep you occupied," Catherine said, her eyes brimming with laughter. "Do you never stop plotting, Angel?"

"That reminds me, you must not call me Angel. I am Miss Brent, Miss Evelyn Brent."

"Very well, Cousin Evelyn."

"I do not really like the name Evelyn, but it is not too different from my own and will match the monogram on my handkerchiefs."

"In case you need to drop one. I do understand. How about Eugenia instead?"

"That is even worse. I have an aunt Eugenia who disapproves of me prodigiously. Evelyn is not so bad. You could call me Lyn for short."

"Lyn let it be. I wish I could eat like that," said Catherine enviously as a large Banbury cake disappeared. "I should soon be fat as a flawn."

Angel looked down complacently at her own trim waist. "Mama says when I am older I shall have to take care if I do not wish to grow plump like her," she consoled, then giggled. "Especially, she says, as Papa is growing to be quite an 'imposing figure.' "

"Mother is as like Aunt Louisa as two peas in a pod, but my papa is positively skinny. It seems most unjust that I should inherit his height and Mother's shape. If I overeat, I too shall be an imposing figure by the time I reach Uncle Frederick's age!"

"Well, I could not swallow another morsel now. I can scarce keep my eyes open. Will you say good night to Aunt Maria and Uncle Clement for me, please?"

"Of course, dear. Come, let me tuck you in. Sleep well, Lyn."

Angel hugged her cousin. "We are going to have a wonderful summer," she announced drowsily. "Good night."

The next day Mrs Sutton took her niece shopping. She and Catherine patronised the smartest shops in Banbury, but Angel was shocked to see how far the provincial styles lagged behind the latest London fashions. She realised that her cousin's dress, which she had thought almost quaint, was considered modish here, though both the Sutton ladies affected the restrained colours appropriate to a minister's family.

Fortunately, she was looking for something very similar. After a wistful glance at a delightful, if old-fashioned, walking dress of jaconet with a peach-coloured sarsnet slip, she turned determinedly to plain muslin in various shades of grey. She was completely oblivious of the startled looks elicited by the housemaid's second-best gown, but Aunt Maria muttered harrassed comments to the dressmakers about schoolgirls who grow out of everything at once.

Catherine managed to persuade her cousin to order one silk evening gown in a delicate lavender.

"I shall feel quite ashamed of my own finery if you are to wear nothing but half-mourning," she pointed out *sotto voce*. "I cannot think that a single gown of coloured silk will give away your secret. And what say you to this blue merino for a cloak and hood? I understand it rains a good deal in the Lake District. See, this is the exact shade of your eyes."

Angel rejected it firmly, choosing in its place a slate grey kerseymere whose subdued hue made her eyes the bluer in contrast, though she did not know it. A shawl of Thibet cloth for cool days was added to her purchases. It was not as fine and soft as the cachemire it imitated, but the ingenious weavers of Scotland had succeeded in imparting to it a silvery sheen that she found irresistible.

The Suttons' gig filled with packages. Thoroughly enjoying herself, Angel bought a parasol for her cousin and a reticule in the shape of a Grecian urn for her aunt. All three ladies were fitted with sturdy walking shoes in preparation for the rough mountain country so enticingly described by Mr Wordsworth.

"And now the milliner's, if you please, Aunt," requested Angel.

A wide-brimmed straw bonnet was first on the list. It took all her resolution to reject a charming confection with coquelicot ribbons and a bunch of cherries dangling saucily, but that hurdle passed, she was easily able to overcome the Suttons' horrified objections when she asked to see some caps.

"But Angel!" cried Catherine, "even I do not wear caps yet!"

"Lyn!" hissed Angel.

"Evelyn dear," said her aunt more calmly, "I cannot think it necessary . . ."

"I am quite determined," Angel assured them, "so pray do not fly up into the boughs. There is no sense in doing things by halves, after all."

Passing over frivolous froths of lace, beribonned gauze, braid-edged crêpe lisse, she chose a pair of French-work cornettes which could be worn alone or under her bonnet, a cottage cap, and a Parisian mob. She tried them on, tucking up her ringlets underneath. Two or three curls refused to be confined, making their appearance at her temples even when she had the milliner tack on broad borders of Honiton lace.

"I wish I had not promised Mama not to cut or dye my hair," she said crossly in the end. "Well, it will have to do. I look a regular quiz in the caps in spite of it, do I not, Catherine?"

Her cousin laughingly refused to answer. Nothing, she thought, could make Angel's delicate features appear less than lovely, but she had no intention of giving her the idea that further efforts to hide her charms were necessary. Who could guess what hubble-bubble notion she might come up with next?

* * *

Mr Sutton planned a leisurely trip northward for the party, as he did not have to be in Barrows End till the following Sunday. They left on Monday morning and travelled via Warwick and Chester, visiting places of interest en route.

Angel managed to stay out of mischief until fine weather tempted them to the coast at Morecambe. Against the advice of a local fisherman, she persuaded Catherine to walk with her across the wide, silvery sands. The tide rushed in with appalling swiftness and trapped them on a sandbank, whence they were rescued, wet and frightened, by the surly shrimp-fisher.

"What an odiously rude man!" Angel exclaimed when he had left them safe on dry land, wringing out their skirts.

"I expect he did not guess that your papa is a marquis," pointed out Catherine.

Angel digested this in silence as they plodded back toward the town. Being plain Miss Brent was more difficult than she had supposed.

The weather changed. When they stopped the following night in the village of Windermere, the long, narrow lake was all but invisible in driving rain. The inn was draughty, the bed lumpy, and the food unappetising. Weary after days of travel, Angel wondered whether she would have done better to spend a dull summer with her parents in London. There was no maid to brush her hair and warm her sheets, and for the first time she felt the lack. When she arose, her dress had not been sponged and pressed, breakfast was lukewarm porridge, and it was still raining.

The long, slow drive over the Kirkstone Pass seemed endless. By the time they reached Barrows End they were all thoroughly depressed, and their first view of the vicarage did nothing to raise their spirits. A small, square, grey stone building with tiny windows shrouded in dingy white net, it was separated from the cemetery surrounding the small, square, grey stone church by a row of gloomy yews. The small, square garden between the lane and the front door was full of lettuces, carrots, peas, and spinach, and the only colour came from the scarlet blossoms of a row of runner beans.

Mr Sutton descended, picked his way up the muddy path, and hammered on the door. After a long pause, it opened a crack.

"I am the Reverend Sutton," the ladies heard him say. "You must be Mrs Applejohn."

"Aye."

"Is your husband here? He will be needed to help carry in our bags."

"Aye." Mrs Applejohn opened the door a trifle wider, revealing herself as a withered, crabbed old body in a black dress and plain white cap. She peered at the waiting carriage, then turned and shouted in a surprisingly strong voice, "John! T'Reverend's come!"

The coachman climbed down from the box and began to untie the luggage, which was strapped all over the vehicle. Mr Sutton returned to the coach, assisted the ladies to alight, and escorted them to the house.

"I hope there is a good fire within," said Mrs Sutton crossly as a large drip made its way down the back of her neck. "Mrs Craythorn warned me that the house had only two bedrooms, but I had thought it larger than this."

The only fire was in the kitchen stove, and round it the ladies huddled while the taciturn Mrs Applejohn went unwillingly to lay another in the front parlour. As soon as she could feel her fingers and toes once more, Angel went to explore. It did not take long. On the ground floor were the kitchen, a single parlour to serve for both dining and sitting room, and a small study. Upstairs were the two bedrooms and a third, tiny apartment, scarce bigger than a closet, which seemed to be in use as a sewing room. Looking out of its window, at the back of the house, she saw a stableyard with space only for a single horse and a battered gig. Beyond, a green meadow sloped down to a row of trees, which she thought might conceal a brook. In the rain, nothing further was visible.

Disconsolately she made her way back down the steep, narrow stair and found the hallway overflowing with damp trunks and boxes. Among them she spotted the portmanteau in which she had packed her new shawl, and kneeling on the bare wood floor, she dug it out.

"I rather think I shall be needing this," she said to herself, shivering, as she draped it about her shoulders. "It will take a very exciting adventure to make up for this!"

=== 3 ===

IN SPITE OF continuing drizzle, the little church of St Braddock was full for the morning service. Parishioners who had not been seen in church since Easter had come to inspect Mr Craythorn's substitute, and more attention was paid to Mr Sutton's sermon than might normally have been expected in a month of Sundays.

Most of those attending were farmers and their families, from a wealthy yeoman with pretensions to gentility to an aged shepherd who had abandoned his flock to the care of his dogs on the mountain just so that he could welcome the "new reverend." Raising her eyes from her prayerbook rather more often than was seemly, Angel was glad to note that the Grisedale family pew was occupied.

It was hard to be sure without staring in a way that must have called forth a reproof from Aunt Maria, but she thought one of the two ladies must be Lord Grisedale's daughter. No mention had been made of a Lady Grisedale, so perhaps the other was a companion, or an aunt. She was too finely dressed to be a governess. With them was a gentleman whose height and breadth of shoulder dwarfed his companions, especially the younger, who was a shrimp of a girl. Not shrimp, Angel corrected herself, remembering the rude shrimp-fisher. Elfin, she decided charitably.

She squinted speculatively at the tall gentleman, then glanced at Catherine beside her. He must top her by a good six inches. Was this the suitor she had resolved to look for? She wondered if he were the disgraced Lord Dominic, now restored to favour. Surely they would wait after the service and introduce themselves!

As Mr Sutton's sermon drew to a close, an errant sunbeam found its way through a high window. It lit on the stone head of a long-suffering hound that had for several centuries been the sole support of the equally stony head of its master, the first Earl of Grisedale. By the time the benediction was pronounced, the ray had moved on to illuminate a carved oak frieze, very ancient, depicting the obscure St Braddock suffering martyrdom in the coils of a gigantic sea-serpent, while angels sang lustily but failed to come to his rescue.

"Do you think that monster lives in Ullswater?" asked Angel with a giggle as the congregation rose from their knees, rustling. "He must be a local saint for I have never heard of him."

"What a very uncomfortable thought!" Catherine whispered back. "I hope it was not a very long-lived monster."

The Grisedale party was the first to leave. Angel noted that the young lady's gown was elegant, but not by any means in the first stare of fashion, while her older companion was so beribboned and beflounced as to leave scarce an inch of her dress unornamented. Angel was about to follow when her aunt laid a hand on her arm.

"We will go last, my dear," she said.

"But Aunt Maria, supposing they leave before we have met them?"

"That is their privilege. You do not wish to force your company upon them, do you, Lyn?"

Reminded of her loss of rank, Angel muttered, "No, ma'am." But she privately determined that one way or another the acquaintance should be made.

The ladies from the vicarage at last made their way up the aisle and emerged into sunshine which, though halfhearted, was dazzling after the gloom of the past few days. They found half the congregation waiting, anxious to meet the vicar's wife. In the church porch, Mr Sutton was shaking the hand of the old shepherd, a hale and hearty fellow with a shock of white hair. As the ladies approached, the old man touched his hat to them and departed. And before Angel could voice her eager questions, Mr Sutton was ushering his family out.

"There are people waiting to meet you," he assured her, his eyes twinkling, and he led them towards the lych-gate, where stood the party from the Hall. Mr Sutton introduced his wife and daughter. "And this is my niece, Miss Brent," he continued. "Maria my dear, Lady Elizabeth Markham, her companion Mrs Daventry, and her cousin, Sir Gregory Markham."

"My *dear* Mrs Sutton," began Mrs Daventry as bows and curtsies were exchanged, "I am *certain* that we will be the *greatest* friends for there are no other *ladies* in this *wild* part of the country and it is up to us to *support* each other, and for all the vicarage is a *shockingly* unsuitable house, I *knew* as soon as I spoke to your *dear* husband that you must be a *lady*, unlike *poor* Mrs Craythorn, I am afraid, and is it *true*, as I have heard, that your own *sister* is the Marchioness of Tesborough?"

"Yes," replied Mrs Sutton shortly. "I beg you will not make it generally known, ma'am, for I do not wish to put on airs."

"*Certainly* I will not, for there is simply *no* one to talk to hereabouts. They are all the most frightful *yokels*, you must know. Of course, I was acquainted with Lord Frederick Brenthaven before his marriage. And your niece is Miss *Brent*? Curious coincidence, but there . . ."

"Brand," said Angel loudly and firmly. "Miss Brand."

Catherine could not suppress a tiny snort of amusement, which she tried to turn into a cough. Lady Elizabeth, apparently totally cowed by her companion's never-ceasing flow of words, did not seem to notice, but Sir Gregory, who had been looking bored, glanced from one young lady to the other with a gaze that was suddenly alert.

Mr Sutton attempted to come to his wife's rescue.

"Maria," he said, breaking in on Mrs Daventry's chatter, "I am sorry to tear you away but there are a great many people waiting to make your acquaintance. Pray excuse us, ma'am."

"I'm sure I had better come with you," announced Mrs Daventry to his dismay, "for since *dear* Lady Grisedale passed away last year I *flatter* myself I have fulfilled *all* her duties and one *must* take notice of the tenants, you know, even if it is the most prodigious *tiresome* thing imaginable, and I would not have you think . . ."

Relieved of the presence of their elders, the young people began to chat, if indeed Sir Gregory could be considered young, for Angel thought he must be at least thirty. She turned her attention to Lady Elizabeth, whose reserve she attempted to pierce, with a lack of success that made her the more determined to accomplish it.

"Your father's elocution is remarkably clear," Sir Gregory remarked to Catherine, after an exchange of commonplaces. "Odd that Mrs Daventry should have misheard Miss *Brand*'s name."

Catherine looked up at him in confusion and muttered an indistinct denial.

"Doing it rather too brown, ma'am. What kind of rig is your little cousin running?" he enquired, with a twinkle in his eye that reminded her of her father.

"You will not give her away?" she begged. "There is no harm in it, I promise you, or Papa would not countenance such a deception."

"So, Lady Evangelina does not wish to be known?"

"Did you recognise her, sir?"

"Not I. I move little in Society, having enough to do at home. More than enough at present. But who has not heard of 'Angel,' Miss Sutton? Come, enough of your cousin. Tell me how you look to amuse yourself at Barrows End."

Angel was broaching the same subject with Lady Elizabeth, having been unable to elicit more than a monosyllable on any other she tried.

"How do you spend your time, my lady?" she enquired. "I think there are not many amusements in the neighbourhood?"

"I like to sew," said Lady Elizabeth in her soft voice. More and more she seemed to Angel like a shy, frightened elf. "And I play the pianoforte sometimes, and sketch a lot when it is fine. There are a great many subjects to be found locally."

"I'm sure there are. I like to sketch and have brought my book. Perhaps we might go out together one day?"

"That would be delightful," Lady Elizabeth agreed with enthusiasm. "And I often visit Papa's tenants too, whatever Mrs Daventry may say."

"She does say a lot, doesn't she?" giggled Angel. "How do you bear her?"

"I have no choice. Papa says I must have someone and that she is as good as the next person, and a relative besides. I let her talk while I think my own thoughts. It is not so very bad, especially when Cousin Gregory is here. He sometimes goes out with me so that I do not need Mrs Daventry."

"Do you ride?"

"Oh yes, often."

Angel was about to remark that she was very fond of riding when it dawned on her that her uncle certainly could not mount her, and Lady Elizabeth might think that she was angling for an invitation. Before she could resolve this dilemma, it was taken out of her hands.

"Do you ride, Miss Brand?" asked Sir Gregory. "My uncle has a great many horses in his stable that are rarely ridden, and I feel sure he would be happy to accommodate you. Do you not think so, Beth?"

"Oh, yes," agreed his cousin, "if you will persuade him."

"Catherine, you do not suppose Uncle Clement will object? This is beyond anything great! Only I do not have a riding habit with me. I daresay I can have one made up in Patterdale." She turned to a discussion of local dressmakers with Lady Elizabeth.

" 'Good morrow, Kate,' " said Sir Gregory, " 'for that's your name, I hear.' "

" 'Well have you heard, but something hard of hearing: They call me *Katherine* that do talk of me.' And that is Miss Sutton to you, sir. I hope you do not mean to suggest that you find me shrewish?''

" 'Oh, Kate, content thee; prithee be not angry.' Not a shrew, Miss Sutton, but I believe I have found you out for a bluestocking, to be quoting Shakespeare with me. Confess!''

"Truth to tell, I have read *The Taming of the Shrew* an hundred times, looking to find all the virtues in my namesake.''

"And what success had you?''

"Little,'' she admitted, "except that now I could recite you the whole play. But you'll not find me reading Kate's homily on obedient wives.''

"Ah, 'tis plain to see you are not married. You will change your tune when you are wed.''

"I doubt it, sir. I do not hold men to be the superior sex.''

" 'That wench is stark mad, or wonderful froward.' Here is the ill effect of too much education, Kate,'' Sir Gregory said, grinning; then, as she frowned, "I beg your pardon—Miss Sutton.''

"I'll not argue with you, sir, for I see that my best arguments will but prove your point. Here comes Mrs Daventry.''

Sir Gregory groaned and clutched his ears, but when the lady came up he was all bored propriety.

"Are you ready to depart, ma'am?'' he drawled in a very different voice from that he had used with Catherine. "Cousin, will you take my arm? The path is slippery.''

Farewells were said, and promises to meet again, and the Grisedale carriage moved off up the lane. Mr and Mrs Sutton were still busy with their parishioners, so Angel and Catherine walked towards the vicarage, nodding in response to the curtsies and tipped hats of the farm folk. As they approached the gate between the churchyard and the garden, a rather stout and florid young man walked up to them, removed his fashionable beaver, and bowed low, dropping his silver-mounted cane in the process.

They stopped and looked at him in surprise as he picked it up and straightened with a gasp, crimson-faced from the exertion, not, as was soon evident, from embarrassment.

"Beg leave to introduce m'self," he uttered with cheerful nonchalance. "Dick Burchett at y'r service. Met the Vicar and his missus just now, y'know. Pa owns Beckside Farm."

Neither Angel nor Catherine could think of any suitable response to this revelation. Fortunately Mr Burchett did not seem to expect one.

"He's a warm man," he explained. "Price of wool's good with the war and all. Sent me away to school and thinks that makes me a gentleman. Keep telling him all I want's to be a farmer; won't listen. Wants to send me to London now, find a toff to marry, but I'm courting Betsy down at Meadow Farm in Patterdale."

Angel dissolved in giggles.

"I'm very happy for Miss Betsy," said Catherine, "but I cannot guess why you are telling us this, Mr Burchett."

"Camouflage," he revealed proudly. "Pa says y'r ma's a lady, so if he thinks I'm courting you, he'll let me bide. Don't mind, do you? Won't bother you much, but you might like to come up to Beckside one day, see the animals. Know ladies like kittens and calves and lambs and such."

"I'm sure we'd be happy to accept your invitation, sir. Wouldn't we, Lyn?" said Catherine severely.

"Oh, yes," gasped Angel. "Love kittens. Have any puppies?"

"Lots." He opened the gate for them, bowed again, and went off with a cheerful wave.

"What an odd young man!" Catherine exclaimed, laughing. "There is certainly no humbug about him. The very soul of candour. I rather liked him. Oh, do look, Angel!" She pointed to the northwest.

The churchyard was completely surrounded by tall yews, and not until they were well into the vicarage garden did the newly revealed panorama become visible. Behind the house, a brilliantly green meadow stretched in the sun down to a stream edged by willows and alders. On the far side, a cart track ran parallel, backed by a stone wall, beyond which more meadows climbed to woodland, then bare fell, then up and up to the towering mass of Helvellyn mountain, huge beyond belief, its summit standing out clear-cut against a pale blue sky.

"I want to climb it," breathed Angel. "Let's go this afternoon."

"Oh, Angel, surely it would take a whole day! I believe there are paths, but one should have a guide, I expect, and take food."

"But it is such a fine day, I hate to waste it. It will probably rain again tomorrow."

"There are certainly shorter walks we might take today. Think of woods and rocky dells and waterfalls. Let's follow our own stream down there, and see where it takes us."

They asked permission over luncheon. Catherine and her mother watched with envy as Angel consumed enough cold lamb and well-buttered bread for two, and finished up with a dish of strawberries drowning in sugar and cream. "May we walk along the stream this afternoon?" she asked between mouthfuls.

No objection was raised to this plan, so after changing their gowns and footwear, the young ladies strolled across the meadow. A pair of brown-eyed cows raised their heads to stare at the intruders, then went back to cropping the lush grass and buttercups.

To Angel's delight, there were stepping stones leading across the water to the track on the other side. She bounced across, while Catherine followed more cautiously. By mutual consent they turned upstream.

On their left, the clear water chattered over its rocky bed. The drystone wall on their right sheltered a myriad flowers: foxgloves, yarrow, campion, and toadflax, purple knapweed and scarlet pimpernel. Butterflies fluttered by and the air was full of the hum of bees and the distant lowing of cattle.

"What did you think of Lady Elizabeth?" asked Angel, after they had walked for a while in silent contentment.

"I hardly spoke to her," Catherine answered. "A quiet little mouse, though pretty enough, with that dark hair, if her face had more animation."

"She had plenty to say when I asked her the right questions, but she is shockingly shy. Of course she never gets a word in edgewise with that odious woman around. I daresay she is out of practice. Her papa sounds monstrous disagreeable too. Only imagine casting off his only son because he ran away to join the army! I am sure she must miss her brother, and her mama too."

"Did she speak of them?"

"No, but she will. I was not with her for longer than ten minutes but already I have her confidence, I think. The poor child has had no friends!"

"Child! She must be quite your age, Angel."

"She is so little and shy, I feel I must protect her."

"An unprecedented feeling, I am sure."

"Well, yes, except that sometimes I try to shield Mama. Only she has Papa to look after her. Of course, there is always Sir Gregory. What thought you of him, Catherine?"

"He is very large and looks sleepier than he is. What is your opinion?"

"At first I thought him fine enough to be your suitor. Do not smile, I told you I meant to look out for a husband for you. He is certainly tall enough! Then I thought him by far too dull, for he just stood there looking bored. But afterward it seemed to me that he was laughing at me, and that I did not like at all. It would be odious to be married to a man who laughed at one."

"Do you think so? He is certainly a great tease." Catherine considered warning her cousin that her disguise had already been pierced, then decided against it.

"I think it very likely that he is sly," Angel suggested, "for he hides behind that bored face and makes you think he is not listening, and then makes fun of you. Of all things, I abhor slyness."

"I do not think him sly, but you may have the right of it. One should not judge on such short acquaintance. Look, we cannot follow the stream any further."

They had walked half a mile or so, and now the track swung to the right and the stream's course continued through a gap in a high stone wall, which barred their path.

"I shall climb over it," said Angel at once.

"Pray do not! You will certainly dirty your gown and probably rip it, if you do not fall and break your leg."

"Oh, very well. Perhaps I can go around the end by the stream."

"Has it not occurred to you that someone built the wall to keep you out?" protested Catherine as her cousin pushed through a tangle of hazel bushes overgrown with sweet-scented honeysuckle.

"It must be Grisedale Hall. They will not mind."

"I daresay you are right," Catherine sighed. "I beg you will not fall into the water."

She made her way around the edge of the thicket and found Angel contemplating the proposed passage. There was a two-foot drop from the grassy bank onto a jumble of boulders of various sizes, most of them wet with spray. They looked alarmingly slippery, but supposing that one managed to stay upright it would be possible to climb past the end of the wall. Until this was accomplished, it was quite impossible to see how high the bank was on the other side.

Before Catherine could protest again, Angel picked up her skirts in one hand and jumped.

"Come ahead," she said. "It's easy." Balancing with her unoccupied hand, she proceeded, and heaving another heavy sigh, her cousin followed.

Three minutes later they were sitting on a conveniently fallen tree trunk. Angel took off her shoe and emptied water from it.

"I came off better than you," said Catherine. "I declare I do not know what comes over me when you propose these adventures. I am by far too old for such pranks."

"Let us walk a little further." Angel bounced up, ready to go. "Oh, Catherine, do not turn your head a minute, but guess what I can see."

"A raging bull."

"No."

"Lord Grisedale's gamekeeper with a shotgun."

"No, guess again."

"I cannot imagine." She looked round. "Angel, a gate! If we had just walked a little further along the track, we might have entered comfortably!"

"It would have been vastly less amusing. Come on."

They had not walked very far when three figures on horseback rode over a rise a quarter of a mile distant, and they recognised Lady Elizabeth and Sir Gregory, with an unknown gentleman. Angel immediately waved and hallooed.

"We cannot speak to them!" cried Catherine. "I do not know how I look, but you are the very image of a ragamuffin."

"Then they will not guess that I am the daughter of a marquis. You are a pattern-card of propriety, not a hair out of place, I promise you."

There was no time for further remonstrances, for already the riders were drawing near.

"Hello," Angel greeted them sunnily. "I thought this must be Grisedale Hall."

"I beg your pardon for trespassing," Catherine added hurriedly, slightly flushed.

Lady Elizabeth was by far too well bred to seem to notice Angel's hoydenish appearance, but as the gentlemen dismounted, the stranger raised a quizzical eyebrow.

"Miss Sutton, Miss, er, Brand, your servant," said Sir Gregory, at his most languid. "Allow me to present Lord Welch."

The stranger made his bow.

"You are visiting in the neighbourhood, ma'am?" he asked Catherine in a pleasant, well-modulated voice. His tightly fitting blue coat, exquisite fawn unmentionables, and glossy, white-topped boots made Sir Gregory look downright casual.

"My father has taken over the parish for the summer, my lord."

"And I am her cousin," broke in Angel. "We walked up from the vicarage."

"It is a beautiful day," volunteered Lady Elizabeth.

"One of my shepherds promised a fine week, according to my bailiff," remarked Lord Welch. "These yokels are amazingly accurate about the weather. I shall probably ride over from Upthwaite daily to pay my respects to the earl." He looked smilingly at Lady Elizabeth, who blushed.

"I am sure there is no need for such diligence," said Sir Gregory, frowning. "My uncle was unable to see you today, and I do not suppose he will do so soon. You would do better to inspect your land while the weather permits."

Angel had noted the blush, but missed the grateful glance from Lady Elizabeth which followed it, directed at the baronet. Scenting opposed romance, she made up her mind to lend her assistance.

"There are a thousand pleasanter things to do on a sunny day," she declared. "We must have a picnic, at least, and go sketching. Do you sketch, my lord?"

"No, Miss Brand, but I am a great admirer of young ladies' talents. Perhaps I might serve to carry your easels?"

"That will be delightful, will it not, my lady?" Angel prattled on, making plans enough for a month of fine weather. Lord Welch obligingly agreed with her every suggestion, and she scarce noticed that Lady Elizabeth uttered not a word except for an occasional faint and unheeded protest. They rambled on, the gentlemen leading their horses; Angel walked between her ladyship's pony and his lordship, and Catherine brought up the rear with Sir Gregory.

"What a minx she is!" that gentleman commented drily. "Angel by name, but no angel by nature. If I had not guessed her secret, I should think her a most encroaching female."

"I am very glad you did guess, or I should be covered in confusion to an even greater extent than I am. Papa had warned me that Uncle Frederick allowed her a great deal of freedom, and that I must watch out for her, but I cannot tell what she will do next, and she does not heed me unless she chooses. There is no malice in her, though."

"I daresay the acquaintance will be good for Beth. She has been too much penned in. I hope they will take to one another."

"Angel declared she was in a fair way to win your cousin's confidence. However, if she continues to press my lord's suit, I fear she is like to lose it fast, is she not?" asked Catherine with a grimace.

" 'Nay, come, Kate, come; you must not look so sour.' Can you not explain to her that your more experienced eye has discerned his company to be unwelcome?"

"I can try, and will if you wish it. And I wish you will not call me Kate. It is not at all proper."

" 'Alas, good Kate, I will not burden thee,' " he said, grinning. "I find it well nigh irresistible, but I am running out of suitable quotations, so I will try to be good—if you will persuade the headstrong Miss Brand not to invite the viscount on all her expeditions. It is deuced difficult to exclude him, with the best will in the world. Perhaps I should explain that there are objections quite apart from Beth's dislike of the man. He has sold off most of his land, and still finds himself in need of her dowry, nor do I think him a man of principle in other matters. Unfortunately, my uncle sees only the advantage of disposing of his daughter without further effort. He is a sick man, and never was inclined to put himself out for his womenfolk."

"You should not be telling me this, sir, I am sure," said Catherine in some confusion.

"Why, Catherine's the sweet soul of discretion! No, I cry pax, and admit that Shakespeare never wrote that line. I think it true, though. Now, shall you turn around and tell Lord Welch what I have said of him?"

"Of course not. But still, you should not tell me. And it is quite unfair to make up quotations. Oh, dear, I really must take Angel away before it is too late. How she ever manages not to be shunned by the Ton, I cannot guess. Lyn! It is time we turned homeward."

"Must we?"

"Yes, Mother will be looking out for us. Good-bye, my lady, my lord."

"Good-bye, everyone!" Angel echoed. "We will see you tomorrow!"

=== 4 ===

LEAVING THE PARK decorously by the gate, Angel and Catherine turned down the track towards the stream.

"I hope you have not made definite plans for tomorrow," Catherine said. "Papa may have arranged something."

"Lady Elizabeth offered to take us for a drive about the countryside. She is going to call in the morning, but if we will not be there I shall write her a note. Lord Welch said he will escort us. They are in love."

"I do not think so, Angel. It seemed to me that Lady Elizabeth would have preferred to avoid his lordship."

"Why, how can you say so? He goes to Grisedale every day only to see her, and when he hinted as much, she blushed. You have no feeling for romance."

"Have you never been pestered by suitors you had rather not see? A sly remark may bring a blush of mortification, not pleasure."

"I wouldn't know. I have never been in the habit of blushing," said Angel coldly. "And why does she receive him if she does not wish to?"

"It would be difficult to refuse a neighbour in this place where there are few, especially as Lord Grisedale favours his suit, I understand."

"I can see that that odious Sir Gregory has set you against Lord Welch. *He* is the sly one. His lordship is charming and amiable, and you shall not persuade me that she does not love him."

"Let us not come to cuffs, Angel. We'll agree to disagree." It

37

did not seem to Catherine a propitious moment to bring up the subject of her forward behaviour. She did not wish to bear tales to her mother, but Angel must be made to realise that manners acceptable in a lady of large fortune and impeccable lineage were enough to sink beneath reproach a female in more modest circumstances.

She set herself to coax her cousin out of the sullens, not a difficult task. By the time they reached the vicarage, they were friends again. They found Mrs Sutton entertaining two maiden ladies from Patterdale who, though not parishioners, had felt it their duty to welcome the new vicar. Angel behaved with such becoming modesty that Catherine almost thought she had imagined the events of the afternoon.

Angel was silent because she was plotting. It was not in her nature to keep her plots to herself, but the presence of visitors did not permit her to reveal them to Catherine. Though unwilling to admit the possibility of being mistaken, she was anxious not to force her new friend into the company of a gentleman she disliked, if such were the case. She must discover the truth as soon as possible, which meant that she must go out driving with them both on the morrow without fail, even if it involved a little prevarication such as an imaginary headache.

No ruse was necessary. When Aunt Maria heard of the projected outing, she insisted that Angel must go.

"I hope that Catherine will bear me company, however," she continued. "I cannot abide these brown serge curtains and had planned to go into Patterdale to choose something lighter. Just a cheap print that can be made over when we go home. And I shall take down all the net too. The house is dark enough without blocking all the windows."

"I will certainly come with you, Mother," said Catherine. "Angel, did you not wish to buy some material for a riding habit?"

"Yes, but it must be grey or brown if I am to keep up my disguise, so you can choose it for me, if you will. Lady Elizabeth says there is a seamstress in Barrows End who can make it up, and your curtains too, Aunt, I expect. But Catherine, you must have a habit also."

"I packed one. How is that for forethought? Or perhaps only wishing."

"There is household shopping to be done too," Mrs Sutton told her daughter. "Mrs Applejohn does not shop, and cooks breakfast only on Sundays, I have discovered. She does not live in, of course, so I expect she will not bring up water in the mornings either. I certainly hope the fire stays in overnight. At least John Applejohn will drive the gig into Patterdale so that we need not disturb your father."

Mr Sutton approved their plans.

"I hope you will hold Wednesday free for me," he added. "I have an introduction to the Vicar of Upthwaite, and I wrote some time ago to tell him that, *Deo volente*, I should call with my family on that day. It will be a pleasant outing if the weather holds fine. I believe he is a *young* gentleman."

"Why, we have quite an acquaintance in the neighbourhood already," said his wife. "Miss Weir and Miss Swenster are a little odd but very friendly, and I shall certainly visit them. What a pity Mrs Daventry is so excessively loquacious. I am afraid she is determined upon instant intimacy."

"We must also pay our respects to Lord Grisedale this week," the vicar remembered. "You will be obliged to see the chatterbox for once, my dear. I daresay she is lonely and in need of an occasional listener."

"Poor Lady Elizabeth has to listen all the time," pointed out Angel.

She was dismayed to find the lady in question seated opposite her friend the next morning, when the landau called for her. Lord Welch, who was riding alongside, handed her in.

"Good morning, Miss Brand," Mrs Daventry began. Not awaiting a response, she proceeded to enquire after the Suttons, deplore the humbleness of the vicarage and its usual inhabitants, comment on the weather, and exclaim in ecstasy over the scenery, which was admittedly worthy of remark.

They drove along beside Ullswater, sparkling blue in the sunshine, its further shore lined with trees and meadows and an occasional farmhouse, beyond which rose the steep fells. Ahead, the lake seemed to stretch forever. Angel despaired of being able to talk to Lady Elizabeth, let alone of persuading her to confide. Only when the lane was wide enough to allow Lord Welch to ride beside them did Mrs Daventry cease chattering.

This, in Angel's opinion, was sufficient reason to appreciate his lordship's presence. On further acquaintance she found him an amusing companion. He was witty and complimentary in a style she was accustomed to in London beaux, and if not precisely handsome, he was not ill-looking. He dressed with as much attention to fashion as was appropriate to their rural surroundings. All in all, she approved of him and saw no reason why Lady Elizabeth should not love him. Perhaps Catherine had herself conceived a tendre for him, she thought, and had spoken out of jealousy. It was not an emotion with which she was personally familiar, but she had read that it did terrible things to the most sensible individuals.

In that case, she decided, if her new friend was indeed not enamoured of the viscount, she would do her best to see that he turned to Catherine.

At last they turned back. More anxious than ever to discover Lady Elizabeth's feelings, Angel endured the return trip in absentminded cogitation which led her nowhere. She could think of ways to escape Mrs Daventry, and ways to dispose of Lord Welch, but to rid herself of both at once was beyond her ingenuity.

Fortunately, his lordship left them in Patterdale, to take the lane leading to Upthwaite. This freed Mrs Daventry's tongue once more, but as she paused to draw breath, Lady Elizabeth steeled herself to interrupt.

"I should like to show Miss Brand the bridge over Grisedale Beck, where I caught a fish once," she said. "If you do not object, ma'am. It is not far from the road and will only take a moment. There is a track just around the next corner."

In no time the two girls were alone together at last, strolling as slowly as they could manage down the cart track.

"Is Upthwaite very far from Patterdale?" began Angel cautiously.

"Three miles, or thereabouts."

"Then it is six miles from Grisedale Hall. That is a fair distance for a daily ride. Twelve miles in all!"

"There is a bridle path over Dowen Crag which makes it much shorter." Lady Elizabeth blushed as she said this.

"Is it a pleasant walk?" asked Angel, pleased with the way the conversation was going in spite of her unwonted discretion.

"Delightful. The hill is very steep, but the view from the top is all one could wish."

"I expect you go there often?"

They had reached the bridge, a small arch of stone with a parapet precisely the right height for leaning on. They duly leant, and gazed down into a pellucid pool where silver glints betrayed the presence of a school of small fish.

"Dom used often to bring me here fishing," revealed Lady Elizabeth with a sigh. "My brother Dominic, that is. We used string and a bent pin, but once I caught a trout big enough to eat."

At any other time Angel would have been more than happy to follow up this lead, but now she was not to be deterred.

"You must often walk over Dowen Crag?" she persisted.

"No, rarely. As you see, Mrs Daventry does not like to walk, so I am confined to our own land."

"That would not stop me!"

"I expect it would not. I fear I am sadly timid. Besides, I should be sure to meet Francis, and I am not permitted to see . . . a certain other person."

Temporarily ignoring the second half of this confession, Angel pounced.

"Then you do not wish to meet Lord Welch?"

"Oh, if only I need never see him again! I have known him since I was a child, and he was an odious bully then. He was older and bigger than we, but there were no other children nearby so we saw a lot of him. Then he went away to London for three or four years, and when he returned three years ago he asked Papa's permission to court me. Papa was delighted because I would not need a Season in London to catch a husband, but I was only sixteen so he made him wait. I managed after a while to persuade Papa that I did not wish to marry Francis, and I think he would have let me go to London eventually, only then Mama died so I could not. Now he is quite determined again that Francis shall have me. And though I have told Francis that I love another and will never be his as long as there is hope, he will not stop pestering me.''

"One must make allowances for gentlemen in love," said Angel largely, fascinated by this outpouring of pent-up feeling. "I will try to distract his attentions from you though. Who is the gentleman you love, Lady Elizabeth?''

"I am forbidden to mention his name, or even to think of him. Miss Brand, I wish you will call me Beth. Lady Elizabeth is such a mouthful.''

"I will then, and you will call me An . . . Lyn. My name is Evelyn but I abhor it, and Lyn is quite pretty, is it not? Beth, will you not tell me?''

"Pray do not ask, Lyn, for I promised Papa not to speak of him—though Papa cannot control my thoughts. We must go back or Mrs Daventry will call after us.''

Deep in speculation, Angel was silent as they walked back to the landau, and had she so desired she could not have fitted a word in during the short drive to the vicarage, as Mrs Daventry was apparently making up for lost time. As the coachman let down the step, Lady Elizabeth took her hand.

"I hope you are not offended with me?" she whispered anxiously.

"Of course not, Beth," Angel assured, kissing her cheek. "Shall we sketch tomorrow if it is fine?''

"Oh, yes, please let's! Will you come up to the Hall? At two o'clock, say? I have a spare easel, or I can send the carriage for you.''

"I shall walk. Till tomorrow then. Good-bye, ma'am.''

Mrs Daventry had half a mind to step in and see dear Mrs Sutton, but Angel hurried to assure her that her aunt was from home. This she soon discovered to be the truth, and Uncle Clement was also absent. Coaxing a luncheon out of Mrs Applejohn, she ate it in the kitchen and was almost done when the gig was heard in the drive to the side of the house.

She dashed out to the stableyard, and embraced Catherine.

"You were quite right," she admitted. "About Beth and Francis. Lord Welch, I mean. The poor man is suffering from unrequited love, which is excessively uncomfortable for Beth. I'll tell you all about it later."

Aunt Maria's purchases were unpacked and examined, and last of all appeared the parcel with material for Angel's riding habit.

"I do not call this precisely grey!" exclaimed Angel, spreading out a length of shot silk.

"It is if you look at it this way. And the blue going the other way is exactly the colour of your eyes."

"Well, it is very pretty, anyway. Will you come with me to the dressmaker?"

"What, at once? Let me sit a little to catch my breath, and a cup of tea would not come amiss. Then I'll come."

The dressmaker's patterns were all at least two years old, but Angel decided that was just as well, as the silk was less sober than she had intended. She had already found her resolution unequal to wearing caps in the warm July sunshine, and instead had pinned her hair up in the least becoming style she could imagine. Being inexpert in the art, she had a tendency to lose several hairpins every time she moved her head, and after sitting on one Aunt Maria suggested that Catherine might help her.

So when the young ladies set off to walk to Grisedale Hall the next day, with the sun still miraculously shining down, Angel's golden locks were pulled severely back behind her ears and confined in a net which she declared, giggling, to be positively spinsterish. The whole was hidden under her plain straw bonnet, which made Catherine's modest fawn ostrich feather look almost frivolous.

Catherine had not wanted to go on the sketching party.

"I was not invited," she pointed out, "and besides, I cannot draw worth a farthing."

"I am sure you are expected, and if you come perhaps Mrs Daventry will not consider it necessary to chaperone us, even if Lord Welch comes. And he probably will, so you can draw him off and it will not matter that you cannot sketch. Please come!"

Catherine was not best pleased to be asked to distract the viscount. She had disliked him mildly at first sight, and Angel's revelations, coupled with Sir Gregory's, did nothing to contradict her opinion of him. However, she resigned herself with a good grace to playing chaperone, and shortly before two o'clock they approached the Hall.

It was an impressive mansion, built chiefly of local stone but with an added portico of marble brought in at great expense from Italy by the previous earl. The great hall of Tudor days had been partitioned into apartments of a more modern size, and the drawing room into which the two young ladies were ushered was comfortably, if not elegantly, furnished in the style of the last century.

From Angel's point of view, the afternoon was every bit as successful as the previous morning's work. She and Beth set up their easels on a knoll overlooking a small lake, or "tarn" as she was told she must call it. She had nobly decided not to press her friend, at least as yet, for the identity of her secret suitor, though she might have been less reticent had she not been certain that she had guessed it. The mention of "a certain person" in relation to Upthwaite village, accompanied by a blush, she added to her uncle's description of the vicar of that parish as a "young gentleman," and the answer was undoubtedly four.

Satisfied with her arithmetic, she did not return to the subject even when Catherine and Lord Welch strolled off together, leaving her alone with Beth. Instead, after privately congratulating herself on the beginnings of a rapprochement between that couple, she encouraged reminiscences of Lord Dominic Markham, which Lady Elizabeth was happy to indulge in. Her father would not hear his only son's name spoken in his presence, and for fear of offending, Mrs Daventry extended the ban to her own conversation, so that only with Sir Gregory could she talk of her beloved brother. And since Sir Gregory disapproved almost equally of his cousin's behaviour and his uncle's reaction, he was small comfort.

"He did have friends in Dom's regiment who sent news of him," she admitted as Angel waxed indignant, "so he was able to tell Mama and me occasionally that Dom was still alive at least. But there has been no word for a long time now, since the battle of Ciudad Rodrigo."

"That was just after Christmas, was it not? It does seem a long time."

"I am glad that Mama died before we ceased to hear of him. She had enough sorrow to bear without that."

"Tell me about your mama."

"She was over twenty years younger than Papa, and she was always frail. When Dom ran off, she took to her bed and gradually faded away. If there had been any hope of seeing him again—but Papa was quite adamant. And then he was taken with a fit of apoplexy, soon after Mama was buried, and now he is practically an invalid himself. At least it means that Cousin Gregory comes more often. He is the heir, you know, if Dom never . . ." Suppressed tears stole her voice.

"I can see that you miss Lord Dominic quite dreadfully. If it would help to talk about him, I should like to hear about when you were children together. I never had any brothers or sisters."

Beth found that there was indeed relief to be found in communicating her memories, and as they sketched she waxed eloquent upon the subject of her brother's endless talent for mischief, becoming cheerful and animated.

Meanwhile Catherine and Lord Welch were strolling along a gravel path around the tarn, whose banks were overgrown with bulrushes and yellow flags.

"Drawing is not one of your chosen pastimes then, Miss Sutton?" enquired his lordship.

45

"As I have no aptitude, I choose not to display my lack of skill, my lord."

"Very wise, no doubt. Lady Elizabeth is an accomplished artist. I daresay your cousin is likewise?"

"Lyn has more enthusiasm than ability, I believe, but you must judge for yourself. If it were not for the opportunity of exercising the critical faculty, I am sure that gentlemen would find little amusement in ladies' sketching parties."

"You have found me out, Miss Sutton, though I do not presume to criticise. The least sign of talent is worthy of admiration, and I am willing to pay it homage."

"Sir Gregory is not an admirer of art, I suppose, or is he occupied about affairs of more weight?"

"Oh, Markham has gone into Derbyshire, I believe. There's no knowing where the fellow will be from one day to the next. A regular here-and-thereian, I assure you."

"His home is in Derbyshire?"

"Yes. A nice piece of property, I've heard, though not to compare to Grisedale. He'll have the lot, you know, if Dominic does not turn up."

"Is not Lord Dominic with the army in Spain?"

"Everyone supposes so, but he's not been heard of since he left, four years ago. Devilish bacon-brained thing to do, begging your pardon, ma'am. He always was ripe for mischief, and the earl kept him tied to his apronstrings up here with nothing to do. Only if he'd thought, he'd have realised that there was a good chance Sir Gregory would inherit."

"He cannot have known that his father would turn him off. It is a most unnatural act! And even then he must have had the title, and I expect the house and park at least are entailed, so it was just a question of the farms and money. A boy mad for the army cannot be expected to consider that."

"I bow to your judgment, ma'am. But soldiering is a chancy occupation, and he never had any love for his cousin. The one a care-for-nobody and the other a prig."

"I do not know Lord Dominic," said Catherine coldly, "but by my first impressions of Sir Gregory I should not describe him as a prig."

"Believe me, prosy as a parson!"

This remark was hardly calculated to win over a parson's daughter, and Catherine had to turn the subject and make a determined effort to be civil as they wended their way back to the artists' station.

On their arrival, Lord Welch pronounced a panegyric on the work of both young ladies. Catherine decided that Lady Elizabeth's picture had considerable merit for an amateur. Angel, however, had always had too many amusements available to apply herself to her pencil, and in this case she had not even been thinking about what she was doing.

"This should be published as a lesson to artists in what to avoid!" commented Catherine tartly.

"I shall give it to you to send to a publisher," offered Angel, unoffended. "It was not at all difficult. I'll do you another one day."

His lordship begged for Lady Elizabeth's sketch, which she unwillingly gave him, and they packed up their tools.

"Shall you come tomorrow?" her ladyship asked Angel hopefully, as they strolled back towards the house.

"I do not know if we will have time, Beth. My uncle wishes us to pay a call with him."

"Never fear, I shall come to keep you company," declared Lord Welch gallantly.

"Pray do not trouble, Francis. I have just remembered that I promised to visit old Mrs Wharton, so I will not be at home."

His lordship looked most disconcerted, being used to have things all his own way. Angel was sorry to see him suffer, though pleased at her protégée's small show of independence. To salve his wound, she chattered to him the rest of the way, and he appeared happy to flirt with her, with many a sidelong glance to see what Lady Elizabeth made of his defection.

Escaping from Mrs Daventry with considerable effort, Angel and Catherine walked homeward along Grisedale Beck.

"I greatly fear that he is still in love with her," Angel confessed.

"You must not expect to accomplish miracles. It will take time to wean him from her," soothed Catherine. Not knowing her cousin's plans on her behalf, she hoped Angel was not herself falling in love with Lord Welch, for she found him less and less amiable.

Angel was glad she took the reflection so calmly. Perhaps the ramble around the lake had assuaged the worst pangs of jealousy, she thought. She must endeavour to throw them together often.

=5=

CLOUDS GATHERED THAT night, and by the morning Helvellyn was invisible again. However, John Applejohn prophesied that there would be no rain before evening, so the Suttons and Miss Brand set off in the gig for Upthwaite.

The valley in which the small village lay ran roughly parallel to Grisedale, from which it was separated by the imposing steeps of Dowen Crag. One branch led to Upthwaite Park, seat of the Viscounts Welch, and the other to the hamlet.

The vicarage turned out to be on quite a different scale from that of Barrows End. It was a pleasant-looking house, facing down the valley towards the lake, and almost large enough to be described as a manor. As Mr Sutton stopped the gig, a lad who had been clipping a hedge came over to take the reins.

"This is much nicer than ours," approved Angel. "Front gardens are supposed to have flowers, not vegetables."

A maid opened the door to them, and as they entered the vicar of Upthwaite came to greet them. He was a tall, grey-eyed young man with clear-cut good looks and a gentlemanlike manner. Angel approved him at once as precisely right for Lady Elizabeth, for among other advantages his calm, composed demeanour would not intimidate that bashful creature.

Introductions were performed, and Mr Leigh ushered his visitors into a delightfully cosy front parlour, whose large windows admitted ample light in spite of the dull day. A second young gentleman, short and dark, was standing at one of them, gazing out at the gay flowerbeds and the long view beyond. He turned on hearing their entrance.

49

"Allow me to present my friend Mr Marshall," said Mr Leigh. "He is staying with me at present. Donald, this is Mr Sutton, who is taking Barrows End parish for the summer. Mrs Sutton, Miss Sutton, and Miss Brand."

Mr Marshall bowed, and Angel saw that a thin white scar ran down the left side of his pale face. She was not sure whether it looked romantic or sinister, but it was certainly interesting. Though he did not speak at once, she felt a kind of inner tension in him, like a tightly coiled spring, and when he moved forward she saw that he limped. Sinister, she decided. How exciting!

When he did speak, it was to ask Mrs Sutton, in a perfectly normal way, whether she had had a pleasant ride from Barrows End.

"I hope you are not too uncomfortable in the vicarage, ma'am," he added. "It is a cramped little house . . . or so I have heard."

After a quarter of an hour of polite conversation, Mr Sutton requested a word with the younger vicar on church business.

"By all means, sir," said Mr Leigh. "Marshall, you will entertain the ladies for me? Perhaps they would like to see the gardens."

"If it would not be too much trouble," agreed Mrs Sutton. "My niece was admiring the flowers when we arrived."

"You are fond of flowers, Miss Brand?" asked Mr Marshall, leading the way outside.

"Oh, yes," Angel replied. "They are so much prettier than vegetables."

He laughed, and as his rather sombre face relaxed, she thought that perhaps he was only *slightly* sinister.

"Undeniable, ma'am," he said.

She hastened to explain about the Barrows End vicarage garden being full of spinach and sprouts.

"Detestable," he agreed solemnly. "It is bad enough to find them on the dinner table, without being faced with them every time one leaves the house."

"Do you think so too? Cousin Catherine *likes* vegetables. Until

I found out, I did not suppose that any person under forty ate them voluntarily.''

"I'll wager you do not feel the same about raspberries. Shall we see if Gerald's canes are ready to be harvested?''

"Do let's. Aunt Maria, Mr Marshall will take us to pick raspberries!''

Mrs Sutton and Catherine were admiring the view.

"Do you go ahead, Lyn,'' she said. "We will follow shortly.''

They found the kitchen garden, and soon Angel's fingers and lips were stained with raspberry juice.

"Your name is Lyn, Miss Brand?'' enquired Mr Marshall, filling her cupped hands. "That must be why you remind me of a linnet.''

"It's really Evelyn, only I prefer it shortened. A linnet is a bird, is it not?''

"A little grey bird with an unexpected voice and a fondness for fruit. Have you never heard a linnet?''

"I have lived a great deal in London,'' Angel explained.

"Judging by your sweeping comparison of flowers and vegetables, you are equally ignorant about flowers, Linnet.''

"I know roses and violets and . . . and daffodils.''

"It is too late for daffodils, but I should like to show you the place where Wordsworth composed his poem. It is by Ullswater, you know.''

"That would be delightful. Perhaps Catherine and I can ride over one day. Lady Elizabeth Markham has said that we may borrow horses whenever we wish.''

"You have met Lady Elizabeth already?'' he asked eagerly.

"Yes, and we are dearest friends.''

"Is she well?''

"I believe so, though not in good spirits. You are acquainted with her then, sir?''

"I am, and I must see her. I don't suppose you would be willing to arrange a meeting, Linnet? There are reasons why I cannot go to Grisedale.''

"Pray do not call me Linnet, Mr Marshall. It is most improper, and my aunt is coming."

The young man groaned and abandoned the subject. When Mrs Sutton and Catherine arrived, he set about picking berries for them, agreeing in an absentminded way to their remarks upon the beauties of the surrounding country.

They returned to the house to find that Mr Leigh had provided a sumptuous luncheon. Angel wished aloud that she had not consumed so very many raspberries, but the others noticed no visible diminution in her appetite.

She was filling her plate for the second time, when there was a deep barking in a distant part of the house. A moment later Mr Leigh's cook-housekeeper flung open the door of the dining parlour.

"Yon dog's ta'en the mutton and willna' gie it up," she announced, very red in the face and flustered. "I'll no hae the baist in my kitchen anither minute! Beggin' your pardon, sir."

"The devil!" exclaimed Mr Marshall, jumping to his feet. "My apologies, Mrs McTavish. She can go outside now. I'll come and rescue the mutton if there is anything left of it."

"Is it your dog?" asked Angel. "I should love to see her."

"She is very large. I shut her in the kitchen lest she should alarm you ladies."

"What is she called? Is she not friendly?"

"She adores people but tends to become overexcited. She is not yet two years old, you see. I call her Osa, which is Spanish for 'bear.' Excuse me, I must go to Mrs McTavish's aid."

"I'll come too," decided Angel. "Catherine, won't you come with me?"

Sighing inaudibly, Catherine rose and followed her cousin to the kitchen. They arrived to find a huge, white, fluffy monster grovelling guiltily on the floor at her scolding master's feet. Seeing them, Osa wriggled towards them, tail wagging madly, and rolled over on her back to have her tummy rubbed. Angel obliged, and after a few blissful moments the dog sat up and licked her face

52

gratefully. Mr Marshall hurriedly produced a handkerchief.

"What kind of dog is she?" asked Catherine. The sound of her voice reminded Osa of her presence, but she escaped with only a wet hand.

"A Pyrenean Mountain dog," her master replied. "They are sheepdogs like our collies, but rather than herding the flocks they guard them from bears and wolves."

"If I saw her coming with belligerent intent, I'd run," confessed Catherine. "She is beautiful though. How fortunate that she likes people!"

"Where did you get her?" Angel wanted to know. "In Spain?"

He hesitated, and when he answered it was with such obvious reluctance that Catherine looked at him sharply.

"Yes, from a Basque *guerrillero*."

Catherine, seeing that Angel was bursting with questions, spoke quickly. "Lyn, we are keeping Mr Marshall from his luncheon, and the remains of mine await me. Come now."

Unwilling but for once obedient, Angel followed her, and Osa's master soon rejoined them.

"I fear the leg of mutton was unsalvageable," he apologised to his host. "Mrs McTavish says we shall have to make do with a Welsh rarebit for dinner."

"I hope you and Mr Leigh will dine with us one of these days," proposed Mrs Sutton. "We go to Penrith next week, but perhaps the following week?"

"I shall be delighted to accept," Mr Leigh assured her, "but Donald does not in general . . ."

"Please come, Mr Marshall," entreated Angel. Ignoring Aunt Maria's frown, she continued, "There is a sad shortage of young gentlemen in the neighbourhood, and we cannot sit down five to dinner."

"An . . . Lyn!" said Mrs Sutton sharply, but Mr Marshall smiled at her and cut off any further reprimand.

"I daresay it might be managed," he allowed, and, as his friend looked at him askance, went on, "Dash it, Leigh, I cannot be

53

forever cooped up, and if we ride over the Crag . . . I shall be happy to accept your invitation, ma'am.''

Angel breathed a sigh of satisfaction.

All too soon they returned to Barrows End and there were chores to be done. Every day her aunt discovered more tasks that Mrs Applejohn adamantly refused to find time for. The girls were set to dusting the front parlour, and as Angel had never done such a thing in her life and had no idea how to go about it, it was a lengthy job.

''I cannot think why Mrs Craythorne wants so many china shepherdesses!'' she said pettishly. ''They are not at all pretty. I should like to take the poker to them.''

''Pray do not,'' begged Catherine, uncertain whether her cousin might take it into her head to carry out her proposal. ''They are hideous, I agree, but I suppose she is attached to them.''

''I know, I'll ask Aunt Maria if they can be packed away, and then we will never have to dust them again!'' She danced out, pleased with her brilliant solution, to return disconsolate a few minutes later. ''She says it is an excellent idea, both because they are dreadful and so that they will be safe from accidents. So when we have finished dusting the horrid things, we are to fetch a box from the stables and pack them in straw. Why did I ever make such a suggestion?''

''Only think how pleased you will be next time we dust,'' consoled her cousin. ''And how delightful it will be to go home in September to a houseful of servants!''

As they worked, they talked about their new acquaintances.

''Mr Leigh is a true gentleman,'' Catherine commented. ''Sensible and courteous, well informed, conversable. I thought him charming and I expect he is an admirable parson. Papa certainly seems to approve of him.''

''Should you like to marry him? He is the very person for you, I am sure. And we are not to see him for two weeks! I must try to arrange a meeting sooner.''

"But Angel, did not you tell me that Lady Elizabeth and he are sweethearts? He would make her a perfect husband, I think, but even if they have no hope of marriage because of Lord Grisedale, you would surely not expect me to set my cap at another female's beloved!"

"To tell the truth, I may have been mistaken," Angel confessed. "I did think Beth was speaking of Mr Leigh, but I did not know then of the other. Mr Marshall asked me to arrange a meeting for him with her so he must be the one she meant."

"Unless he spoke for his friend, or perhaps they are rivals," suggested Catherine, hiding a smile.

"That would be altogether too confusing! How should I know which one to help?"

"You had much better leave them to their own devices, my dear. I hope you did not offer to bring Mr Marshall and Lady Elizabeth together?"

"N-no, for you and Aunt Maria came, and there was no opportunity."

"Thank Heaven for small mercies! You had decided though, I take it, that he would be an equally unexceptionable suitor?"

"Well, no, not really. In fact at first I thought him prodigious sinister, with that dark hair and the scar and the limp. Then he turned out to be pleasant enough, but I think perhaps he is too lively for Beth."

"An intense and forceful young man, I agree."

"He might frighten Beth. Osa would if he did not."

"Not necessarily. She is not alarmed by horses."

"True, but I do not think him right for her. And he is not tall enough for you, for I am sure he does not top me by more than an inch."

"Then you are free to pursue him for yourself. With discretion, I beg!"

"If I find Beth does not love him, then I just might," said Angel, her voice full of mischief.

The next morning it was raining. It was Angel's turn to carry up hot water, so when the church clock struck seven Catherine reached out and poked her, across the narrow space which separated their beds.

"Time to get up, sleepyhead," she said cheerfully, and snuggled down again.

Angel yawned and groaned and muttered, then, resigning herself to the inevitable, she threw back the covers, shivering. She put on slippers and a wrap, looked out at the rain and groaned again, then trudged down the narrow stair.

The stove was stone-cold.

Until this week, Angel had scarcely been aware that hot water did not appear by magic in her ewer every morning. The fact that a fire must be carefully tended to provide it had been quite beyond her ken. She considered giving up and going back to bed until the Applejohns arrived to deal with the problem, but the previous evening her uncle had read her a mild scold on her unwillingness to do her share of necessary chores. She decided to demonstrate her desire to comply. She would light the fire.

It took her five minutes to work out how to open the fire-door. She peered in, and could see nothing but grey ash. No sense in trying to relight that. There was a stack of wood beside the black iron stove, so she pushed in as much as would fit on top of the ashes and looked about for a tinderbox.

She had never had any occasion to strike a light, but she had seen it done and it had not looked difficult. After a few tries she became proficient, to her delight, in striking flint against steel. The tinder began to glow as a stream of sparks fell onto it and soon a brimstone match flared up. Quickly she thrust it among the wood in the firebox. It went out. Three successive attempts ended the same way, and Angel sat down with a sigh to rest her aching hands and decide what to try next. By now she was determined not to be beaten.

Her wandering gaze fell upon a box of wood on the other side of the stove: thin sticks and twigs, shavings and dried heather. Of course! One must light smaller pieces first, and they in turn would light the larger logs. It was the work of a moment to pull out a couple of thick sticks and substitute a packed mass of kindling. She lit a match, set it to the bone-dry wood, and quickly slammed the door as it flared up.

With another sigh, of satisfaction and exhaustion, she sat down again to wait for the water to heat. A sudden thought made her jump up to check that the kettles were full. All was well, she need not go out in the rain to fetch water.

Quickly recovering her energy, Angel set about preparations for breakfast. That was one chore she had escaped so far, for Aunt Maria had decided it was more trouble to teach her to cook than it was worth. How surprised and pleased her aunt would be, she thought with a smile. Her eyes were burning, so she stopped setting the table and rubbed them. Perhaps the water was warm by now. She went over to the stove and was about to test the kettle with her hand when a puff of choking black smoke belched up into her face.

Coughing and wheezing, eyes streaming, Angel made for the door. Groping blindly she found the latch, opened it, and stumbled towards the stair, followed by clouds of pungent fumes.

''Help!'' she wailed.

It was some time before she calmed down enough to give a coherent account of her misadventure. By then Uncle Clement, a handkerchief held to his nose, had shut the kitchen door, opened the windows and the back door. The rest of the house was clear of all but a faint, pervading smell of woodsmoke, and a grumbling John Applejohn had been persuaded to rake out the stove.

At last Angel dried her tears, caused, she insisted, entirely by the smoke. She raised her soot-streaked face and red-rimmed eyes, and described precisely what she had done.

''Goose,'' said Aunt Maria kindly, hugging her. ''Air is necessary for combustion, you know. You have to rake out the ashes so that air can flow in through the grating, and then put no more wood than will allow it to circulate.''

''Don't tell me!'' Angel clapped her hands to her ears. ''If it happens again on my day, we will just have to wash in cold water."

"Hot or cold, you had better wash your face soon," advised Catherine. "You look for all the world like a climbing boy. We are going to see Lord Grisedale today, and what he'd think if he saw you now doesn't bear dwelling on. He'd certainly not guess your true identity!"

=6=

WHEN ANGEL AND the Suttons were ushered into the drawing room at Grisedale Hall, they found only Lady Elizabeth and her companion awaiting them. A footman announced that his lordship would see Mr Sutton immediately. The vicar excused himself and followed the servant, whereupon Mrs Daventry launched upon a complaint about the climate of the Lake Distict.

"It is *raining* again!" she announced in case they had not noticed. "I declare I do not know how it is to be *borne*. Three days of sunshine we had and I *quite* expect that that is all we shall see this *summer* for they say this is by far the *wettest* part of the kingdom and I am sure . . ."

Mrs Sutton and Catherine closed their ears and sat with glazed smiles on their faces, thinking their own thoughts and occasionally murmuring unintelligible comments, which seemed to satisfy Mrs Daventry. Angel had managed to seat herself and Beth on a sofa at some little distance, and they talked quietly together.

In view of the presence of the others, Angel hesitated to attempt the subject of Messrs Leigh and Marshall, so she did not even mention the previous day's visit. Instead she described her mishap with the stove, eliciting a laugh from Beth that brought Mrs Daventry's monologue to an abrupt halt.

". . . and I *assure* you in Norfolk it is very different— Why, the girls are laughing! Pray *what* did you tell her to make her laugh so, Miss Brand? I *dearly* love a joke myself."

Seeing Angel about to answer and afraid of what might emerge, Mrs Sutton hastily interrupted. "I am sure it is nonsense, ma'am, and not worth repeating. The silliest things amuse young ladies. I expect you remember that from your youth, as I do.''

This called forth an oration on Youth, followed by a series of reminiscences which nearly sent Catherine to sleep. She could not imagine how anyone who had had such a dull childhood was able to recall it in such minute detail. As she stifled her fourth yawn and wondered whether the fifth would escape her, the footman returned. His lordship requested the pleasure of the company of Mrs and Miss Sutton and Miss Brand.

The ladies rose, shook out their skirts, and followed him. Angel wondered why the summons had thrown her into high fidgets. By all she had heard the earl was an irascible old gentleman, but he was not an ogre and had no reason (as yet, she qualified) to rip up at her. Besides, he was merely an earl and Papa was a marquis, though she could not tell him so. It must be an uneasy conscience as to her intentions towards his expressed wishes for his daughter's future, she decided. But she was no dependent of his, to be bound by his wishes. She dismissed her misgivings as the footman threw open a door and bowed them through.

The room they entered was hot and gloomy. A huge fire roaring in the hearth was the only lighting, and heavy crimson drapes covered the windows, while the walls were panelled in dark wood and the only furniture was a number of leather-upholstered armchairs. In one of these Angel at last distinguished a small, hunched, elderly gentleman who, she realised to her surprise, must be Lord Grisedale, as the only other person in the room was her uncle. For no reason she could think of she had expected someone much larger.

She examined him with interest as she made her curtsy, and decided he looked bitter, surly, and miserable. The latter, she thought, could be cured at least in part by dousing half the fire and throwing open both curtains and windows. She herself was already hot and sticky and uncomfortable, and the air had a musty smell as if it had been breathed too many times.

''I beg your pardon, ma'am, for not rising to greet you,'' said his lordship to Mrs Sutton, sounding not in the least apologetic. "My physician has placed strict limits upon my freedom of movement."

"Pray do not let it concern you, my lord," she replied.

"I do not, I assure you. Are you quite comfortable at the vicarage? It is not as commodious as you expected, I daresay." The words were unexceptionable, but the tone of the earl's voice was malicious and provoking.

"It suits us very well for the summer. The surroundings make up for all the deficiencies."

Angel was full of admiration for the way Aunt Maria managed to give as good as she got without being impolite.

"Ha!" grunted his lordship. "Well, I am tired. You may go." They murmured good-byes, dropped curtsies, and were halfway to the door when he called harshly, "Wait! Gregory tells me the girls like to ride. They may borrow horses as long as a groom rides with them. Good-bye."

"Thank you very much, my lord," chorused Angel and Catherine. They curtsied yet again, and fled. Mr and Mrs Sutton joined them at a more decorous pace, and they all breathed a sigh of relief as the footman closed the door behind them.

"It is kind of Lord Grisedale to mount us," said Catherine, who was looking somewhat pale. "Papa, I feel a little dizzy."

"I'm not surprised," hissed Angel as the vicar lent his daughter a supporting arm. "My head was swimming in there, and I *never* faint."

Mrs Sutton decided that her daughter needed fresh air, so they soon made their farewells.

"I hope I never have to enter that room again," asserted Catherine in heartfelt tones, as they drove homeward.

"He is not a conciliating person," said the vicar mildly, "but he has had a deal to bear. I do not think his doctor's advice is sound."

"Certainly not!" snorted his wife. "Light and air and moderate exercise would do both body and temper a world of good, and so I shall tell him if I see him again. I am only sorry I was too taken aback by his manner to do so this time!''

Between pouring rain, chores, and the preparations for the trip to Penrith, Angel did not see Beth that weekend except to nod to her in church. So appalling was the weather, with howling gales that took a couple of slates off the roof and lashed the tall yews into an alarming frenzy, that Mrs Sutton considered postponing the outing. However, there were a number of household items, unobtainable in Patterdale, without which she could manage no longer.

When they left, late on Monday morning, downpour had diminshed to drizzle, and by the time they reached Penrith, a few promising patches of blue sky were visible. Angel was happy to find that a previous guest at the Gloucester Arms had been Richard III. She shuddered in anachronistic dread when permitted a peek into the wainscoted chamber where the wicked king had once laid his weary head, even though Catherine insisted that he had been much maligned.

The room they shared was also lined with elaborately carved panelling. Angel was immediately convinced that somewhere among the oaken roses, leaves, and bunches of grapes a secret catch must be concealed, one which properly manipulated would move aside a section of the wall to reveal a hiding place.

"It is forever happening in novels," she pointed out as she prodded and twisted in vain. "There will be a niche containing a manuscript with the confession of some awful deed, or perhaps a lost will. No, I know! Mary Queen of Scots stayed nearby, so there must have been a hiding place for Papists in Penrith. I'll wager there is a priest's hole behind this.''

"If so, I hope you find it," said Catherine generously, laughing. "But come now, Angel. Papa and Mother will be waiting.''

Between shopping and sightseeing, Angel had no leisure to investigate until the following evening. Sleepy after an entire day in the open air, they all decided to retire after dinner. Catherine helped Angel to undress, then thought of something she wished to say to her mother.

"I won't be long," she said. "Do you lock the door when I leave, and I will knock when I return."

Angel went straight to work hunting for the secret hiding place. Catherine's amusement had deterred her before, so now she seized the opportunity offered by her cousin's absence and poked and prodded and twisted. She was beginning to give up, when she pressed the centre of the umpteenth flower and distinctly heard a grinding noise.

Breathless with excitement, she pushed harder. Slowly, so slowly, an entire panel swung noisily aside, and there before her opened no mere paper-stuffed niche but what must surely be a fully fledged priest's hole. That would show Catherine!

She was in half a mind to wait to explore until the sceptic's return, then she thought of a better idea. She would hide in the tiny room, push the door nearly shut, and make ghostly groans and wails. Taking her candle to make sure of a good light, she stepped over the sill and looked around. There was nothing to see but bare, whitewashed walls, no skeleton, no ancient parchment scribbled with cries for help, not even a dry water jug and a crust baked hard with age. Still, it was a priest's hole.

Catherine must surely return soon. Angel shut the door, all but an inch-wide gap. It moved much more easily closing than it had opening. There were footsteps in the corridor, followed by a knock upon the chamber door. She had forgotten that it was locked. So much for her plan! Hurrying to let her cousin in, she stumbled against the panel, felt it move smoothly under her hand, and heard a solid click as it slid into place.

"Bother!" she said aloud, and looked for the latch. The blank wall stared back.

The muffled sound of knocking came to her straining ears. A swift glance around convinced her that the other walls were equally featureless.

"Help!" she shouted, beginning to feel dreadfully closed-in. The knocking paused, then resumed slightly louder. Catherine must surely be calling to her by now, but she heard no voice. How long would it be before the landlord permitted her uncle to have the door broken down? Would they be able to hear her directions as to how to open the panelling? Could she even remember which flower it had been? How long would the air last in this coffinlike room?

"Panic will get you nowhere," she told herself sternly. "Calm down and look more carefully."

The floor was wooden, a simple parquetry pattern in pale oak. Oak parquet in this hidey-hole? Angel studied it more closely. One rectangle was of a darker hue.

Heart in mouth, she knelt and pressed it. There was a familiar grinding noise, and a section of the floor folded down to reveal a steep stairway.

Angel gasped. Well, it was not precisely what she had been looking for, but any port in a storm. Candle held high, she started downward.

At the bottom was a square of floor scarce two feet wide, surrounded by the horribly familiar whitewashed walls. The floor was of plain boards. She sat on the bottom step, set her candle on the floor at her feet, and leaned forward to rest her head despairingly in her hands.

The riser of the lowest step was carved, with three roses just like those in the inaccessible chamber above! Not pausing to wonder whether she might emerge in her nightgown in a taproom full of tipplers, Angel crouched on the tiny floor and pressed the center of the left-hand flower. Nothing happened. Perhaps it worked the trapdoor above. She tried the middle flower. Silently the riser of the second step swung down. In the cavity it had concealed were two bulging leather bags.

At any other time, Angel would have been wildly excited. Now the need to escape was overwhelming. She pressed the third knob.

The wall to her right slid aside and there, caught in the act of loosening his cravat, stood Sir Gregory Markham.

"Good evening, Sir Gregory," said Angel.

The baronet had had a tiring day. He had left his Derbyshire estate early that morning and ridden all day, arriving at Grisedale Hall late in the afternoon. There he had found that his uncle's bailiff had left undone an extremely urgent piece of business, so, stopping only for a bite to eat, he had ridden on to Penrith. The only thing in the world he wanted was to step into the steaming hip-bath that awaited him and rest his saddle-sore limbs. The bootboy had pulled off his boots and left with them. And then a hole appeared in the wall of his chamber and through it stepped Miss Evelyn Brand, née Lady Evangelina Brenthaven, only daughter of the Marquis of Tesborough, in her nightgown.

For a moment he stared at her in disbelief, then he exploded.

"What sort of damned silly lark is this, young woman? Get out!"

"I can't," said Angel, rather annoyed. "I do not know how to open the door upstairs, and you cannot expect me to wander about the inn like this."

"You appear to be doing just that!"

"Well, but I did not mean to. I found a priest's hole and got locked in."

In spite of himself, Sir Gregory was interested. He listened attentively as the whole story came out.

"And I nearly forgot," Angel closed, "there are two bags of treasure in there. At least I think they must be treasure. Wait a minute, I'll get them."

A few moments later she emptied onto the dresser a gold crucifix encrusted with rubies and emeralds, a gold chalice set with diamonds and pearls, and a pile of gold and silver coins stamped wtih the profile of Queen Elizabeth.

They stood and looked in silent awe. Then Angel sighed and broke the trance.

"And now we have to smuggle you back to your chamber before anyone finds out you have been in mine, you tiresome child," said Sir Gregory brusquely. "I suppose I shall have to go out and see what is going on. Wait here, and don't open to anyone but me. Dash it, I've no boots!" Casting a darkling glance at his unwanted visitor and a longing one at his rapidly cooling bath, he went out.

He was gone for a good quarter of an hour. Angel had time to pass from indignation to new wonder at the jewels, and then to worry, before he returned.

"I spoke to your uncle," he reported. "They were on the point of calling the landlord but had not yet done so. We will go up your secret stairs and see if I cannot find the catch."

"I'm taking the treasure," Angel announced belligerently.

"You don't trust me with it?" For the first time since she had burst in upon him, Sir Gregory looked amused. "By all means, take it, but hurry. I shall go ahead."

As she scooped the money back into its sack, she heard him mounting the hidden steps, which creaked under his weight. When she joined him at the top he was looking around at those bare, bare walls. The room seemed even tinier with his large figure in it.

"I hope they only sent small priests to England," said Angel, squeezing out of his way.

"How did you open the trapdoor?"

She showed him the block of darker wood. The rest of the floor was all of the same paler shade.

"I can't see anything else," he admitted helplessly. "There is nothing for it, you will have to wrap yourself in my coat and go through the corridors and up the main stair."

"You could fetch my clothes for me."

"And stand outside the room in my stockings while you dress? No, the less coming and going there is, the better. I hope you are not going to be difficult," he added as she pouted, "or I shall put you over my knee and spank you."

"You would not dare!"

"Try me, Miss Brand."

Angel's resistance collapsed. Then a thought struck her. "It will not be the least use for me to go up," she pointed out gleefully, "for the key is locked in the chamber and we still cannot get in!"

Already halfway down the stair, Sir Gregory groaned.

"I wash my hands of the whole business. You may borrow my coat to go to your aunt's room and then I leave the matter in your hands."

"You are the most odious man I have ever met! Oh, there must be a way to open that wretched door! The priest was supposed to be hidden, not imprisoned. Why should the exit be so difficult to find?"

"Suppose the lower entrance was found, it would delay the searchers and perhaps give the fugitive time to escape."

If Angel had not disliked him thoroughly by this time, she would have applauded this ingenious theory. As it was, she snorted disbelievingly. "I'll look one more time," she sighed, and went back up.

This time she saw the answer as her eyes reached the level of the floor. The grain of the wood ran lengthwise on all the rectangular blocks but one, where it went across. Sir Gregory must have been standing on it last time she came up, and looked down on from above it was scarcely distinguishable. In a pet she stamped on it, and a moment later stepped out into her chamber.

The next morning, when the gaping landlord had been informed of his inn's newly discovered tourist attraction, and the cross, the chalice, and the Elizabethan money had been turned over to the nearest magistrate, Mr Sutton thanked the baronet for his part in the adventure.

"It was sheer luck," he said, "that she entered the room of someone who respected her innocence."

"Believe me, sir," responded Sir Gregory, "the only danger she was ever in from me was that I might wring her neck."

Though she did not hear this, Angel was angrier with him than ever. It had been thought wise that her name should not be publicly associated with the business in any way, so Sir Gregory had reaped all the glory.

"It is most unjust!" she stormed to Catherine. "I suppose if there is a reward for finding the treasure he will get that too."

"He will certainly turn it over to you. Angel, tell me, do you *never* consider the consequences of your actions?"

"What's the point? I was trying to be helpful when I lit the stove and all I did was fill the house with smoke. And this time I was kicking up a lark and I found a treasure! So you see, it is no use whatsoever considering consequences."

To that, Catherine found no answer.

= 7 =

"ANOTHER GREY DAY!" groaned Angel at breakfast on Friday. "It is too bad! I vow it is enough to give one the megrims."

"Are you meeting Lady Elizabeth today?" asked her aunt.

"This afternoon, perhaps. She is busy this morning. And when I was with her yesterday that odious Mrs Daventry never left us for a moment, and then Lord Welch came, so we scarcely exchanged a word. Catherine, will you go for a walk with me?"

"Not this morning, Angel. I have some mending to do and I want to read a little more of the history of Richard III that I bought in Penrith."

"History! How dull! I wish I had a novel by me."

"I must go to Patterdale this morning," said Aunt Maria. "Should you like to come with me?"

"I suppose so," replied Angel ungraciously, then, seeing the beginning of a frown on her uncle's forehead, "I beg your pardon, Aunt. Yes, I should like to come. Are you going to visit the Weird Sisters?"

"If you mean Miss Weir and Miss Swenster, I shall probably drop in for a few minutes. Mrs Applejohn mentioned that they had called while we were away."

"Did not Miss Weir say that they read a great many novels? Perhaps they will lend me some." Angel brightened.

John Applejohn drove them to Patterdale in the gig. A couple of hours later, when Mrs Sutton was ready to return, Angel begged to be allowed to walk home.

"I'd like to go down to the lake for a few minutes first," she said.

Her aunt looked dubious. "I cannot think Louisa would like me to let you walk alone about the countryside."

"It is only a half hour's walk, and it is so quiet here. Please, Aunt Maria?"

"Well, if you will not do anything bird-witted, Angel."

"I promise. Thank you."

She waved good-bye and strolled down the village street towards Ullswater. Following a path that wound among the trees, she came to a clearing at the water's edge. A coal-black horse was tethered to one side, and looking around for its owner, she saw Mr Donald Marshall sitting on a rock on the shore, gazing moodily across the lake, his dog stretched out beside him.

"Good morning, sir," she called cheerfully.

He started, then turned round, while Osa bounced up and came to meet her.

"Miss Brand! I did not hear you coming."

"I beg your pardon if I startled you." She advanced towards him across the daisy-studded grass, one hand on the dog's huge head.

"No matter," he bowed. "Are you alone?"

"Yes, and I promised my aunt I would not do anything bird-witted if she allowed me to walk on my own."

"Would she disapprove of your stopping to talk to me? Do you often do bird-witted things?"

"*I* do not think so, but I do fall into scrapes quite frequently. I expect she would not like me to be alone with a young man with whom I am scarce acquainted."

"Then do not tell her, Linnet."

"I shall not, unless she asks. Then I shall say first that Osa was with us for chaperone, and then that you call me Linnet so I can not help but be bird-witted when I am with you!"

"When you are not being gooseish," he agreed, laughing.

"Well, since birds are à *la mode* today, it seems, will you play ducks and drakes with me?"

"You mean skipping stones? I have seen it done but I've never tried. Will you show me?"

"Find some flat pebbles and I will engage to teach you the art."

They wandered along the shore, denuding it of suitable stones. Osa chased the first few they threw, she looked so hurt and embarrassed when they sank, leaving her no trophy to return to her master, that he found a stick and kept her busy with that, to the disgust of a family of mallards, which fled squawking for shelter. Each time the dog emerged from the lake she shook herself vigorously, and as she was not only large but shaggy, the humans were soon somewhat damp.

"How lucky it is warm in spite of the clouds!" exclaimed Angel, turning her back on the fifth shower.

"Yes, or poor Osa would be chilled to the bone. That water is icy."

"Believe me, I know!"

Angel's pebbles were soon skipping three or four times regularly, but try as she might, she could do no more. Mr Marshall, with effortless superiority, sent his bounding six or even seven times into the air from the lake's surface.

"Now watch this," said Angel at last. "This stone is a perfect shape, and if it does not do better for me I shall likely take a pet and never play again. Watch!" She flung it across the water. "There, it did five!" she crowed, and turned her laughing face to him.

He laughed too, but there were lines of fatigue about his mouth and his scar was scarcely whiter than his cheeks. "That last jump was more of a slide," he said, "but we will allow it this once."

"It was a very good jump! You look tired. Is your leg hurting? We had better sit down for a while."

"I am perfectly all right." His face was suddenly rigid, his mobile mouth taut. "We will go on."

"Oh, don't be bacon-brained!" begged Angel vulgarly. "I do not mean to offend you, but if you are in pain and will not admit it, it is you who are being bird-witted. Besides, I may never throw five jumps again and I wish to stop while I am ahead. Do sit down! Osa has more sense, look at her."

He relaxed slightly and smiled with an effort. "Very well, Miss Brand. Here is a convenient rock. Will you be seated, ma'am?"

"Thank you, kind sir. Pray join me, will you not? What a delightful view!"

"Yes. Tell me, Linnet, do you always say precisely what comes into your head?"

"Usually," she admitted, "though I can be discreet if I choose, I promise. But I cannot abide humbug."

"And you consider that I . . . ?"

"Why, yes! You were trying to prove yourself something that you are not, and it was not even anything of importance."

"I see what you mean. Though to me it is important. I have not yet grown used to being a cripple, you see."

"A cripple? Is that how you see yourself? Then it is no wonder that you are blue-deviled. Lord Byron limps just as badly, and he is the most sought-after gentleman in London, and odiously conceited too. Or so I have heard," she added hastily, remembering her rôle. "Did you . . . No, I shall now show you how discreet I can be and not ask you if you were wounded in the Peninsula, for Catherine said she thought you did not like to talk of it. I know: if *you* will promise to be discreet, I shall tell you what happened to me in Penrith."

Swearing secrecy, crossing his heart and spitting and hoping to die, Mr Marshall declared his eagerness to hear the tale. He proved a most satisfactory listener, expressing appropriate horror when the door clicked shut, thrilled at the discovery of the treasure, and disgusted with Sir Gregory's cavalier attitude.

"Gregory always was devilish prosy," he assured her, "or so Gerald says."

"I still think it quite abominable that everyone should be told it

72

was he who found my priest's hole. Though I daresay it would not do to have people know I was in his chamber in my nightgown. We should have thought up a way to keep that secret. It was a famous adventure though, was it not?''

"Indeed, yes! Would that it had been I who awaited you at the foot of the stairs! Of all the things I wished to do when I was a child, finding treasure is one I have never accomplished.''

"I expect we might discover another if we tried," Angel suggested hopefully. "It would not be so alarming with two of us. And if Osa was there, I should not be afraid at all.''

The dog, hearing her name, sat up and put her damp, heavy head in Angel's lap. She looked up adoringly.

"Here, Osa!" ordered Mr Marshall. "Miss Brand is just beginning to dry out.''

"I was. Perhaps I had better start homewards before she decides to soak me again." Angel stood up and brushed several long white hairs from her skirt. She saw that he was rising with difficulty from his low rock seat, and wanted to help him, but restrained herself. So as not to embarrass him, she watched the ducks diving for food.

When she turned back to him, he was picking a posy of pale blue flowers.

"I'll wager you don't know what these are," he said with his boyishly engaging grin. "No, I'll not tell you, but I'm sure you can find someone who will. Here.''

"They are very pretty, even without a name. Such a delicate shade of blue. I'll pick some of those little red flowers to go with them.''

"They will close their petals if you do. That is scarlet pimpernel, and it does not like to be picked.''

"I've heard of that. I thought it only opened if it was fine. Perhaps we will have a sunny afternoon.''

"If so, the clouds had better blow away soon. It must be near two o'clock already.''

"Oh, dear, do you think so? They will never let me walk alone again!" cried Angel. "I did so mean to be good. I did not know it was so late." As Mr Marshall pulled out his watch, a distant church clock struck one and she sighed in relief. "That is not quite so bad, then, but I daresay Aunt Maria will ring a peal over me."

"It is entirely my fault," apologised her companion. "Let me set you on your way. Thunder will carry two with ease."

"Thank you, but I should be foolish beyond permission to ride through the village with you when I do not intend even to tell my aunt I met you! I may be bird-witted, but I am not a complete numbskull."

"And I may be bacon-brained," he responded with a grin, "but I am not so lost to all sense of propriety as to propose to take you up behind me on a public street. There are half a hundred ways to pass around Patterdale without seeing a soul."

Angel had considerable difficulty arranging herself securely on Thunder's rump.

"Skirts are so silly," she said crossly. "In breeches it would be the easiest thing in the world. I do not feel very safe with no reins to hold."

"You must put your arms about my waist."

"Oh." She obeyed. "I have a lowering feeling that I should not be doing this. I am certain Mama would say it is quite improper, except perhaps in an emergency, which this is not."

"It is, if you do not wish to find yourself in the suds for dawdling. Cheer up, Linnet, and consider that I cannot even kiss you while you are behind me, so it cannot be so very shocking."

"Oh." Angel considered. His slight body was strong and supple in her arms, very much alive. A sudden warmth flooded her cheeks, and she was glad he could not see her. She *never* blushed. "Do you . . . do you wish to kiss me?"

"Any young man who is not half dead always wishes to kiss a pretty girl."

"That is not very complimentary!"

"Why not? I said you were pretty, didn't I?"

"I do not think you can have had much opportunity in Spain to practise complimenting females," she said kindly.

74

"True. May I practise on you? You must correct me when my efforts fall short of perfection."

"If you wish. I have had a great deal of experience, so I am sure I shall be able to help you. Oh, look! Someone has carved 'HER' on that tree. I've seen that before, and scratched on rocks too. It seems such an odd thing to write."

"It is short for Herbert. There is a halfwit of that name who lives in a hut on the mountain above Upthwaite. Someone once taught him to write his name and that is all he remembers of it."

"Learning even that much must have been an important event in his life if he still goes about scrawling it everywhere. It is quite an achievement for an idiot."

"He is not totally witless. I believe Welch occasionally makes him do a day's work for his rent and has made a fair carpenter of him when he can be pinned down. In fact Gerald told me just the other day that he had been working fairly steadily, under threat of having his house demolished about his ears. Poor old Herbert is greatly attached to the tumbledown shack."

"I expect it is all he has, and in this climate he certainly needs it!"

"Do not malign our climate, Miss Brand. The sun is coming out this minute, as foretold by the pimpernels. And I must set you down here, I fear. If I take you closer someone may see us. Follow this track and you will very soon come to Grisedale Beck. Then it is but a few minutes walk to the vicarage. Good-bye, Linnet."

"Good-bye, sir, and thank you for the ride." She stroked the horse's nose. "Thank you, Thunder. And good-bye, Osa, wherever you are!"

"After rabbits, I expect. I hope your aunt will not be out of reason cross." He waved, set Thunder at the low stone wall, and cantered away across the meadows, where she saw Osa join him.

Angel sighed, for no reason she could explain, and set off homeward. She had not gone far before she heard hooves behind her on the stony path and turned to find Lady Elizabeth and Sir Gregory close behind her. The baronet smiled at her in the sardonic way she particularly disliked, while Beth greeted her with delight.

"Lyn! How glad I am to see you! We have had such a dull morning visiting tenants."

"Good afternoon, Miss Brand," said Sir Gregory, dismounting. "Are you walking alone?"

"Just up from the lake," Angel replied, immediately defensive. "Uncle Clement said I might."

"Are you tired?" asked Beth. "I am sure you might ride Cousin Gregory's horse the rest of the way."

"Certainly not. It is no distance. Beth, do you know what these flowers are? I found them by the water."

"Why yes. They are forget-me-nots."

"Oh. I am afraid I have sadly crushed them." She regarded them thoughtfully but did not throw them away. "I went with Aunt Maria to see Miss Weir and Miss Swenster," she went on after a moment. "They have lent me half a dozen novels, and they said you may borrow them too, if you wish, when I am finished."

"I should like that of all things, but do not give them to me when Mrs Daventry is by. She thinks young ladies should read only sermons and essays and histories."

"Catherine actually enjoys histories. It is very strange! She was reading about Richard III only this morning."

"Have the Suttons recovered yet from the alarms of Penrith?" asked Sir Gregory. "Your aunt in particular was quite distraught when you disappeared, I believe."

Angel had not considered this aspect of the episode and was not pleased to have it pointed out to her. "They are all very well," she said shortly. "I suppose you have told Beth all about it, as I could not yesterday."

"No, I was certain that you would wish to present your version of the story. If you choose to do so now, I promise I will not interrupt."

With a disbelieving glance, but glad of the opportunity, Angel launched into a description of her adventure for the second time

76

that day. Sir Gregory was as good as his word, leading his mount in silence and with an infuriating air of boredom, which was displaced by an even more obnoxious twitch at the corner of his mouth when she waxed eloquent on the subject of his unco-operative attitude.

Fortunately Beth's breathless admiration made up for her cousin's odious cynicism, and the dénouement coincided with their arrival at the stepping stones behind the vicarage.

". . . And I stamped on the square, and the door opened at once," Angel narrated. "Oh, here we are home already. Will you come in, Beth? Then I can tell you how *he* stole my treasure, and besides, if you are with me Aunt Maria will not scold me for being late. I will walk back to the Hall with you later, so Sir Gregory need not stay."

"I believe I should pay my respects to the vicar," said that gentleman, calmly ignoring his dismissal. "Come, Cousin, let me take your bridle to cross the stream."

As Angel had planned, her arrival with Lady Elizabeth and Sir Gregory silenced all remonstrances. She hoped her aunt would assume she had been with them all the time. Mrs Sutton rang for a pot of tea, and conversation turned upon the return of sunshine and the prospect of a sunny weekend.

"Should you care to go for a ride, Miss Sutton?" Sir Gregory asked Catherine. "You have not yet taken advantage of my uncle's stables, and if it is fine tomorrow we might perhaps go up to Braddock's Force. It is not very far, and I think you would enjoy it."

"What is Braddock's Force?" demanded Angel. "Is it named after Saint Braddock?"

"You will have to ask Beth," he told her. "I know only that it is a delightful spot at the end of a pleasant ride."

"'Force' is our local word for waterfall," revealed Lady Elizabeth. "Saint Braddock is supposed to have lived beside it and practised exorcising frogs and newts before he attempted to drive the monster from Rosshead Tarn."

"Then the picture in the church is not of Ullswater?" asked Catherine. "I am so glad! I quite thought I should have to forgo boating on the lake, for I've no wish to be swallowed by a sea-serpent. A visit to the Force does sound like an attractive outing. Should you like to go, Lyn?"

"If my aunt and uncle permit," said Angel, a show of submission that impressed no one.

"As long as Sir Gregory will be present there can be no objection," the vicar decided. "But does Lady Elizabeth wish to go?"

"Oh, yes! It seems like forever since I was up there, and it was always one of our . . . my favourite places. Miss Sutton, are you able to come up to the Hall now to choose a mount?"

Angel and Catherine changed into their riding habits and the four of them walked up the lane, John Applejohn having been sent ahead with the horses. As usual when the four were together, Angel and Beth soon had their heads close, leaving Catherine to entertain the baronet. Angel had qualms about letting her cousin bear the whole burden of conversation with that disagreeable gentleman, but she simply had so much to say to her friend that there was no alternative.

Seeing the girls deep in a discussion of the novel that Beth had just finished, Sir Gregory turned to Catherine.

" 'Come, Mistress Kate, I'll bear you company,' " he said.

"Why, sir, you are out of character. It was never Petruchio who said that."

"No, it was Hortensio, I believe, but I must seize my lines where I may."

"Shakespeare had other Katherines, I think."

"But only one worth knowing: the princess of France in *Henry the Fifth*. And I'll not woo in broken French. Besides, the relevant bit is not in verse and therefore devilish hard to remember."

"You prefer verse, sir?" asked Catherine, passing hurriedly over the first part of this speech, which was obviously meaningless.

"If I am to get it by heart. Not for reading. Miss Brand mentioned that you are engrossed in a history of Richard III?"

"I am, but I cannot imagine why she should comment upon it."

"Merely to decry your taste in literature."

"I must point out to her that it would do my reputation as a bluestocking no good to be found reading the kind of novel she enjoys."

"You *wish* to be known as a bluestocking? Fie, fie, Miss Sutton!"

"One must have some sort of reputation, I suppose, and that will do as well as any. You have your own, sir, I am sure."

"Certainly. Ask your cousin and she will tell you I am a starchy, cross-grained slow-top with a deplorable tendency towards antiquated notions of propriety. In short, a horrid creature, and stricken in years to boot."

"Politeness bids me deny that she would say so, but honesty forbids! I hope you do not mind it. She does not know you well."

"If you do not share it, her opinion is nothing to me."

"That is not how I should choose to describe you, no."

"Then how?"

Catherine laughed. "There are many possibilities. How like you 'a mad-brain rudesby'? Or perhaps 'one half lunatic, a mad-cap ruffian'?"

"Hoist by my own petard," he sighed. "I believe you have been studying in preparation for just such an opportunity. Away with the Shrew! Let us talk of Hunchback Richard."

When they reached the Grisedale Hall stables, they found Lord Welch there, on the point of departing. He gladly turned back and offered his advice on the most suitable mounts for the young ladies. At the sight of him, Sir Gregory's mask of boredom had descended once again, and as he declined to voice his views, the viscount's suggestions were accepted. Miss Sutton was soon mounted on a safely sluggish bay hack and Miss Brand on a rather more lively roan, and they trotted through the park accompanied by Lady Elizabeth and his lordship. A suddenly remembered errand had called Sir Gregory into the house.

Once more Catherine was left with the gentleman, and this time Angel had no qualms about abandoning her. She had few opportunities for winning Lord Welch's regard away from Beth, and Angel hoped she was making the best use of every moment with him.

The viscount rode beside Catherine and made sporadic comments with perfunctory courtesy, but it was plain to her that his thoughts were riding ahead with Lady Elizabeth. Her dislike of the man spurred her to attempt to aid the girl by drawing his attention to herself, and after several false starts she found that the subject of gambling was one in which he was passionately interested. This, she suspected, must be the root of his need for Beth's dowry. In fact he spoke, complainingly, of large losses at the gaming tables.

"Of course there are no end of card-sharps in London," he explained to her, "and I'll wager half the ivories at Watier's are loaded. Otherwise I must have won. I challenged a pair once, but somehow they substituted good dice and I was forced to apologise. I got my own back though."

"I beg your pardon?"

"Revenge, I took my revenge. I hired a bunch of bully-boys and had that cheating liar beaten half to death."

The cold-blooded satisfaction with which he said this chilled Catherine and drove all possible responses from her lips. Lord Welch did not seem to notice her silence. He rattled on about games of hazard, macao, whist, and faro, long past and surely forgotten by the rest of the participants, congratulating himself on his minor successes, blaming his losses on trickery.

Angel, looking back, was delighted to see the couple deep in conversation. Later, as she and Catherine walked homeward, she asked what they had talked of.

"Nothing of interest," said her cousin shortly.

Something private, thought Angel, satisfied. "And what did

you speak of with the odious Sir Gregory? Why does he call you Kate? Not even Aunt Maria calls you that.''

"It is a silly joke, my dear. I wish he would stop it but he will not, and it is not worth teasing myself over.''

"He is quite the most provoking man I have ever met! I am very glad I thought to invite Lord Welch to come with us to the waterfall, are not you? *He* is a true gentleman.''

=8=

TO ANGEL'S RELIEF, Saturday was not merely fine but cloudless. She sang over her morning chores, trying to sound as she imagined a linnet might, until her uncle thrust his head around the study door and begged her to stop.

At midday Sir Gregory and Lady Elizabeth arrived. Angel and Catherine joined them, and soon they were riding up a bridle path between bracken thickets, then into the dappled shade of the woods. The plash and tinkle of an invisible stream mingled with the songs of a multitude of birds.

A keen horsewoman, Angel was content just to feel the animal moving beneath her and to soak in the green-tinted sunlight, the odours of growing things and leafmould. A lizard skittered from a rock beside the path; a jay flashed blue from tree to tree, screeching a raucous warning of their approach; a pair of red squirrels chased each other through the gnarled branches of an ancient oak. The theatres and ballrooms of London seemed far away.

In spite of her father's huge estates in Kent, Angel had spent most of her life in the metropolis. The marquis's involvement in politics had never allowed him to absent himself from the seat of government for long periods, and her mother could not bear to be parted from either husband or child. Angel had always enjoyed her brief stays in the country but thought it would be dull to live away from the amusements of the city.

On this perfect day, she began to wonder if it would really be so tedious. Beth seemed perfectly content and was never unoccupied, and *her* life was exceptionally circumscribed. Angel compared the beauty of her present surroundings with her memories of dusty, grimy London in July, where the only place to ride was the over-familiar parks, or streets full of smells from gutters and back alleys that made one gasp for fresh air. She breathed deep, filling her lungs with the scent of a honeysuckle vine running rampant over rocks and bushes.

Sir Gregory, who was in the lead, called back that he could see Lord Welch waiting for them ahead, and soon Angel saw him, standing beside his horse at a branching of the ways. Once again she noted his smartness, in contrast to the baronet's casual dress. In fact he was the most fashionable gentleman of their acquaintance in Westmorland, precise to a pin. It did seem a pity that Beth could not return his regard.

The viscount broke the spell of the quiet woods with his inconsequential chatter Angel responded, and the two of them soon fell behind.

"Let's catch up," she suggested. "I don't want to be last to see the waterfall."

"It will wait for us. We don't want Lady Elizabeth to think we are hurrying after her. In fact, I'd rather she thought we were dallying together."

"You mean you want to flirt with me to make her jealous? I don't believe you will succeed. She has not the least idea of marrying you."

"Oh, she'll come around. After all, she knows no one else in the least degree eligible, though she pretends to be in love with some imaginary fellow. To make herself interesting, I suppose. She'll get tired of it and then we'll tie the knot quick as winking. Won't hurt to make her worry a bit."

Angel was dubious, but he seemed very sure of himself, and he had known Beth forever while she had met her two short weeks ago. Perhaps she did intend to marry him in the end. No one could blame her for inventing a romance to brighten a dull life.

But what then of Mr Marshall, who had been so anxious to see her? Though he had not mentioned the matter when they met by the lake. Was it for Beth's sake that he wished her to teach him to pay compliments to ladies?

Angel shied away from the thought and urged her horse faster up the slope.

Braddock's Force was a series of falls, none high, which tumbled from pool to still, brown pool. The banks were set with mossy rocks, their crevices green with maidenhair ferns, while over the white foam of the cascade leaned a rowan tree laden with scarlet berries. Angel was delighted with the scene.

If St Braddock had indeed lived here, it was so long ago that his dwelling had merged back into its surroundings. They found a number of flat stones which might once have been part of the hermit's modest shelter. Seated on them in comfort, they consumed the excellent picnic provided by Sir Gregory.

The baronet had apparently made up his mind to tolerate the viscount for the duration, and his lordship avoided harassing Beth by either his attentions or deliberate neglect, so they had an agreeable time.

Lord Welch was in fact somewhat in awe of Sir Gregory, who in spite of his lower rank had years and inches in his favour. He found Sir Gregory's usual air of cynical boredom intimidating. As long as the earl favoured his suit, a mere cousin was not a serious stumbling-block in the way of his possession of Beth's fortune, but he thought it only commonsense to take every opportunity to turn him up sweet. It was always possible that the old curmudgeon would pop off the hooks before he persuaded my lady to toss her cap over the windmill, and then the baronet would hold the pursestrings. In fact, if she did not soon abandon her freaks and fancies, Lord Welch would find himself without a feather to fly with. He needed that dowry and he needed it soon.

Exerting himself to please, Lord Welch succeeded to the extent that Beth lost most of her nervousness, Sir Gregory and Catherine for once found his company pleasant, and Angel, denied her usual throng of admirers, went so far as to wonder momentarily whether she should pursue him on her own account. He would not have been pleased had he known how quickly she dismissed the notion. It seemed laughable when she recalled how recently she had rejected Damian Wycherly's offer.

The trouble was, she thought, that of the four young gentlemen known to her in this part of the world, none showed signs of admiring her wholeheartedly. Which led to the lowering reflection that her charms were more solidly based on rank and fortune than she had supposed. Perhaps she should purchase a feather, just a small one, for her bonnet?

As they rode back down the hill, Angel announced that, since Lord Welch was going that way, she wanted to ride up Dowen Crag.

"Should you mind riding further, Miss Sutton?" Sir Gregory asked. "It is not more than half a mile, but the way grows steep."

"Fortunately it is my horse's limbs and not mine which must bear the burden," said Catherine. "I should like to see the view."

So they accompanied Lord Welch up the track, which soon left the trees and grew rocky. On one side rose a grassy slope, while to the other the gently falling hillside became steeper as they proceeded, until the path skirted the rim of a precipice.

At last they reached the top. For the last hundred feet the cliff had grown shallower, till there was a drop of a mere fifteen feet or so, with a steep bracken-grown slope at its base. At the very highest point of the path, partly concealed by bushes, a huge slab of rock hung out over empty air. Lord Welch dismounted and walked out on it, followed by Beth and Angel.

"That looks shockingly dangerous," Catherine said. "Lyn, stay away from the edge, I beg of you."

"It has been here throughout living memory," Sir Gregory reassured her. "I suppose one day it will succumb to wind and rain, or rabbit burrows perhaps, but we must hope it will hold yet a while."

"Do come, Catherine," urged Angel. "You cannot see the view properly from there."

"Will you live dangerously?" asked the baronet with a smile, and when she nodded he helped her dismount and tied the horses beside the others.

She took his arm, wondering why she felt so unwilling to venture out upon the rock. She had never been afraid of heights, nor fearful beyond reason of physical danger. Determination overcame disinclination and she stepped forward to join her cousin.

The effort was amply repaid. The green hillside fell away towards Patterdale, and beyond stretched Ullswater, sparkling impossibly blue beneath the blue vault of the cloudless sky. Its farther shore was too distant to make out details, but on the near side they could clearly see a pony trap in the village street. Turning to the south, the beginnings of Grisedale wound into the hills, and to the north lay Upthwaite's valley.

"Think what you must be able to see from the top of Helvellyn," breathed Angel. "Catherine, I am quite resolved that we must climb to the summit one day. Have you ever been up there, Beth?"

"No, for when Dom went I was only twelve and he said I was too little."

"The only sensible thing he's ever done," commented Sir Gregory drily, earning a black look from his cousin.

"Lord, I remember that!" exclaimed the viscount. "He and I and Gerald Leigh did it together. We didn't wait for a fine day and the mists came rolling in when we were halfway down. We had to spend the night in an old shepherd's hut. Dashed lucky you were not with us, Beth! Well, I must be on my way, but if you're planning an assault on Helvellyn, count me in. Good-bye, ladies."

With a bow and a wave he swung up on his horse and rode off towards Upthwaite, leaving Sir Gregory to help the ladies mount and to escort them down the path in the opposite direction.

"What a delightful day," mumbled Angel as she snuggled down in her bed that night. "I hope you have not fallen in love with Lord Welch, Catherine. He is quite determined that Beth shall marry him."

"Never fear, Angel. I can assure you that I have not conceived the slightest tendre for his lordship."

"It will have to be Mr Leigh for you after all, I think. Good night." She fell asleep with the happy recollection that Mr Leigh and Mr Marshall were coming to dinner on Monday.

That same evening, Mr Marshall had interrupted his friend in the polishing of his sermon for the next day.

"I'm going to ask her," he announced abruptly, limping into the vicar's study.

"Ask who what?" enquired Mr Leigh tolerantly.

"Ask the Brand chit to help me meet Beth. I cannot endure this waiting much longer."

"I am not at all sure why you did not do so when you met her the other day. You told me you conversed for several minutes."

"I very nearly did ask, only she seemed reluctant that first time and I did not wish to press her. But this delay is intolerable."

"Patience never was your long suit. However, in this case I believe you are right."

"Your cursed religious scruples will not force you to throw a rub in my way, then?"

"I told you, the case is quite different. Think you she will oblige?"

"There's no knowing what she will do. She seems to act always on impulse."

"Then you are birds of a feather."

"Damn . . . Dash it, Gerald, do not preach at me! I never could abide it! I have done my best to turn her up sweet, so perhaps she will oblige."

"I hope you are not playing fast and loose with her," said the vicar rather sternly. "Have you no liking for her apart from her possible usefulness to you?"

"Lord, I did not say that. She's a pretty little thing under those quakerish garments, and she has a certain . . . *je ne sais quoi*. I didn't tell you that she rang a peal over me when I would not ad-

87

mit that my leg hurt. Called me bacon-brained and a humbug! She has a certain style to her."

"An odd little creature, but with more to her than meets the eye. You'd not consider asking the cousin? I'd wager she would be of more practical assistance."

"Possibly, but I think her straitlaced, and since she does not know the whole story she might well disapprove of acting as a go-between. No, I'll stick with Mistress Linnet, for in spite of her dress she's not one to disapprove of anything but humbug!"

Early Monday evening, the two young men rode over Dowen Crag towards Barrows End. It was an inclement evening, not precisely raining but with the air full of an all-pervading dampness. They both turned up their collars and pulled their hats down low, and the horses stepped with care on the slippery rock path.

Coming down into the Grisedale woods, they met Lord Welch, on his way homeward and equally swathed against the weather. He greeted the vicar with laconic carelessness, and glanced uninterestedly at his companion, who hunched his shoulders, hiding his face deeper in shadow. Neither the weather nor friendship invited lingering. It did not suit the viscount to associate with one who must earn a living.

Nor was Gerald Leigh eager to seek Lord Welch's society. He and Mr Marshall continued without pause down the hill to the vicarage.

Stabling their horses, they entered the house through the kitchen. Mrs Applejohn looked up from the pot she was stirring. Her rosy cheeks paled, she reached out one hand and seemed about to speak, but at a scarcely perceptible shake of Mr Marshall's head she closed her mouth firmly.

"Will you tell Mrs Sutton that Mr Marshall and I are come," requested Mr Leigh, removing his wet hat and coat and hanging them on a chair. There was nothing like a visit to Barrows End vicarage to make him appreciate the comfort and convenience of his own.

With her usual taciturnity, the old housekeeper clumped out, returning in a moment to indicate with a jerk of the head that they should go on into the house. Since that first start she had not looked at Mr Marshall, and now she returned to her pots and pans without a word.

"You were right," said Mr Leigh as they stepped into the hall. "It is unbelievable just how close-mouthed these people can be."

"Mrs Applejohn is a paragon of reticence. I'd not trust others so far."

They found Mrs and Miss Sutton and Miss Brand awaiting them in the parlour-cum-dining-room. Flowered chintz curtains and the removal of half a hundred china shepherdesses had done much to brighten the apartment, but on this gloomy day candles had already been lit and a cheerful fire lent an air of cosiness to the domestic scene.

Catherine had a book in her lap, Mrs Sutton was knotting a fringe, and Angel was struggling with some mending. As they entered she jumped up, happily abandoning her task.

"I am so glad you are come!" she cried. "I vow I have pricked my fingers with that odious needle a dozen times in ten minutes."

Mr Marshall took her hands, and while his friend greeted the other ladies, he examined them intently.

"No permanent damage, I think," he said with a sigh of relief, raising one to his lips. "I shall buy you a thimble."

"I have one, only it gets in my way. I had a thousand times rather dust than sew. It is the most tedious occupation imaginable. Good evening, Mr Leigh. Uncle Clement was called out to a deathbed. Is it not a horrid thing?"

"One of the perils of our profession, Miss Brand, as pricked fingers are a hazard of your sex. Miss Sutton does well to prefer a book."

"Catherine finished her mending hours ago, while I was out riding. Besides, she does not tear things as often as I do."

This brought a general laugh.

"I am particularly careful," Catherine admitted, "because I am no fonder of mending than you are, Lyn. Mr Marshall, will you take a glass of sherry?"

Mr Sutton came in before they had finished their drinks. Angel showed signs of wishing to interrogate him about his dying parishioner and had to be quashed by her aunt.

"All right, Aunt Maria," she submitted amicably. "It is just that there is a positively gruesome deathbed in the novel I am reading and I wished to know if—"

"What are you reading, Miss Brand?" queried Mr Marshall hastily, and was soon deep in a discussion of a number of the more lurid offerings of modern authors. He and Angel found themselves in perfect agreement on a preference for wicked noblemen over mad clerics.

Mrs Applejohn brought in a tureen of green pea soup, and they moved to the table. When a roast leg of lamb made its appearance, Angel enquired after Osa.

"I persuaded Donald not to inflict the brute on you," revealed Mr Leigh.

"She's not a brute!" said Angel indignantly.

"I hope you did not leave her in the kitchen?" Mrs Sutton asked with a smile.

"No, I tied her in the stable," Mr Marshall assured her. "Mrs McTavish has not yet forgiven me for that mutton, I fear. I have to go on my knees to beg for scraps for Osa."

After the meal they returned to the parlour half of the room, and studiously pretended to be unaware of Mrs Applejohn clearing the table. Mr Sutton offered the gentlemen brandy and port, which was accepted on condition that the ladies should not feel obliged to withdraw. Mr Marshall was wondering if he had been overoptimistic in supposing that he would have a chance to speak privately to Linnet, when her uncle was once more called away and Mrs Sutton went to see him off.

Relying on Mr Leigh to entertain Miss Sutton, he abandoned his scarcely touched brandy and turned to her cousin.

"Miss Brand," he began, "I have a particular request to make of you, which I have mentioned before. I hope you will not think me impertinent to apply to you a second time."

"You mean about Lady Elizabeth? I wondered if you would ask me again. I did not like to do anything until I was certain you were in earnest."

"Very much so, Linnet. It is imperative that I see her. I cannot tell you more, but I assure you that I mean no harm. In fact, she will be excessively grateful to you if you will help to arrange a meeting."

"Without anyone else finding out, sir?"

"Yes. I know it looks odd, but there are circumstances which render it impossible for me to approach her openly. I am not merely knocking up a lark, I promise. Linnet, help me!"

Surprised by the desperation in his tone, Angel abandoned her reservations, which truth to tell had more to do with jealousy than considerations of propriety.

"I will," she declared. "Give me a few days to persuade her. Can you meet me on Friday, so I can tell you what goes on?"

"Of course. Down by the lake?"

"No, on that big rock at the top of the path over the Crag. No one will see us there, except from so far away they won't be able to see who we are. And we can see anyone coming."

"The Crag then. At noon, if that suits you. Linnet, you don't know how grateful I am." He took her hand and was going to kiss it, but she pulled it away from him.

"I wish you will not call me Linnet," she said crossly.

Meanwhile, Catherine was talking to Mr Leigh about the possibility of boating on Ullswater.

"I'd be happy to lend you my rowboat," he said, "but it is too small to carry more than three."

"You are an oarsman, sir?"

"Yes indeed. My mother lives on the other side of the lake, and I row across to see her every week, unless it is stormy. It is considerably shorter than riding around, and I enjoy the exercise."

"Then when we find a boat, we will hire you to go with us!"

Mrs Sutton came back into the room, the tea tray was called for, and the young gentlemen soon took their leave. Catherine and Angel went up to their chamber and heard the men talking as they saddled their horses.

"Curse this rain!" came Mr Marshall's voice. "I'm going back over the Crag."

"Don't be a fool! It is pitch dark, you'll break your neck."

"I've no mind to ride six miles and get soaked to the skin. I know the way like the back of my hand. You go around and I'll be waiting for you. Good-bye!"

There was the sound of horses going in opposite directions, and then silence.

"What a reckless young man Mr Marshall is," commented Catherine.

"Yes," agreed Angel sadly. "I was beginning to like him, but he is in love with Beth after all. Oh, well, there is always Damian Wycherly!"

9

THE NEXT DAY the ladies of Barrows End vicarage had an invitation to take a dish of tea with Miss Weir and Miss Swenster in Patterdale. It was a pleasant day, with a balmy breeze blowing and high wisps of mare's tail lending interest to an otherwise azure sky. Having completed their shopping, they sent John Applejohn home with their purchases in the gig and proposed to walk back after their visit. Even Mrs Sutton, to whom exercise was usually anathema, declared that the weather was too fine to waste.

The Weird Sisters, as Angel had christened them in an unexpected burst of erudition, lived in the end cottage of a row. It was slightly larger than its neighbours and this, together with its immaculate garden and genteel inhabitants, lent it a certain status. Tall, thin Miss Swenster, an aspiring poet reputed to have "a way with words," had named it Rose End, and short, plump Miss Weir never tired of pointing out the clever pun as she showed visitors around her rose garden.

When the Suttons and Angel arrived, she was busy clipping deadheads off the bushes.

"Oh, dear!" she exclaimed, bustling up to them. "Is it three o'clock already? Not that I mean to suggest that you would not arrive on time! Is it not a delightful day? Perhaps you would like to see my roses before we go in? The sun brings out their perfume, I always say. Let me cut a bouquet for you to take home. There are plenty, I assure you. Rose End we call our little house, you know, and at the end of the row too. So clever of dear Tabitha!"

Still chattering she led them into the house, and Angel wondered why her endless talk was so much less irritating than Mrs Daventry's. They sat down to tea in a charming drawing room with French windows onto the garden, and as she consumed cucumber sandwiches and seedcake, Angel told Miss Swenster how much she was enjoying the novels she had borrowed.

"And Lady Elizabeth would like to read them too, if you are sure you can spare them so long," she added.

"Of course, of course," twittered Miss Weir. Her friend's reputation seemed to be based at least in part on the rarity of her speech. "The poor little lady, I declare she is no better off than poor Princess Charlotte, and how the Prince Regent can behave so monstrous unkind is more than I can understand!"

"Why, what has he done?" asked Catherine. "Papa will not have any newspapers in the house while we are on holiday, you know."

"He has forbidden Princess Charlotte to see her mother! Is not that unnatural in a husband and father? When I think how the poor Princess of Wales must feel to be separated from her only child, it makes my heart bleed, indeed it does." Miss Weir dabbed at her eyes with a tiny wisp of lace. "Did you ever hear of such a shocking thing, Mrs Sutton? The ways of the male sex are quite incomprehensible to me, I am glad to say, but . . ." She prattled on, and Angel ceased to listen, turning to a pile of copies of the *Gazette* which she found upon an occasional table at her elbow.

The talk of goings-on at Court had whetted her appetite for news of her own circle, daily trivia being the sole content of her mother's letters. She was turning to the gossip column to see who was staying where and with whom, when her eye was caught by the heading "Announcements."

"A betrothal is announced," said the first, "between Lady Anne Ardsworth, daughter of the Earl and Countess of Ardsworth, and Lord Damian Wycherly, eldest son of the Duke and Duchess of Medcliff." It could not be true! Admittedly, Damian had confessed under pressure that he was merely "fond" of her, but that was scarce six weeks ago. How could he do this to her?

She turned quickly to the gossip page, which was full of little else. "Having been rejected by the cruel Lady E. B., better known as A.," it began, "Lord D. W. has found consolation in the arms of Lady A. A." At least they acknowledged that he had proposed to her first! Angel read no further but sat in a daze, answering at random when spoken to.

Mrs Sutton noticed her distraction and brought their visit to an end as quickly as politeness allowed. Angel recovered her composure sufficiently to thank their hostesses and bid them a courteous farewell. Then they were out in the street and walking towards Grisedale.

As soon as they left the bustle of the village street, Mrs Sutton and Catherine turned to her with questions hovering on their tongues.

"Damian is going to be married!" she burst out. They looked blank. "Lord Wycherly! Damian! He asked me to marry him just last month and I refused him!"

"But Angel, if you love him, why did you refuse him?" asked Catherine.

"I don't love him!"

"Then why are you thrown into high fidgets?"

"How can you ask? It is hardly complimentary that he is so easily consoled. Everyone will say he never really loved me."

"To whom is he betrothed?" asked Aunt Maria quietly.

"To Anne Ardsworth. A silly, fluffy female without an idea in her head. It does not bear thinking about!"

"Have you thought how she must feel? To her it must seem that everyone is saying he only asked her because he could not have you. A most uncomfortable position to be in."

"Oh." Angel paused. "I had not considered. You are right, Aunt Maria, I should not like to be in her shoes for anything."

"Do you know her? Then I think you had better write to her

and wish her happy. If you are not sure what to say, I expect Catherine or I can help, unless you had rather consult your uncle.''

''N-no, I can do it. Must I really . . . ? Yes, I suppose I must.''

Angel was very quiet the rest of the way back to Barrows End, and the beauty of the day was lost on her. As soon as they reached the vicarage, she found pen and ink and sat down to compose a letter. It took her some time, but at last she was satisfied. She showed it to Catherine.

''Do you think it will do?'' she asked as her cousin finished reading it.

''Certainly. It is generous of you to say that Lord Wycherly did not love you, Angel.''

''It's true. He told me that he worshipped me and then that he was deuced fond of me. That's not love, is it?''

''I don't think so,'' said Catherine cautiously. ''I do not believe it is what I should look for in a husband.''

''Nor I. Well, I hope they will be happy together, but you know, that leaves me at a stand. I quite expected Damian to be waiting for me if I did not find romance this summer.''

''You are not yet at your last prayers, my dear. And do not tell me again that you will be nineteen in September. Spare the feelings of your aged cousin.''

''I quite think you and Mr Leigh will make a match of it. You were talking to him forever yesterday, were you not? He will suit you much better than Lord Welch. You do like him?''

''He is an estimable gentleman. Now come and show your letter to Mother. She will be pleased with it, I know.''

For the next two days rain fell in a deluge. Placid Grisedale Beck became a torrent, and Angel saw nothing of Beth. However, they had been invited to Grisedale Hall to dine on Thursday, and in the middle of the afternoon the rain miraculously faded away. They drove up the muddy lane between wet hedgerows and meadows gleaming in the evening sun.

Lord Grisedale was in the drawing room to greet them, along

with his daughter, her companion, and his nephew. Although he did not rise as they entered, he seemed to be in a better humour than on their previous visit. Angel soon decided this was due to the malicious pleasure he took in bullying Beth and Mrs Daventry. Nothing either of them did or said met with anything but unqualified disapproval, nor did their silence please him.

The burden of making a show of conversation was taken up by Mrs Sutton and Sir Gregory, who endeavoured to attract the old man's attention to themselves. His disagreeable comments were met by the baronet with polite boredom, and by the vicar's wife with tart rejoinders which at first seemed to infuriate him, but at last surprised a crack of laughter from him. Angel thought his laugh sounded rusty from disuse.

Once again, Angel was filled with admiration of the way her aunt handled the provoking old earl, and she resolved to copy her when her turn came to endure his megrims, as it inevitably did.

"Come here, girl," ordered his lordship, glaring at her from under his beetling brows.

She went to stand before him and performed her best curtsy.

"My lord?" she enquired.

"What have you and Eliza been up to together?" he barked.

"*Beth* and I have not seen each other since Monday, sir, because of the rain." She knew her friend hated to be called Eliza. Lord Welch sometimes did so to tease her.

"Bah! I did not ask when you last met, but what sort of mischief you have been leading her into! She never had an ounce of pluck in her. Always followed D . . . other people about like a tantony-pig."

"Papa!" whispered Beth pleadingly. "Pray do not—"

"Be quiet, girl! You, what's your name, answer me."

"I've not led her into any mischief, sir, and it's not fair to call her hen-hearted just because she does not get into any on her own."

"Saucy chit! If you were mine I'd—"

"Uncle," interrupted Sir Gregory with an air of ineffable

weariness, "I believe you wished to speak to Mr Sutton about the Sperlings?"

Angel was rather annoyed with him. She felt she was doing quite well and was sure she could have thought up an excellent retort for whatever dastardly suggestion Lord Grisedale came up with. Resuming her seat beside Beth, she smiled at her with satisfaction.

"I am so sorry," murmured Beth. "That he should speak so to a guest! He only did it to put me to the blush, you know. You were so brave to—"

"Elizabeth!" roared her father. "Either hold your tongue while I am speaking or leave the room!"

Mrs Sutton did not find the prospect of conversation with Mrs Daventry sufficiently appealing to risk calling down that wrath upon her head, and the room became so quiet that everyone was soon perfectly cognisant of the Sperlings' business. It was a great relief when dinner was announced.

Lord Grisedale took in Mrs Sutton, and the vicar gave his arm to Lady Elizabeth. Sir Gregory followed with Catherine, leaving Angel and Mrs Daventry to tag along behind. Angel thought disconsolately of her mother's perfectly arranged dinner parties, where no lady could conceivably be left without a partner.

They ate in state at an unnecessarily long table which made it necessary to speak loudly in order to be heard by one's next-door neighbour. Angel did not even try, concentrating instead on the excellent food. Her uncle, on her left, did no more than throw her an occasional encouraging smile, and Mrs Daventry, seated between her and Lord Grisedale, uttered no more than four words during the entire meal.

"Pass the salt, please," she requested.

"Don't interrupt, woman," snapped his lordship, who was conversing quite happily with Mrs Sutton.

The vicar had calmly moved his chair down the table until he was close enough to Lady Elizabeth to talk quietly with her. A scandalised footman hurried to bring his plate and a multiplicity of knives, forks, spoons, and glasses after him. He soon had Beth looking more cheerful, but she did not attempt to speak to Catherine, on her other side. Catherine was in any case being adequately entertained by Sir Gregory. He said something that made her laugh, and thus inadvertently brought the earl's unwanted attention upon her.

"What's the joke, miss?" he roared down the length of the table. "Come on, speak up! What are you laughing at?"

"A *bon mot* of Sir Gregory's, my lord," she answered composedly.

"If it is so funny, I want to hear it. Speak up, girl."

"I fear it would be incomprehensible out of context, sir. I cannot repeat our entire conversation."

"Not fit to be aired in public, eh? You ought to be ashamed of yourself, young woman. In my day . . . " He went back to his discourse with Mrs Sutton, and not a moment too soon. Catherine had not lost her composure, but both her mother and father had been on the point of intervening, and on Sir Gregory's face was a look of anger such as she had not thought that cool gentleman capable of expressing.

Lady Elizabeth was almost in tears with embarrassment. With a smile of apology to the baronet, Catherine joined her father in soothing her ruffled sensibilities, and soon the girl had recovered her complexion sufficiently to give a sign to the ladies to withdraw. They needed no second invitation.

Mrs Daventry started talking the minute they were out of hearing, drowning Beth's apologies.

"The haricot was tolerable good, was it not, my *dear* Mrs Sutton, but the sirloin was *sadly* overdone and I do think the leg of pork was on the dry side also, which . . ."

She seemed oblivious of any unpleasant occurrences beyond the imagined spoiling of a few dishes. It suddenly struck Angel that the reason she did not mind Miss Weir's chatter was that that little lady was as cheerful as Mrs Daventry was censorious.

This reflection brought back a memory of Lord Wycherly's perfidy, and it was in brooding silence that Angel took her seat on a sofa beside Beth, as far from the others as possible.

"I fear you are much offended," said Beth hesitantly. "Papa is quite outrageous. Pray do not suppose that it is directed particularly at you, for he is the same to everyone."

"Is he? Then I am surprised that anyone visits you at all. Oh, Beth, do not cry, I beg you. I shall not desert you, I promise, so do not fall into the mopes."

"It is unbearable, Lyn. I do not know how I survived before you came, nor how I shall when you leave. I would even marry Lord Welch to escape from here!"

"He told me you would in the end. He thinks you are pretending to be in love with someone else."

"How dare he! Just because the man I love is too honourable to seek to see me against Papa's wishes! I have not met him since Francis came home from London, so he knows nothing of the matter."

"That is three years ago, you were only sixteen! Have you never seen him since then?"

"Not to talk to, only to exchange bows. But I could tell by the way he looked at me that he still felt the same. Lyn, what shall I do? I cannot marry Francis, I cannot stay here, *he* will not take me without my father's blessing. What shall I do?"

"Beth, Mr Marshall wants to see you! He must have realised how chuckleheaded it is to stay away for such a nonsensical reason. He asked me to arrange a meeting, so—"

"Who? What are you talking about? Who is Mr Marshall?"

"Why, Mr Leigh's friend!" Angel exclaimed. "Your—"

"Mr *Gerald* Leigh?" queried Mrs Daventry, who had paused for breath at the wrong moment. "The vicar of Upthwaite? There *was* a time, you know, when he was quite an *admirer* of dear Lady Elizabeth, or so the *earl* tells me, but that is all past, for his father was only the *fourth* son of a *baron* so you see he is *quite* ineligible, though I daresay he is entitled to be considered a gentleman and of course his *mother* is a *Cranbourne* and may hold up her head with the *highest* but there, the son must earn *his* living for there is only the house and *no* land, and I believe a *small* amount in the Funds but not enough to live upon with any degree of *elegance*, and with no rank, fortune is *essential* though even were he rich as *Golden Ball* he could not aspire to the hand of a female in Lady Elizabeth's position. Lord Grisedale was *forced* to give the young man quite a *set-down*," she went on in a lowered voice to Mrs Sutton.

Angel turned her attention back to Beth, and was shocked to find her pale and shaking. Catherine also noticed her agitation and came to see if she could be of any assistance.

"Beth, what is it?" asked Angel urgently, but softly, clasping her hand.

"Nothing, it is nothing," she said, on the edge of tears. "Pray do not . . . I must . . ."

"I think you must retire to bed," suggested Catherine. "It has been a shockingly difficult evening for you, my dear. We will make your excuses if you wish to go, or perhaps you would like Lyn to go with you?"

"No. Thank you. Please do not . . . Pray excuse me, I am very tired." Lady Elizabeth managed to bob a curtsy to Mrs Sutton on the way to the door, then disappeared without another word.

It was all they could do to stop Mrs Daventry following her. The vicar's wife absorbed Catherine's brief explanation: "Tired, nerves overset," and set herself to soothe the anxious companion. In this she succeeded so well that by the time her husband and Sir Gregory joined them, the lady's tongue was rattling on as fast as ever.

Like his daughter, Lord Grisedale had retired. It was generally agreed that in the absence of both host and hostess the party should break up. Sir Gregory seemed reluctant to see them go, but he acquiesced with a good grace.

"Shall we see you tomorrow?" he asked Catherine, under cover of Mrs Daventry's chatter, as he helped her with her wrap. "I hope tonight has not given you an ineradicable distaste for our society."

"Pray do not regard it, sir. It is for us to hope that Lady Elizabeth will not hold us to blame for her discomfort."

"I should be sorry to think my cousin so lacking in discernment. We shall, then, go on as before? 'I am sure, sweet Kate, this kindness merits thanks.' No, do not tell me Petruchio demanded thanks when he spoke thus. Take it as I mean it, for I do thank you. Miss Brand, will you come and see Beth tomorrow?"

"Of course, if she wishes to see me," Angel assured him. "I'll come in the afternoon, unless she writes to say not to. I hope she is feeling better by then. Good night, Mrs Daventry."

"Good night, Miss Brand. I trust you will remember what his lordship said to you."

"I certainly shall, ma'am, I certainly shall."

Catherine heard these words with an uneasy feeling that there was more to them than was obvious. She hoped Angel would confide in her, in her usual candid manner, but her cousin prepared for bed in a thoughtful silence.

Angel was pondering Lord Grisedale's attack on her. It was most unjust in him to suggest that she had been leading Beth into mischief. However, having been blamed before the fact, her conscience was much easier about her future plans, of which his lordship would undoubtedly disapprove. Only how was she to persuade Beth to meet Mr Marshall? It was very odd that she denied knowing him, and whatever had come over her when Mrs Daventry had been disparaging Mr Leigh? Not to mention the fact that she had earlier asserted that she was prepared to marry Lord Welch!

Angel was thoroughly confused. She would have liked to consult Catherine, but she had told Mr Marshall she would keep his request secret. Lying in the dark, her head buzzing with speculations, she decided that he must allow her cousin to take part in their plans. And to convince Catherine that his aims were innocent, his friend Gerald Leigh, a clergyman she had described as estimable, must also be involved. Between the four of them, surely they could bring about a meeting with Beth.

And then perhaps she would find out just who it was that Beth was in love with!

The next morning, Aunt Maria was overwhelmed by the speed with which Angel completed her chores. She would have to walk up the Crag and she did not know how long it would take, so by half past ten she was ready to go. With fingers crossed behind her back, she asked her aunt if she could go for a short stroll on her own along the track by the stream. Mrs Sutton, busy folding and counting linen with Catherine, agreed absentmindedly.

She hurried down the meadow and over the stepping stones. Brilliant sunshine was already drying the muddy banks of Grisedale Beck, and the stony track was easy going. She noticed scarlet pimpernels everywhere, raising their bright, tiny faces as if to confirm that it was a fine day.

By the time she had struggled up the bare, rocky path, she was hot and thirsty. She went out on the overhanging rock and looked down towards Upthwaite. The distant sound of a church clock told her it was only half past eleven, so she moved back to the shade of some bushes by the path, and sat down to wait.

Scarce ten minutes later Osa bounded up to her, saluted her wetly on the cheek, and rolled over, moaning her need to have her chest scratched.

"You big baby," said Angel, petting her. "Where's your master?"

He was not far behind.

"Where is your horse?" he greeted her, dismounting and throwing Thunder's reins over a bush. "Don't tell me you walked all this way? I must have been half sprung to have suggested this place! I had not thought . . ."

"You hardly drank anything, it was I who suggested it. You said by the lake. I had not thought, either, that I could not go off on my own on a horse! Never mind, the walk is not so bad if I had not been hurrying. There were pimpernels and lots of other flowers. I am determined to learn their names."

"Did you ever find out the name of the flowers I picked you?"

"Yes, I did. Mr Marshall, Beth acted as if she does not know you! It is very odd, but I was not able to talk to her about it; we were interrupted. Is it really Mr Leigh who wants to see her?"

He groaned and dropped his head in his hands. "I had not thought! Of course she would not recognise my name."

"If you do not know each other well enough to have exchanged names, I cannot guess why you are trying to meet her in this surreptitious manner! It seems to me, sir, that you never do think," said Angel in condemnatory tones.

"I do know her! I've known her for . . . for years and years. And I daresay Gerald would *like* to see her, but I *must*. If you do not trust me, will you take his word that I have no dishonourable intentions?"

"I do trust you, so don't climb up on your high ropes. I have a plan, only Catherine will have to be in it too. And I think it would be a good thing if Mr Leigh is also, because he is respectable and a minister. Now listen . . ."

Twenty minutes of lively argument served to work out the details of their conspiracy. Angel pledged herself for Catherine's cooperation, and Mr Marshall for the vicar's.

"I must go," said Angel at last. "I told Aunt Maria I was just going for a stroll. Osa, take your head off my feet."

"I'll take you halfway on Thunder," offered Mr Marshall.

"No, thank you; with two of us he would probably go off the cliff."

"I can lead him."

"Humbug! It would take me twice as long to get home, and for all I know you would be laid up for a week. Good-bye, Mr Marshall. We'll see you tomorrow."

He gazed after her with amused exasperation till she disappeared among the trees.

=10=

TO ANGEL'S SURPRISE, Catherine was perfectly willing to help bring Lady Elizabeth and Mr Marshall together, even before she had been assured of Mr Leigh's approval. She suggested that Sir Gregory should be included in the party; after all, he disapproved of Lord Welch as a suitor for Beth and might be relied upon to take his cousin's part.

"How can you say so?" responded Angel. "I should never rely on him to be anything but a marplot. Swear you will not tell him."

"Very well, I will not. That means we must persuade him as well as Mrs Daventry not to accompany us on Monday."

"That's easy. Only wait and see. But you must dispose of her."

They were walking up the track to Grisedale Hall as they talked. They found Lady Elizabeth in good frame, though paler than usual. Angel immediately proposed a horseback outing for the following Monday, and her friend listlessly acquiesced.

"I thought we might ride into Patterdale and look about the shops," Angel went on, peeping from the corner of her eye at Sir Gregory. "I have a ribbon to be matched and I need some lace and a new pair of gloves, and if I can find some sprig muslin I like I may buy enough for a dress, and, oh, a thousand things. Shall you come with us, Sir Gregory?"

"Thank you, ma'am, I believe I shall be fully occupied about the estate on Monday," he replied.

Angel shot a glance of triumph at Catherine.

"I shall try to match *my* ribbon also," declared Mrs Daventry, "so we will take the *carriage*, though whether it is worth the effort in *Patterdale* for the shops are *quite* beneath one's notice if there were anything better within reach, and I declare one may compare shades *hour* after *hour* . . ."

"It is a tedious business," agreed Catherine quickly. "If you care to entrust me with your ribbon, I shall do my best to match it for you. I daresay the shops will be excessively busy on Monday."

"My *dear* Miss Sutton, I cannot *possibly* ask you to take on such a *wearisome* task in my behalf, *indeed* I cannot, it would be the *outside* of enough, though a *younger* person does not feel the *strain*, I believe, as does a *mature* person . . ."

"I shall be happy to do it, ma'am. I have few errands of my own and it will occupy the time while I wait for the girls. We *mature* ladies know how long they take, giggling over every little thing and endlessly changing their minds."

"If you are *quite* certain it will not be an *imposition*, Miss Sutton. I will fetch the ribbon immediately."

"Bravo!" congratulated Angel *sotto voce* as Mrs Daventry sailed out. She and Catherine exchanged grins.

"If I were a suspicious man," complained Sir Gregory, "I should suspect that I succumbed rather more easily to similar tactics. It is not a flattering reflection!"

With a guilty look, Catherine said breezily, "You must allow young ladies a few secrets, sir."

"And *mature* ladies?"

"Mature ladies also. It is a beautiful day, I should very much like to stroll about the gardens."

"Allow me to accompany you," he offered with alacrity. "Being of mature years, I suppose we can dispense with a chaperone? We will leave the *young* ladies to their secrets."

The prompt reappearance of Mrs Daventry did not allow Angel to indulge in any confidences. As with so many of her visits with Beth, the rest of their time together permitted nothing more intimate than an exchange of sympathetic smiles.

As she and Catherine walked home, she came to a sudden decision.

"If nothing comes of this meeting," she announced, "Beth shall come and stay with me in London this winter, even if I have to abduct her. Between her papa and her companion and her cousin, I do not believe she will survive another year at Grisedale Hall!"

The next day they met Mr Marshall and Mr Leigh in the woods, where anyone crossing the Crag would not see them. Catherine found she was relieved after all to find that the young vicar was lending his support to the venture.

"I was sure it was the right thing to do," she explained to him, "but those two hotheads are ripe for any harebrained fetch. I am glad I shall not be the sole voice of reason."

He regarded her quizzically. "I think you know more than you have been told, Miss Sutton," he said. "You have a discerning eye. Is anything hidden from you?"

"Only your feelings, sir, into which I will not pry."

"I will tell you this much, as a warning: I am not absolutely certain that I can be relied upon to act reasonably, under certain circumstances. You must be my anchor as well, if you will."

"I shall do my best, Mr Leigh, and hope that your conception of reason is not too different from mine."

"Am I to take that as a warning?"

"Under certain circumstances, yes," she replied with a laugh. "I find I am eager for this confrontation. Let us see if the others have agreed upon the time and place."

Final arrangements having been made, they parted. Angel was pensive on the way home, but when they reached the stepping stones across the beck, she stopped on the middle one, turned precariously to face Catherine, and announced:

"Mr Marshall loves Beth and Beth loves Mr Leigh. I do not see how we will ever sort it out."

"It will all work out in the end, Angel," Catherine assured her tranquilly. "Pray do not make me stand on this stone any longer, or I shall certainly fall in!"

* * *

Sunday seemed endless, and Monday morning's chores a thousand times more tiresome than usual. At last Beth arrived at the vicarage, accompanied by a groom leading two horses.

An hour later, their shopping completed in record time, Angel persuaded Beth to take them to see the place where Wordsworth saw his "host of golden daffodils."

"Should you like to go, Miss Sutton?" Beth asked.

"I should like it of all things, Lady Elizabeth. It is a perfect day for such an outing."

"Call her Beth, Catherine," said Angel impatiently. "She has been wanting you to this age but did not like to ask because you are so much older."

"Lyn, you have a positive genius for making me feel like a granny, or at least an aunt! Beth, you will call me Catherine, of course. You are right, it is much more comfortable."

The groom was sent home with their purchases. In view of Catherine's advanced years, even Beth agreed that there could be no objection to the three of them riding together.

They trotted down to Ullswater, and Beth led them along the path where Angel had met Mr Marshall. The shallows at the lake's edge were alive with mallards, coots, and moorhens, and farther out a family of swans sailed majestically, admiring their own reflections in the still water.

Soon Beth remarked that they were near their destination. Deciding that she must have some warning of what lay ahead, Angel told her they were meeting Mr Leigh.

Pale as a ghost, Beth pulled up her horse. "Lyn, I cannot! I promised Papa—"

"Never to speak of him. That is what you told me. It *is* him then! You did not say you promised not to speak *to* him."

This sophistry left Beth speechless.

"Did you ever give your word not to meet him?" asked Catherine gravely. Beth shook her head. "Well, I daresay Lord Grisedale assumed you would not, but one cannot be bound by other people's assumptions, especially when, if you'll pardon my speaking so, he is given to unreasonable and extravagant demands.''

"Beth, you will not be such a wet-goose as to ruin his life just because your papa is a knaggy old gager!''

"Lyn, where did you come by such an expression?'' demanded Catherine, and even Beth smiled faintly.

"You are very persuasive,'' she admitted. "There will be someone else there also?'' Almost as if she did not realise it, she had set her horse walking again.

"Yes, Mr Marshall. You said you do not know him, but he is very insistent that he must see you. Mr Leigh is coming just to reassure you, because he is a parson so you can trust him.''

"I should trust Gerald if he were a tinker!'' Beth assured her fervently. "If he thinks I ought to see Mr Marshall, I will do so, though I cannot imagine . . .''

They came out of the shade of the woods into a wide, grassy clearing dotted with huge old oaks. Mr Leigh was sitting alone on a fallen tree trunk, but Angel saw that Thunder was tethered beside his sorrel gelding. The young man rose when he saw them and came towards them.

Catherine and Angel dismounted but Beth, who had stopped in mid-sentence on catching sight of him, sat in the saddle as though transfixed. His face as pale as hers, he went to her, took her hand in both his, and looked up at her. After a moment of silent communion, he lifted her down.

"There is someone here to see you,'' he told her, holding her hands. "He is waiting in the woods.''

"You will not leave me alone, Gerald?''

"Not unless you wish it, and I think you will. Come, Beth.''

He led her down a path that was little more than a rabbit track. Angel strained her eyes to see from the brilliant sunshine into the deep shade, but could make out nothing. They heard a sudden, wordless cry of joy from Beth. Then Mr Leigh returned to where they waited.

"I beg your pardon for not greeting you,'' he apologised, now rather flushed. "Let me tie your horses. Will you sit down upon this log? I have spread a rug over it."

"How very thoughtful, Mr Leigh," Catherine approved.

"I do not understand at all," confessed Angel as the vicar led their mounts to the other side of the clearing. "It seemed quite clear for a moment that he and Beth are in love with each other, only then he took her to Mr Marshall and it does not appear to vex him in the least that they are alone together. Does she wish to marry both of them, like a Mohammedan?"

"I believe the Mohammedan men take several wives, and not the other way about," Catherine pointed out with a sympathetic smile. "I know you are confused, Angel, but you will soon discover the whole, I am sure."

Mr Leigh's return silenced Angel's demand for an explanation. They conversed in a desultory way upon topics of general interest, in which none of the three seemed to have any interest whatever. At last they heard the rustle of approaching footsteps. Swinging round, Angel saw the missing pair embrace, before they came arm in arm to rejoin the party.

The joy on Beth's face was overwhelming, and quite unlike the pale hesitancy with which she had greeted Mr Leigh. She sparkled, thought Angel, and she almost danced up to them, while Mr Marshall, his arm about her waist, had a look of relaxed happiness very unlike his usual tense bearing. His limp was scarcely noticeable.

"Why did not you tell me?" cried Beth. "All these months I did not know if he was alive or dead!"

"I have not seen you," reminded Mr Leigh gently.

"I guessed," said Catherine, "but how could I tell you when I might have been wrong?"

"I've not the least idea what you are talking about," grumbled Angel. "Will someone please enlighten me?"

Mr Marshall took her hand. "You mean you truly do not know, Linnet? I was certain you must at least suspect."

"Suspect what?" she demanded, pulling her hand away in exasperation. "I vow I shall never speak to any of you ever again."

"Why, this is Dom!" explained Beth soothingly. "My brother, Lord Dominic Markham."

"At your service, Miss Brand," said Lord Dominic, and bowing low, he repossessed himself of her hand and raised it to his lips.

For once, Angel was speechless.

Catherine broke the brief silence. "I am loath to end this happy occasion," she said, "but we have been gone a long time, the groom returned without us, and we must be on our way."

"When shall I see you again, Dom?" asked Beth. "Tomorrow?"

"Yes, I don't see why not. We can meet on Dowen Crag. Gerald?"

"I cannot see Lady Elizabeth again," said Mr Leigh with uncharacteristic harshness, turning away. "Her father has forbidden it."

"You came today," pointed out Angel, who had by now recovered her voice.

"That is different. I regard his disinheritance of Dominic as unreasonable, indeed iniquitous. However, he does have the right to decide that I am not an eligible suitor for his daughter."

Beth pulled on his arm until he was forced to face her. "What you do with your life is for you to choose," she said quietly, "but will you ruin *my* life just because my father so decrees, when you have said yourself that he is unreasonable?"

"Beth, in this case he is not unreasonable. I am not worthy of you, you deserve a husband of rank and fortune, someone who can offer you—"

"If you abandon me again, I shall marry Francis Welch. Papa will make me, and I shall have no motive for resisting."

"Welch wants to marry you?" asked Lord Dominic, interested. "You could do a lot worse, Beth."

"How can you say so!" exclaimed Catherine and Gerald as one.

The vicar went on, "After your long absence, Dom, you cannot know what sort of man he is."

"You never did like him," said his lordship dismissively. "He's a bit of a rattle but a good enough fellow. Daresay Beth likes him well enough.''

"*I* like him," put in Angel.

"Well, I do not," stated Beth firmly. "But I shall have no alternative.''

Gerald groaned. "Miss Sutton, explain that I cannot honourably continue to see her. I must not . . ." Again he turned away, his face despairing.

"Fustian!" said Catherine. "I warned you not to trust to my ideas coinciding with yours. Male notions of honour are a deal too nice. My advice is to court her without secrecy, short of visiting the Hall, and when Lord Grisedale comes to hear of it, count on Sir Gregory to pull you through.''

"Oh, yes!" cried Beth, and flung herself into Gerald's arms in such a way that he was forced to choose between embracing her and letting her fall.

"Gregory!" snorted Lord Dominic. "As well rely upon a spavined nag to win you a wager as on that prosy, preaching flat to be of the least assistance.''

"He does not like Lord Welch," Catherine informed him, "and besides, Mr Leigh is a fellow preacher.''

He looked at her suspiciously, but she preserved a serious demeanor. Reluctant though she was to break up the reconciliation between the vicar and his beloved, time was passing and the last thing they wanted was to invite questions about their long absence. She pointed this out, and at last they all mounted and headed back towards Patterdale.

Lord Dominic, assured of meeting his sister the next day, was content to ride ahead with Miss Sutton and Miss Brand, leaving the reunited couple to follow. He guided the party from the lakeside to the lane.

"I don't suppose we shall meet anyone who might recognise me," he said carelessly, "and we can ride abreast here and talk." He was in a gay mood and kept his companions well entertained, giving Angel a lesson in the nomenclature of the flowers by the wayside as they rode.

They went slowly, and when they were halfway to Patterdale they heard the thud of hooves coming up behind. Lord Dominic drew back into the shadow of a tree and pulled his hat down, but the rider who appeared was arrested by the sight of Beth and Gerald and did not notice him.

"Lady Elizabeth!" cried Lord Welch. "What the devil are you doing with Leigh?"

"It is none of your affair, Francis," responded Beth defiantly.

"It most certainly is, when we are practically affianced. Not to mention the fact that your father has strictly forbidden you to see him. I wonder what the earl will have to say to this little escapade?"

"If you tell Papa, I shall kill myself before I marry you!"

"And if I don't, you will run off with the parson!"

Catherine decided it was time to intervene as Gerald seemed to have been silenced by his uneasy conscience.

"Good afternoon, Lord Welch," she said, riding back.

"Oh, Miss Sutton . . . I had not seen . . . I beg your pardon, ma'am. Good afternoon."

"Might I make a suggestion?" she offered. "If you do not inform Lord Grisedale of this meeting, Lady Elizabeth shall continue to receive you and permit you to court her as usual. Surely you can rely upon your manifest advantages to win her hand, *if* she is able to see Mr Leigh regularly instead of dreaming of him in an unrealistic way."

The viscount considered her proposal. He was determined to have Beth willy-nilly, but it would be much pleasanter if she was agreeable, and vanity dictated that given a choice she would inevitably choose him. Besides, he could always tell Lord Grisedale at a later date if it seemed advisable.

"Very well," he grunted. "Hullo, Markham. Coming out of hiding?"

Lord Dominic who, with Angel, had joined them, looked abashed. "You don't sound surprised," he said.

"Oh, I've known it was you staying at the vicarage any time these three weeks. I daresay half the country knows. I don't suppose anyone is brave enough to tell your father, even should they wish to. Don't worry, I shan't give you away."

"I said you were a good fellow, Welch. It's deuced uncomfortable hiding out, and if everyone knows anyway I shall get about more. Don't want Gregory to find out, though, so I'll stay away from Grisedale."

"Come over to Upthwaite Park sometime," invited Lord Welch. "We'll take out a gun after rabbits if you like."

The two young men rode on together talking of sport. Brushing aside Beth's thanks, Catherine urged the others to follow.

"I've no mind to have to think up excuses," she declared.

Lord Dominic and Gerald Leigh had to leave them at the turning to Upthwaite, but the viscount rode with them to Barrows End. Thus provided with an unexpected excuse for their lateness, Angel was more inclined than ever to look upon Lord Welch with a favorable eye. And no one could accuse him of bothering Beth, she thought, for he had not addressed a single word to her all the way home.

Of course, if Beth preferred Mr Leigh, that was her own affair, but it was odd to choose a solemn parson over a dashing peer. Admittedly she was not in the least tonnish. Simply not up to snuff, Angel decided sadly, though she had the sweetest disposition imaginable and more resolution than one might give her credit for.

At least the meeting had cleared up one mystery.

"I am very glad," she said to Catherine as they went upstairs, "that Lord Dominic is not in love with Beth after all!"

═11═

"DICK BURCHETT CALLED again while you were out," said Mrs Sutton at dinner. "He does not seem disturbed to find you always gone when he comes, but you will not wish to give offense, I know. I told him I thought you had no other engagements on Friday and could visit Beckside Farm then."

"Burchett?" queried Angel, her thoughts far away. "Oh, I remember. The odd one we met after church that first Sunday."

"Of course we will go," agreed Catherine. "He is so very unpretentious one cannot help but like him."

"I promised to pay a visit to Mrs Burchett," her mother added, "so I will come with you."

"Unless the invitation is for ladies only, I believe I will join you," proposed the vicar. "Apart from Lord Grisedale, Mr Burchett is the only landowner in the parish, and I should not like him to feel slighted."

"Papa, I think you should put in a word for, was it Miss Betsy? It does not seem fair that the son should be kept from his true love because the father sets himself on high form."

"Or a daughter!" added Angel with unexpected vehemence. "People are always talking about splendid matches and eligible connections, and all that really matters is loving each other. If I fell in love with, with, oh, say with Dick Burchett, I should not be in the least sorry to have whistled Damian down the wind."

"I must hope you will not do so, my dear," said her uncle, "for much as I sympathise with your views, I should find myself at a loss to explain it to your parents."

"Not to mention Miss Betsy," Catherine pointed out.

"Well, I will not, for I do not like him above half, but I daresay it will be amusing to see the farm, so I will tell Beth I cannot see her on Friday."

"How is Lady Elizabeth?" asked Mrs Sutton. "I'm afraid she was sadly out of frame last Friday, though she seemed well at church. Her father's manners must be a constant source of mortification to the poor child."

"She was happy as a grig today. Aunt Maria, would you say that a minister is a respectable alliance for an earl's daughter?"

"As the granddaughter of an earl myself, I can hardly deny it, Angel. Of course, my papa was merely a second son."

"Well, he was my grandfather, so you cannot expect me to concern myself with that."

"May I enquire where this sudden interest in genealogy is leading?" requested the vicar.

Suddenly aware that she was jeopardising a secret not her own, Angel clapped her hand to her mouth.

"I think you had best not, Papa," said Catherine calmly. "I can assure you that Angel is not at present contemplating marriage with a clergyman."

"*My* father is a marquis," Angel pointed out.

Mr and Mrs Sutton exchanged amused glances, and kindly allowed the subject to drop.

Angel and Catherine walked up the Crag with Beth the next day. It was cloudy, and much cooler than the last time Angel had accomplished the climb, but she swore the path had grown steeper in the interim. Lord Dominic, waiting with his dog at the top, grinned heartlessly as they flopped down on the great rock to catch their breath.

"If we are to meet here often," he said, "we shall have to take a groom into our confidence. Who usually rides with you, Beth, Abel? We can trust him. He'd have come to Spain with me if I'd let him."

"Pray tell us about Spain, Lord Dominic," Angel begged, and then remembered, "Oh no, you do not like to talk of it, do you?"

"That was when I thought it would give me away. And while we are on the topic, would you both please call me Dom, as Beth does? Then if anyone overhears, they will think you are saying Don, for Donald."

"What they will think is that we are a pair of forward hussies!" declared Catherine tartly. "Very well, Dom, are you going to entertain us with your exploits in the Peninsula?"

Judging by his stories, Lord Dominic's exploits consisted largely of a series of outrageous pranks. Catherine supposed he had seen serious fighting since he bore the evidence, but either he thought the tale unfit for delicate female ears or he did not wish to boast. Though he spoke of manoeuvres and bivouacs, bloodletting was never mentioned.

Angel was enthralled. She was eager to find out at which battle he had been wounded, and only refrained from asking outright because she was afraid it might distress Beth. No considerations of delicacy would hold her back next time she was alone with him, she vowed to herself.

Later, she did Beth another service by asking why Mr Leigh was not present.

"I hope he has not changed his mind about the propriety of seeing Beth?" she asked.

"No. Whenever he mutters about it, I tell him it would be downright dishonourable to hedge off after raising her hopes, and I threaten to call him out if he so much as mentions the possibility. Can you imagine it—a duel between a cripple and a parson?" He laughed, but there was a tinge of bitterness in his voice. Osa raised her great head and licked his hand consolingly.

"Then why did he not come?" Beth wanted to know. "Dom, he does . . . he is fond of me, is he not? I simply assumed that he still felt . . . that he wanted . . ."

"Don't worry, goosecap, he's head over heels in love." Lord

Dominic hugged his sister. "If you are so set on getting riveted, you'll have to understand that his time is not his own, nor yours neither. He has parish business today. He'll be here tomorrow if you can come."

"Oh, yes!" she cried joyfully. "Lyn, will you come? And Catherine?"

Angel agreed with alacrity, but Catherine cried off, pleading other business. She was unwilling to find herself cast permanently in the rôle of chaperone, and her opinion of Mr Leigh's good sense and high principles made it seem unnecessary when he was to be present. Whenever she thought about it, she was staggered by the way Angel's advent in her staid life had transformed it. Instead of assisting her father in his work and studying her books, her chief occupations at home, here she was aiding and abetting the clandestine meetings of a pair of star-crossed lovers, and concealing a Prodigal Son from his irate father. And surely the general atmosphere of reckless abandon was explanation enough for the way she so often found herself silently repeating Richardson's dictum, that no young lady can be justified in falling in love before the gentleman's love is declared.

She had always been of the opinion that no one blessed with a modicum of intelligence could quarrel with that!

The next day, while Catherine attempted to pick up the threads of her usual pursuits at home, Angel and Beth rode up Dowen Crag, accompanied by Abel. Unwarned, the groom was so overwhelmed by the sight of Lord Dominic that he went red as a beet and sat on his horse with his mouth open, unable to produce a sound. By the time he had recovered enough to greet his master properly, not an easy matter as Osa was delighted to meet a new friend, Beth and Gerald were wandering down the path arm in arm and deep in conversation.

"We'll go down to the dingle," Dominic told the groom. "Do you go out on the crag and watch for the enemy. You remember our whistle?"

"Aye, Master Dom. This be jist like th'owld days!''

"Keep an eye on the horses, Abel, and mum's the word. Miss Brand, let me show you where we used to fight off Red Indians in my youth.''

As they followed the others, Angel seized her chance.

"I did not like to ask you before where you were wounded because I thought it might distress Beth,'' she began.

"I see that you do not mean to spare me now that she is not by! I . . . I do not like to talk of it, Linnet.''

"You are a great deal too sensitive about the whole business,'' Angel declared severely. "If you never talk of it you will brood, and then you will become just such another cross-grained old surly-boots as your papa.''

He smiled with difficulty. "You may be right. I was used always to be merry and devil-may-care, and now I find myself . . . oh, wishing, for one, that I had not blithely whistled down the wind half of my inheritance.''

"I expect you are growing up, too,'' she reflected, then coaxed, "Do tell!''

"This I received at Corunna,'' he said, fingering the scar on his cheek. "It was not long after I joined up, and I have never been so frightened in my life, before or since. I was only nineteen then, you see. But it turned out to be nothing. The others were both at Ciudad Rodrigo, in January.''

"Both? Your leg and what else?''

"I took a ball in the lung, Miss Inquisitive, and then a Hussar came along and broke my leg with his sabre for good measure. I was in the hospital at Lisbon for three months, then another month in London before I came to Upthwaite.''

"I wish I had known you for I would have come to nurse you, or at least to visit. It must have been horrid.''

"That is not precisely the word I should have chosen, Linnet, but you have the general idea.''

"What did the London doctors say?''

119

"That the bone had shrunk and I must limp forever, though the pain should mostly fade away in a year or two. And to avoid catching cold like the plague."

"Does your chest hurt?"

"Only when I cough. They warned me that it will cause trouble in the winter. There, can you blame me for calling myself a cripple?"

"Yes. You have all your limbs, you are not bedridden, you can even ride a horse!"

He caught her to him in a sudden hug and as quickly released her. "You make me feel better in spite of myself, Linnet. I must learn to count my blessings. Well, here is our dingle. Is it not as wild as the forests of North America?"

The dingle was a circular depression in the hillside, its entrance hidden by a hazel thicket. In its shelter grew a tangle of bushes, brambles, and small trees, and dog-roses bloomed everywhere, scenting the air. The branches of the tallest tree held the remains of a wooden fort, and Gerald was standing hands on hips regarding it sadly. He turned as they picked their way through the jungle.

"Look what wind and weather have done to our refuge," he said, pointing. "It is shockingly dilapidated."

"I do believe it has shrunk," Lord Dominic added critically. "I cannot imagine how four of us fitted into that."

"Possibly we have grown," suggested Beth.

"Miss Brand, let me show you the spot where we used to have our campfire," offered Mr Leigh. "It is just through here, if I remember aright."

He held aside a curtain of ivy, and Angel made her way through a green tunnel into a glade backed by the wall of the dell. In its centre, a circle of blackened stones bore mute witness to years of use.

"Did you ever cook here?" she asked the vicar.

"I'd not call it cooking. We made toast and boiled water."

"I thought your home was on the other side of Ullswater. Is not that a long way to come for a day's play?"

"I used often to stay at the Hall when I was a child. The earl is my godfather, believe it or not. And when I was older I rode or rowed—r-o-d-e or r-o-w-e-d. It is not so far. As I told your cousin, I go over every Thursday to see my mother. She is something of an invalid and does not go about."

"Does she like visitors? I am determined to take a boat trip before we leave Westmorland, and it would be delightful to have such an object in view."

"Why, yes, she does enjoy callers and has very few. My boat will not hold more than two or three, but it is not difficult to hire a larger vessel. Think you your uncle and aunt might like to go?"

"Certainly," Angel pledged them.

"Then I will see what I can arrange."

"Does Lord Dominic row?"

"He used to. I had not thought to wonder whether he could now. I shall have to persuade him to give it a try. An excellent idea, Miss Brand."

Crashing through the undergrowth, Osa warned them of his lordship's approach. Dominic emerged from the shade and they saw that he was very pale.

"Beth wants to see you, Leigh," he said in a strangled voice.

Gerald Leigh glanced questioningly at Angel. She gave him a quick nod. His tall form stooped to pass under the low boughs as Dominic sank down on one of the fireplace stones and dropped his head in his hands. Unmindful of the soot, Angel sat beside him, her hands tightly clasped in her lap. Osa came and licked them, and then went to lie panting in the shade, head on outstretched paws, her dark brown eyes watchful.

"Linnet?"

"Yes, Dom, I'm here."

His lips moved but no words emerged. He cleared his throat, the sound loud in the stillness of the glade.

"My mother died while I was in Spain."

She was silent. He must have known this before now; something further was troubling him.

It came in a sudden torrent. "Beth told me she fell ill right after I left. Nothing specific, but she grew weaker and weaker and lost interest in everything. She lived for news of me. I never wrote, not once, not a single line. Gregory had me watched, damn him, and told her now and then that I was still alive. Beth says that even when my father swore he'd never let me set foot in the house again, Mama hoped, but when she heard nothing from me, for so long, she gave up the struggle and died. I killed her. I killed her as surely as if I had put a pistol to her head and pulled the trigger. I did not think . . ."

His body was shaken by hard, dry, racking sobs, tearing his heart out. Angel could find no words, so she put her arms around him and held him close. As he calmed, she began to say what came to her mind.

"She was always frail, Beth said, and your papa was as much to blame as you. More, for he was there and saw what his decision was doing to her. And he was older and should have been wiser."

"But you do not hold me blameless." His voice was exhausted.

"No. You should have written, sent a message, something. You were heedless and inconsiderate, both faults which I share with you, I fear. But you could not have imagined that your omission would have such a dire effect."

"Mama was never strong. As sensitive as Beth, without Beth's inner strength. I should have guessed what it would do to her. Linnet, you said maybe I was growing up at last. This is part of it, isn't it? Learning to accept the guilt and bear it and go on."

"And learning to forgive your father, perhaps."

"You are very wise, little Puritan. My father was never able to take back anything he had said, to change his mind or compromise. He thought—still thinks, I suppose—it a sign of weakness. Once he had threatened to cast me out if I joined the army, nothing this side of the Day of Judgement could alter his decision."

"And once you had said you would in spite of him, nothing could alter yours?"

He was silent for a moment. "Perhaps. It is a weakness to be unable to confess that one was wrong, is it not? I am learning, Linnet."

"Do not learn too fast, or you will grow old before your time! And do not snap my head off if I say that you are very tired and I am going to ask Mr Leigh to fetch Thunder." Angel stood up and looked down at his grey face.

"Will you come back?"

"If you wish." As she left, Osa went to sit beside him, and on her return she found him absently fondling the dog's shaggy white head and staring into the middle distance. "Mr Leigh went out on the path and put his fingers in his mouth and whistled," she told him with a giggle. "I never thought to see a parson behave so! Abel popped up out of nowhere and Mr Leigh positively bellowed at him to bring the horses, so they will be here in a minute. Promise me you will not brood? About anything?"

"I will try, I promise. You know, I was used to think you a hubble-bubble romp of a female, but I find I have had to abandon my notions. You are candid and compassionate and commonsensical and . . . and comforting and courageous."

"It won't last," said Angel blithely, and they went to join the others.

As if to prove her words, she challenged Beth to a race when they reached the farm track at the bottom of the hill. Her hat blew off and had to be rescued from a blackthorn bush by Abel, and she arrived at the vicarage pink-cheeked, with her golden ringlets tumbling to her shoulders.

Beth went in with her to pay her respects to the Suttons, and they found Sir Gregory, ostensibly calling on the vicar on business, ensconced in the parlour with Catherine and her mother. He raised his eyebrows at her dishevelled appearance. She was certain that if he had carried a quizzing glass he would have examined her through it.

"A pleasant ride, Miss Brand?" he enquired, with something more than casual interest, she thought. At least, any display of interest was a change from his usual world-weary manner.

"Thank you, yes," she replied shortly, and turned away. "Aunt Maria, I beg your pardon for appearing in this state. I did not know you had a visitor. Pray excuse me while I tidy myself."

"A moment, Miss Brand," requested the odious Sir Gregory. "Am I correct in supposing that you have been racing? I thought so. I wish to be certain that you understand how dangerous these hills can be. There are unexpected precipices, falling rocks, hidden bogs, and other hazards for the unwary or those not familiar with the area."

"I am not so chuckleheaded as to gallop where I do not know the terrain," she retorted hotly. "We were down on the track by Grisedale Beck."

"I beg your pardon, ma'am. If you ride out tomorrow, I will come with you and show you a more convenient place to stretch your horse's legs."

"That is not at all necessary. I am sure we do very well without you."

"Lyn!" said her aunt sharply. "That is no response to make to Sir Gregory's kind offer."

Beth took a deep breath and intervened. "She did it for me, Mrs Sutton. Cousin Gregory, I have been meeting Gerald Leigh in secret."

"Only twice," Angel put in quickly, before Beth could reveal Lord Dominic's presence to the enemy.

"I see," said Sir Gregory. "I had wondered if the fellow had enough backbone to defy my uncle."

"Gerald is not craven!" denied Beth with indignation.

"He has antiquated notions about being honourable," Angel explained. "Positively Gothic, in fact."

"Gregory, you will not stop me seeing him, or tell Papa?"

"Has Miss Brand persuaded you that I am an ogre, Beth? I always thought him the man for you, and though I cannot approve of clandestine meetings, I must admit that at present I see little alternative.''

"Just what I thought,'' agreed Catherine.

"Are you in this too, Miss Sutton? And you, ma'am?''

"Not I,'' said Mrs Sutton. "Though I must confess to strong suspicions.''

"And will you acquiesce in concealing the matter from the earl? If you have other views I shall be happy to hear them, for this is not the kind of situation in which I can call myself an expert!''

"I do not know the young man well, but both Catherine and Clement consider him an unexceptionable, highly principled gentleman and I would accept the judgement of either. If his conscience permits him to court Lady Elizabeth under these conditions, I for one will not cavil. Besides,'' she added frankly, "Lord Grisedale has not behaved towards me with such civility that I feel obliged to uphold his rights.''

"Bravo, Mother!'' murmured Catherine.

"So you see,'' Angel called them back to the original object of the discussion, "you need not come with us tomorrow, Sir Gregory.''

"You have abandoned your desire for a good gallop, Miss Brand? No, no, you shall not escape so easily. I planned to challenge you to a race.''

"Your horse is twice the size of mine!''

"But he carries twice as much. Come, you shall choose any horse in the stables that is safe for a lady, and may choose any horse for me that will bear my weight. I'll wager a pair of gloves against a handkerchief.''

"Done!''

Catherine offered to accompany Angel to the Hall next day, to pick a mount and decide on a course. The race would be held on Saturday, as the visit to Beckside Farm was set for Friday.

"I'll take you over to Upthwaite on Friday, Beth,'' promised Sir Gregory. "I suspect I ought to have a chat with Mr Leigh fairly soon.''

Beth looked panic-stricken, but Angel was equal to the occasion.

"You had better write him a note saying you are coming," she suggested quickly. "I have recently discovered that vicars are vastly busy gentlemen."

Her uncle came into the room in time to hear this.

"You are indeed right, Lyn," he agreed mournfully. "We are unconscionably overworked. I am come to tell you, Maria, that all is arranged for our little holiday in Ambleside next week!"

Sir Gregory and Lady Elizabeth left soon after. As the baronet was taking his leave of Catherine, she asked him what had possessed him to challenge her cousin.

"I thought you did not like her above half," she said.

"The impulse of a moment," he replied. "It may serve to keep her out of mischief for a few days. I do not dislike the child, though I fear she still thinks me odiously interfering."

"An ogre," she smiled. "I will see you tomorrow."

As soon as the visitors were gone, Angel started counting days. Tomorrow to the Hall, Friday to Beckside Farm, Saturday the race, Sunday church, and Tuesday they were leaving for three days in Ambleside.

She absolutely had to see Lord Dominic on Monday, or it would be over a week!

═12═

THE ONLY SADDLEHORSE in the Grisedale stables that could carry Sir Gregory was his own grey charger, Atlas.

"He was chosen for endurance, not speed," the baronet soothed Angel. "Come and pick a mount for yourself. There is not a great deal of choice, I fear."

There was not. Angel was about to indulge in scathing comparisons with her father's stables when the arrival of Lord Welch saved her from giving herself away. He agreed absolutely with her judgement.

"I told you the roan would suit you best," he pointed out. "It's no racer though. Tell you what, I've the very nag at home. I'll bring her over tomorrow for you to try. A sporting little mare, she is."

Angel accepted with alacrity, though it meant postponing the race for a full week. Sir Gregory's suggested racecourse she rejected out of hand, but at last they found a spot she considered eligible, if not ideal.

When they returned to the house, she managed a moment alone with Beth.

"Here," she said quickly, "will you give this letter to your brother tomorrow? I know you will not see him, but leave it where he will find it. I have addressed it to Mr Donald Marshall."

"If you wish." Beth was dubious. "Why ever are you writing to Dom?"

"If I do not see him on Monday, I shan't be able to till next Friday." It was so obvious to Angel that she could not go so long without speaking to him that she was unaware that it might require some explanation. "We can meet them both on the Crag. Beth, I have an idea! Should you like to come with us to Ambleside? I'm sure my uncle and aunt can have no objection."

"Oh, Lyn, I should like it of all things! It is so long since I have gone anywhere. But even if Papa agreed, Mr and Mrs Sutton will not want another to take care of."

Catherine and Sir Gregory reappeared at that moment, and agreed to use their influence on the Suttons and Lord Grisedale respectively. Sir Gregory even managed to persuade his lordship to lend the Grisedale carriage. Angel was invited to spend Monday night at the Hall, and in the morning the two girls would pick up the rest of the party in Barrows End.

In the meantime, the visit to Beckside Farm took place. The Burchetts welcomed them with open arms. Dick and two small sisters awaited them at the farmyard gate and escorted them to the house.

"Mind your slippers, ladies," he advised genially. "Pa had a path laid down but it keeps vanishing. Told him it would. Can't keep beasts out of the yard."

"Do you still have kittens?" Angel demanded. "And calves and chicks and . . ."

"Foal born two days ago. Chicks getting big, but kittens still cuddly. In the kitchen here. Come in, do."

Mrs Burchett was setting a kettle on the hob.

"Now, Dick, your pa said to take the Reverend round to the parlour," she reminded, wiping her hands on her apron and bustling forward. "Good day, Mrs Sutton, it's a right treat to see you here. Good day, sir; good day, young ladies."

"May we see the kittens first?" asked Angel.

"O' course, Miss Brand. Jenny, Nora, stop gawking and find them dratted kittens! Always underfoot they be, now they's a-growing older."

Catherine and Angel cooed equally over the kittens and the shy little girls, then Dick took them on a tour of the farmyard. They returned to find Mrs Sutton ensconced at the kitchen table, which was now loaded with food.

A cold ham took pride of place, flanked by cakes and loaves fresh from the oven, slabs of golden butter, a mutton pie, a large bowl of strawberries and another of cream, honey, preserves, and pickles. Mrs Burchett was frying bacon and sausages, and as they came in after washing at the pump, she began breaking eggs into another skillet.

"This," Mrs Sutton announced, "is tea!"

Mr Burchett had taken the vicar off to the parlour for a man-to-man chat. Nora was sent to fetch them, and soon they were all seated round the munificent spread.

"Ye'll ask a blessing, Reverend?" requested Mrs Burchett.

Some two hours later, the Craythorns' unfortunate horse drew the gig back down the hill. Besdies the increased weight of the passengers themselves, the vehicle was loaded with farm produce they had been unable to refuse.

"I never want to move again," groaned Angel. "If that was tea, I wonder what they eat for dinner? No wonder they are all so large and jolly!"

"Yes, even Mr Burchett cheered up after his third slice of ham," agreed Catherine. "Papa, did you speak to him about Dick's Betsy?"

"I believe I have prevailed upon him to regard her with complaisance," the vicar said.

"Good," said Angel. "I expect they will soon be married and I shall give them a wedding present. The piglets were adorable. What a pity they grow up to be pigs!"

The next day, Lord Welch brought his mare Star over to Grisedale Hall. Angel tried her paces and was delighted with her. However, Beth had disappointing news. She would be unable to go up Dowen Crag on Monday, as Mrs Daventry insisted that she rest in preparation for Tuesday's travelling.

Undeterred, Angel told her she would like to go riding anyway, with just the groom. She coaxed Aunt Maria into letting her take an hour away from the packing to get a breath of fresh air, and when Abel arrived she was ready. Together they rode up Dowen Crag, in spite of Abel's shaking his head and tutting.

"Her'd bring Old Nick hisself around her thumb," he muttered admiringly to himself. "Master Dom don't have a chance."

No one was there when they arrived. Angel went out on the rock and looked towards Upthwaite, but it was several minutes before she saw a horseman top the valley's rim, and then it was a solitary rider. A white speck accompanied him: Osa.

"You're late," she accused impatiently when at last Lord Dominic appeared. "Beth couldn't come and I only have a few minutes. Where's Mr Leigh?"

"Called out on an emergency. I waited to see if he would return in time to come. I didn't know you were in a hurry, Linnet."

"No, I'm sorry I was twitty. I've just realised that we have been here four weeks already and there are only four to go. Beth has all the time in the world."

"For what?"

"Oh, for adventures and things," said Angel vaguely.

"Poor Linnet, is your usual life so dull? I must try to arrange some excitement for you. I know, how about a moonlight tryst? There's a full moon tonight. We could meet by the lake."

"Someone might see us. Why not up here? If it's moonlight it won't be dangerous."

"I was not serious! You cannot possibly come out alone at night to meet me! Indeed, you should not be here now."

"No, I should be on my way back, so we will have to arrange this quickly. I will tell Beth I am coming to meet you and ask her to come too for propriety's sake. I am to spend the night at the Hall, you must know. And you will persuade Mr Leigh to come for the same reason. If neither knows the other will be there, they are more likely to agree, do you not think?"

"Probably." Lord Dominic entered into the spirit. "We should meet at midnight. But I do not want you riding up the Crag at night. We will wait where the path leaves the woods. How will you get horses?''

"Oh, I had not thought."

"That sounds familiar. Abel! Miss Brand and Lady Elizabeth will need horses tonight at eleven. See that they are provided.''

"Aye, sir . . . What, Master Dom? Nay, 'tis not seemly for my lady to ride out at such an hour!''

"Please, Abel," coaxed Angel. "We do not mean mischief, but Lady Elizabeth was not allowed to come out today and she will not see her brother for another four days if you do not help.''

The groom was at last won over and sworn to secrecy. Angel hurried home bursting with excitement, which she had considerable difficulty in hiding from her aunt and cousin. The rest of the busy day seemed endless, but finally the moment came when she took her overnight valise and set off for the Hall. Not even the prospect of dining with Lord Grisedale, Mrs Daventry, and Sir Gregory could dampen her spirits.

"She's up to something," Catherine told her mother. "Thank goodness she is out of my hands for this evening. I can even find it in me to hope that the earl carries out whatever threat it was he started to make!''

It was some six hours later that Catherine was awakened from her dreams by a noise she could not at first identify. Then it came again: a handful of pebbles rattling against her window. The casement was open, and several stones thudded to the floor.

Too sleepy to be alarmed, she threw back the covers and went to the window. Leaning out, she saw clearly in the bright moonlight a large figure that could only be Sir Gregory. He was stooping to pick up another load of pebbles.

"Psst!" she hissed. "What in the world are you about?''

"Miss Sutton, I must talk with you," he hissed back. "Pray come down at once.''

"Sir Gregory, I cannot! I am . . . I was asleep.''

"Get dressed. I need your help, Kate.''

She disappeared, and he waited impatiently until the back door opened and she came out. She had scrambled into a gown, but had not taken time to put up her hair. It flowed in a rippling river to well below her waist, cloaking her in mystery, while the pallid light lent an enigmatic air to her features.

"Kate!" he murmured hoarsely, moving towards her with both arms outstretched.

She stepped back. "If you call me that, I shall go in," she threatened breathlessly.

"Miss Sutton, I beg your pardon. Blame the moon. Did you not call me once 'half lunatic'? The goddess steals my wits: 'O, be thou Dian, and let her be Kate, and then—' "

"Enough! Was it for this you called me down?"

"No, indeed! You have made me forget my errand, which is, I think you will agree, of some importance. Your cousin and mine have slipped out of the house and away, an hour since. Have you any idea where they might have gone?"

"Oh, dear, I knew Angel was up to something! Let me think. She and Beth are used to meet . . . Mr Leigh upon Dowen Crag. Perhaps they are there?"

"I cannot believe Leigh would be so unprincipled as to invite Beth out at night! If this is so, he must look elsewhere for support."

"Do not be angry with him. I'll wager this is largely Angel's idea. We must go after them at once."

"I have brought you a horse. 'First kiss me, Kate, and we will.' "

"Sir, you take advantage of me!"

"Shamelessly. Come here." Taking her in his arms he silenced her protests with his lips, a brief, gentle kiss that left her shaken to the core. She looked up at him as he released her, but his face was unreadable in the moon's uncertain light. "Come," he said roughly, and led her to where he had tethered the horses. Atlas whinnied softly as they approached.

In a dream, Catherine let him toss her up onto the bay. They splashed across the gleaming beck and cantered down the track. The balmy night air lifted the weight of her hair and she felt as if, like the moon above, she floated serenely in a pool of light.

Sir Gregory led the way up through the woods, where the scent of honeysuckle hung heavy. They rode in silence but for the soft thud of hoof on leafmould, the distant hoot of an owl, the faint rustles of small night creatures. As they passed, a badger looked up unafraid from his hunt for grubs, his striped face visible only because he moved. A horse neighed.

A horse neighed! Sir Gregory reined in Atlas, and Catherine, once more rudely awakened, pulled up her bay beside him.

"It must be them. Who else would be up here?"

"Come," he said again, and taking her bridle rode out from the sheltering trees onto the bare hillside. Hooves struck stone.

Four startled faces turned to meet them.

"Cousin Gregory!" breathed Beth.

"Dominic!" Sir Gregory was stunned into silence. Before he recovered the use of his tongue, Lord Dominic was on his feet and limping towards him.

"You didn't expect to find me here, Cousin," he said belligerently.

"I might have guessed that only a combination of you and Miss Brand could be responsible for this escapade." The baronet's voice expressed resigned forbearance, but Catherine thought she detected an undercurrent of excitement.

"It was all my idea," Angel declared. "I told Beth I was meeting Dom . . . Lord Dominic, and she came as a chaperone."

If Sir Gregory's lips twitched, it was indistinguishable in the moonlight. He turned to the young clergyman.

"Leigh?"

"I too was brought along to play propriety. I did not know Lady Elizabeth would be here. I had intended to insist that Miss Brand return home at once, but when I got here . . ." He shrugged helplessly.

"Moon madness! Miss Brand, I have no control over your actions, but I hope that as a guest at the Hall you will heed my request to return thither immediately. Beth, come.''

As Sir Gregory helped the girls mount, two shamefaced young men converged on Catherine with muttered apologies.

''There's no harm done, I think,'' she told them. ''At least you had the sense not to let them ride up the Crag in the dark. Good night.''

She turned her horse to join the others.

''I shall do myself the honour of calling at Upthwaite vicarage in the morning,'' the baronet announced in a carrying voice, and the four of them rode back down the hill.

''Cursed interfering busybody,'' growled Lord Dominic. ''I only hope it gave him a nasty shock to see me alive and well.''

''He'd have been within his rights to have thrashed me soundly,'' pointed out Mr Leigh.

''Not when I had a hand in your meeting Beth. I'm her brother, after all.''

''He should have thrashed you too!'' was the vicar's response.

=13=

CREEPING UP THE stairs, Catherine saw that her parents' chamber door was open and a candle lighted within. With a sigh she stopped tiptoeing and was about to knock when her mother called:

"Catherine? Pray come in, dearest."

She went and sat on their bed.

"Angel, I take it?" queried Mr Sutton, sitting up with his nightcap askew.

"Yes, Papa. All is well now."

"Enterprising young lady. What has she been up to now?"

"She persuaded Lady Elizabeth to a midnight rendezvous with Gerald Leigh and . . . Mr Marshall."

"You mean Lord Dominic Markham, do you not?" her mother asked with a smile.

"I thought you must have guessed, Mother."

"There is a definite likeness between brother and sister, though not obvious perhaps. And the strange coincidence of names."

"Dom Markham becomes Don Marshall," mused the vicar. "It must have made things easier at first, when the alias was new to him."

"Angel never guessed, you know. Even after Dom and Beth met, she had to have the relationship explained to her."

"Catherine, do you wish me to speak to her?" asked her father. "I know you offered to take her wholly in charge yourself, but she is a more difficult ward than I had anticipated. I fear Louisa and

Frederick have spoilt her abominably. If you feel her to be a burden, or that you cannot cope with her starts . . ."

"She is not always easy, Papa, but she is so good-natured. She was vastly apologetic tonight. As usual, she 'had not considered.' She wished to take the whole blame, and when I asked if she would spend the rest of the night here at home, she said she must go to the Hall 'to protect Beth.' And they had taken a groom with them, though he ran off when we arrived, so she had some concern for safety."

"She has many good qualities," agreed Mrs Sutton, "and I daresay she will grow out of her thoughtlessness. She is not so much lacking in consideration for others as simply impetuous. Well, if you think you can manage the little minx, let us get some sleep, for we have a journey tomorrow."

"Good night, Mother. Good night, Papa." Catherine kissed them both. "I promise I'll come running if I need help, and I thank you for your confidence in me."

Returning at last to her chamber, she wondered momentarily whether that confidence was justified. Had she acted sensibly in riding off into the night alone with a gentleman she had known scarce a month? A gentleman, moreover, who had taken advantage of her in such a disgraceful fashion.

Even the memory of that kiss could not keep her awake. The moment her weary head touched the pillow, her eyes closed, and the next thing she knew was her mother shaking her.

She yawned all through breakfast. When the Grisedale coach arrived, bearing two lively, chattering young ladies apparently none the worse for the night's adventures, she was much inclined to think that perhaps Angel's opinion was correct. She was growing old.

Lord Grisedale's team was also lively, "rarin' to go," said the coachman, and he declared that he was equally happy to go jauntering about "for 'is lordship don't scarcely even leave the 'ouse nowadays." With such an attitude the Kirkstone Pass was no obstacle, and they were soon driving along the well-wooded banks of Lake Windermere.

"It's even prettier than Ullswater!" exclaimed Angel.

"Yes, indeed," agreed Mrs Sutton. "The islands lend a delightful perspective to the scene."

"Ullswater is much more beautiful!" said Beth hotly, defending her home district. The farther behind they left her father, her companion, and her unwanted suitor, the more she lost her shyness.

They spent the night in Ambleside, and the next day went to Grasmere to watch the St Oswald's Day rush-bearing procession.

"It is a very old custom," explained Mr Sutton, "dating from the days when churches had no wooden floors. Once a year the people of the parish would gather rushes and strew them on the floors to make a sweet-smelling carpet."

"Only once a year?" asked his wife disapprovingly. "That's no way to keep house! They must have been quite foul by the end of the year."

"I daresay, my dear. Of course, in these modern times the whole business is merely an excuse for a holiday."

"Where are Angel and Beth?" Catherine interrupted. "Oh, dear, she *promised* not to think up any mischief."

The girls had disappeared into the crowds of spectators, but it seemed unlikely that they could come to serious harm. Besides, at that moment a brass band appeared at the end of the street, so it was impossible to search. The band was followed by villagers carrying 'rush-bearings.' These were emblems of rushes woven into elaborate designs: harps, stars, serpents, and other traditional patterns. Then came Morris dancers in colorful costumes and jingling bells, accompanied by fiddles and pipes.

Closing the procession was a haywain piled high with fresh rushes and drawn by garlanded girls in white dresses, wearing flowered crowns and surrounded by cheering children. Angel was never able to explain just how she and Beth had joined the decorative maidens, but they both confessed to having enjoyed themselves amazingly.

"I suppose no one who knows you is likely to have seen you," sighed Mrs Sutton philosophically. "But it has me in a puzzle to know how you manage to fall into such adventures, indeed it does."

After this excitement, the glimpse they caught of Mr William Wordsworth and his family was an anticlimax.

The next day they drove back over the Kirkstone Pass. Even Angel felt as if she was coming home when they reached Patterdale and turned up the lane towards Barrows End. Mrs Applejohn actually welcomed them, and Beth was persuaded to stay and dine before continuing to the Hall. She found it difficult to express her gratitude for having been included in the expedition.

"I cannot remember when I have so enjoyed myself," she assured them fervently. "Though in general my life has been much more interesting since you came to the vicarage."

"So has mine," muttered Catherine.

"Tomorrow?" whispered Angel as they parted.

"Two o'clock. They swore to be there. Till then."

Promptly at two, Beth arrived with Abel and the horses. Catherine had been half inclined to insist on going with them, but there was a great deal to be done at home. She felt disinclined for housework, yet no more eager to ride up Dowen Crag, where she would be an unwanted fifth.

So listless was she that her mother commented on it.

"I do hope you are not coming down with something," she said anxiously.

"No, Mother, I am merely tired. I suppose I am spoiled by our holiday."

Mrs Sutton was not satisfied. "Go and lie down, dearest," she directed. "There is nothing I cannot do without your help. We cannot have you falling ill."

Catherine felt no inclination to retire to bed, but it was easier than arguing so she obeyed. Alone in her chamber, she could no longer suppress the memory of Sir Gregory's kiss, and it was impossible to deny that she had behaved to him in a free and easy way which had invited disrespect. In future she would be on her guard, she promised herself. She would treat him with formality and avoid being alone with him. And in a little over three weeks she would be leaving Westmorland and need never think of him or face him again.

To her own surprise, she found herself weeping uncontrollably, and when her mother looked in half an hour later she was fast asleep.

Meanwhile Angel was endeavouring to coach Lord Dominic in the gentle art of complimenting ladies. It was an occupation that involved a great deal of giggling.

His lordship alternated between the laconic and the overelaborate. From the simple statement that Angel was pretty as a primrose, which led to a brief discussion of spring flowers, he moved on to a eulogy of her eyes in which mountain tarns figured largely.

"And icy as they are, colder yet is the glance of displeasure from my Linnet's eyes," he rhapsodised, "which freezes my heart till her smile comes like a sunbeam to warm to life once more the—"

"No, no," Angel stopped him. "That is much too involved and long-winded. Why, I know girls who would be half asleep before you reached the end of your sentence."

"Perhaps I had best stick with the flowers. Your cheeks have the delicate tint of the wild rose in June."

"That's very pretty," she applauded. "Go on."

He continued, comparing her laugh to a mountain stream, her lips and teeth to raspberries and cream.

"Excellent! Much less commonplace than cherries and pearls."

"Much more tempting, too," he said audaciously.

Angel thoroughly enjoyed the lesson, but the only compliment she cared for was spoken before it began, as soon as Beth and Gerald wandered off.

"I missed you, Linnet," Lord Dominic had said simply.

They could not meet again till Monday, because Saturday was the day set for the race. Angel wished she had not accepted Sir Gregory's challenge. However, she had committed herself, and now not even the way time was rushing by could make her back down.

She went up to the Hall in the morning alone, as Catherine was otherwise occupied. After enduring for half an hour Mrs Daventry's complaints about "young girls *forever* off jauntering about the countryside," she was more than happy to welcome Lord Welch when he arrived with her mount.

Beth, having been spared his attentions for several days, also greeted the viscount with complaisance. Sir Gregory was called from his business, and the four of them rode out to give the racecourse a final inspection.

Lord Welch, heartened by his reception, was very attentive to Beth. At first she accepted his solicitude patiently, but his proprietary air became so marked that it began to distress her.

Sir Gregory was about to give his lordship a sharp set-down when Angel noticed her friend's discomfort and took a hand. She drew off the viscount with a coquettish question and he, in accordance with his policy of blowing now hot, now cold, responded with alacrity.

He continued to flirt with Angel at luncheon, under Mrs Daventry's disapproving eye, until Mrs Sutton and Catherine arrived to watch the race. They took Mrs Daventry up in the gig, and everyone made their way to the course.

Sir Gregory offered Angel a head start of a length, but she refused indignantly and was punctilious about making sure Star's nose was precisely level with Atlas's. The huge grey charger towered over her mare but in no wise diminished her eagerness for battle.

Lord Welch, who had appointed himself master of ceremonies, loaded his pistol with a blank shot, pointed it skyward, and fired.

Atlas got off to a slow start, but once he was in full stride it became obvious that Star had no chance. The big horse took the lead and kept it all the way in spite of the filly's gallant efforts. Sir Gregory wondered momentarily whether to hold back, but guessed that Angel would be furious if she realised. He abandoned the gentlemanly impulse and won by a length and a half.

Angel took her defeat with cheerful equanimity, upon which he congratulated her.

"I'm glad you did not let me win," she said. "It was Atlas's race all the way. He's a beauty. Of course, if I had my own horse here . . . I mean, if I could have had a larger choice . . . Oh, never mind. You won fair and square and I owe you a handkerchief. I hope you do not want it embroidered with your initials?"

"No, Miss Brand, I'll not ask that of you."

This response inclined her to think that he was perhaps not quite so odious as she had supposed. She was about to tell him so when Beth came up.

"That was vastly exciting!" she declared. "Lyn, will you race against me now?"

This time, Angel won the race by half the length of the course. Beth's horse cast a shoe at the midpoint, and regretfully she pulled up.

"Another day perhaps," consoled Sir Gregory.

"Come up before me and I will give you a ride to the Hall," offered Lord Welch.

Beth gave him a freezing look.

"I should not dream of doing anything so improper," she said haughtily. "Mrs Sutton will certainly take me up in the gig." And turning her back on him, she walked away.

The viscount was furious. "Little vixen should be whipped at the cart's tail," he muttered, forgetting how close he was to Sir Gregory. "Once we're hitched I'll soon bring her to heel!"

"Did you speak?" enquired Sir Gregory, at his most urbane and leaving no doubt that he had heard every word.

"I'm going to see the earl. I've news for him he'll be grateful for."

"I think not. His lordship is far from well, as I believe I have mentioned before, and I cannot permit him to be disturbed."

"Devil take me if I intend to ask your permission?"

"The servants have orders to allow no one near my uncle without it."

"The iron fist in the velvet glove, eh? Everyone knows you have the old man penned up until you get what you want from him, but there's one person you haven't reckoned on, jailer!"

"I prefer 'guardian,' " said the baronet coolly, "and believe me, there is no one I have not taken into account. Ah, Miss Brand! Lord Welch is on the point of departure, so if you do not mind dismounting, I will do likewise and we may walk together. Unless, sir, you wish to leave Star to be rubbed down and sent over later?"

"I'll take her," growled his lordship, and was soon trotting homeward, leading the mare, while Angel begged a ride on Atlas.

"I don't need a sidesaddle," she assured Sir Gregory. "I have even ridden astride before now, though it is not possible in skirts."

"I am sure it is easier without," he agreed gravely.

=14=

ANGEL WOKE UP on Monday to the shocking realisation that only three weeks remained of her sojourn in Westmorland. What is more, it was raining, and the freedom of the past two weeks of unprecedented fine weather would undoubtedly be curtailed.

Not that the light drizzle could prevent today's meeting on the Crag, but it was bound to make it uncomfortable and short. Angel hoped the others knew a more sheltered place.

Lord Dominic, Gerald Leigh, and Osa were waiting for them at the edge of the Grisedale woods.

"The track is slippery," explained Dom. "We did not want you to ride up there. Beth, do you remember the place we used to call the Cave? We thought we'd go there."

Leaving the horses in Abel's charge, they pushed through the dripping undergrowth until they came to a rocky hollow. A tiny rill here formed a deep and rather sinister-looking pool, to one side of which a low cliff leaned forward protectively. The ground beneath was dry, well carpeted with pine needles, and though the pines shut out the light and made the place gloomy, they also added their shelter from the rain. They sat down, and Osa joined them, smelling strongly of wet dog.

Beth and Gerald went a few paces farther; their voices were drowned by the chatter of the stream and the constant drip of rain from the trees by the pool.

"It looks like a good place for a murder," remarked Angel with a shiver, and to counteract that impression she gave a lively account of Saturday's race. "So I walked back to the house with Sir

Gregory," she concluded, "and he was charming. I think I have misjudged him."

"I doubt it," said Dominic. "He can bring the ladies around his thumb, I daresay. Look at the way Beth dotes on him! But he is a high-handed, prosy bore at bottom."

"Catherine thinks you resent him because he is older than you and was always allowed to be more independent."

"Fustian! A slow-top like Cousin Gregory doesn't know how to make use of independence anyway. And she is another female he has brought round his thumb! Besides, he is out to feather his nest with my inheritance."

"Well, you are not doing anything to get it back, are you? It is two weeks since we brought Beth to meet you and you are not an inch closer to seeing your father."

"There's no hurry. I shall come about, never fear. What would you have me do, ride up to the Hall and demand admittance?"

"You might ask Sir Gregory for help."

"He came over to Upthwaite while you were away and offered his assistance. Pitching it rather too rum, and so I told him! We had a flaming row."

"And said a thousand things you did not mean, I'll wager, and now you cannot take them back."

"Are you taking his side against me, Miss Brand?"

"No, of course not. But I do think you are being cloth-headed. However, I don't mean to quarrel with you. Let us talk of something else. Do you think it will rain all week?"

"Who knows?" said Lord Dominic gloomily.

"I hope it does not, for I want to climb Helvellyn."

"I cannot do so. It may rain for a month, for me."

"You are monstrous disagreeable this morning! We shall ride up as far as possible, and you can come that far."

"It is all arranged?"

"Well, we decided this would be a good week for it if it turns out fine. Mr Leigh! Has Beth told you we are going to climb Helvellyn?"

144

The vicar stood up and helped his beloved to rise.

"Yes," he said, coming over to them. "If it clears up, of course. I thought I had best go to see my mother tomorrow in case Thursday turns out to be a good day."

"Good. Ask her if we can all come to see her next week. I spoke to my aunt and uncle about it and they would be happy to make her acquaintance. Uncle Clement suggested next Monday, if it is fine."

"This rain ruins everything," complained Lord Dominic.

"I shan't see you tomorrow then, Gerald?" asked Beth.

"No, love, but why don't you and Miss Brand persuade Miss Sutton to chaperone you to the vicarage on Wednesday? Perhaps she could find some parish business of her father's to make it unexceptionable."

"I never thought to hear you suggest such a thing, Leigh!" exclaimed Lord Dominic. "Three young ladies to visit a male household!"

The vicar flushed. "Do you think it improper? I suppose you are right. I had thought that as she is your sister, and with Miss Sutton . . ."

"I think it a splendid plan," Angel assured him, "and quite unexceptionable. We will see you on Wednesday. Come, Beth, before he changes his mind." Giggling, the two girls pushed their way back through the bushes and were soon out of sight.

Lord Dominic had difficulty rising and limped heavily as the gentlemen followed.

"This cursed dampness!" he muttered.

"You *are* in a bad skin," commented his friend. "Cross as a bear at a stake."

"I know, I know, don't rub it in. I suppose that is why no mention was made of coming to see *me* tomorrow."

"Does that rankle? I daresay you are right."

"I haven't seen Beth for nearly four years, and now she is so taken up with you she scarcely speaks to me!"

"I have not seen her in nearly as long," reminded the vicar.

"But I am heartily sorry if you are offended. She means no harm, you know, and loves you as much as ever. Only falling in love, being in love, is quite different."

"So I gather from the way you are abandoning your antiquated notions of propriety. No, I am not vexed, though I should be, I daresay, had I not Miss Brand's company, ramshackle minx that she is. Devil take it, I believe Thunder is going lame!"

They were halfway up Dowen Crag by now. Lord Dominic dismounted and found a stone deeply imbedded in his horse's hoof. Neither of them was carrying anything which might serve to remove it.

"You cannot ride him in that state," said Gerald, swinging down from his sorrel gelding. "Here, take Rusty."

"I shall walk."

"Come, Dom, don't be—"

"Dammit, leave me alone!"

He set off up the path. Relieved of his burden, Thunder moved more easily, but his master was soon staggering, until at last he had to stop and cling to the saddle.

"Windmills in your head," remarked Gerald dispassionately, dismounting once more. "Get up."

"Gerald, if you were anyone else I'd kill you for being here."

"Yes, cockerel, except perhaps for Miss Brand."

"Oh, she'd never have let me make such a cake of myself in the first place. *Adelante, amigo!*"

Having already strained his leg, Lord Dominic found the rest of the ride painful and exhausting. To his fury, he had to be helped into the house. Mrs McTavish fussed over him unbearably until, in order to escape her ministrations, he retired to his chamber. Mr Leigh dined with him there, went off to fetch some cards to keep him amused, and came back to find him fast asleep.

He woke late next day, just as his friend was about to leave to visit his mother. His leg was much improved, his spirits not at all. He went to see Thunder.

" 'Tis healing nicely," assured the vicar's manservant, who

counted stablework among his varied duties. " 'Tweren't big, but sharplike, the stone, and worked in right deep. 'Twon't do to ride 'im a couple o' days yet."

"Thank you, Forrester," said his lordship, and tipped the man a shilling. The act reminded him of another of his worries. A lieutenant's pension was a mere pittance, and he could not go on sponging on Gerald forever.

Besieged by blue devils, he toyed with the elaborate luncheon Mrs McTavish had prepared to tempt him, and then retired to the study. A half-full bottle of brandy caught his eye and he poured himself a glass although, usually abstemious, he had no real intention of drinking it. He sat down and gazed blankly at the drizzle beyond the window, rolling the glass between his hands. Osa sat beside him, her head on his feet, but for once she brought no comfort.

Linnet was right, he must do something. And he had quarrelled with her for saying so. The memory was so disturbing that he began to examine his feelings for her, then quickly dropped the thought. Supposing, just for the sake of argument, that he found he was falling in love with her. As a penniless cripple he could have nothing to say to her, though in her presence his injuries seemed unimportant. What an enchantress she was, a provoking, mischievous, outspoken darling.

Cripple! he reminded himself fiercely, and gulped down the brandy. He had eaten very little and it went straight to his head. He sat in a haze of half-thoughts until an insistent knocking at the front door roused him. He vaguely remembered that Mrs McTavish had gone marketing and it was the maid's afternoon off. He had not drunk enough to impair his balance to any noticeable degree, so he went to answer the door, if only to stop the noise.

To his distant surprise, he found on the doorstep the idiot, Herbert, who made a habit of carving three-sevenths of his name on every available surface.

"What can I do for you?" Lord Dominic enquired amiably.

"Where at's t'vicar, yeronner?"

"He is not at home, Herbert. Can I help you?"

"T'vicar's to come to Uplands Farm right quick. 'Tis a 'mergency, yeronner."

"Mr Leigh is out."

"T'vicar, he've got to come. Been't you t'vicar, yeronner?"

"No, Herbert, he is not here. He cannot come now."

The halfwit began to snivel.

"I dassn't go back wi'out t'vicar," he insisted piteously. "Please, yeronner, I dassn't—"

"Oh, very well, I will come and explain, and perhaps I can be of assistance. Do you wait here while I fetch my horse."

"Oh, aye, yeronner, I c'n wait!"

Still feeling somewhat fuzzy behind the eyes, Lord Dominic donned coat and hat and headed for the stables. He was nearly there before he remembered that he could not ride Thunder. The horse whinnied hopefully when he recognised his master and the dog. Dom took a windfall apple from a sack and presented it with a word of apology. He saw that Rusty was in his stall. Gerald must have walked down to the boat rather than leave the sorrel standing in the rain.

"Forrester!" he shouted. The man appeared. "There is an urgent call for Mr Leigh, and as he is not here I shall go to see if I can do anything. Saddle Rusty, if you please."

" 'Tis rainin' yet, sir. Ye'll not want to go out."

"I'm not made of marchpane, man! Don't be an old woman."

"Aye, sir." Hoping that his lordship would return before he had to explain to the vicar why he had let Lord Dominic ride out when he was obviously on the go, Forrester saddled the gelding. "Ye'll not be riding up t'Crag?" he asked anxiously.

"No, to Uplands Farm." Dominic led the horse out, mounted, and called to Herbert. The manservant watched them cross the fields, Osa bouncing ahead, and shook his head in puzzlement. Now why would Mrs Norman over to Uplands send the simpleton on such an errand?

Lord Dominic, not being thoroughly acquainted with the

Norman household, did not ask himself that question, but he was wondering what quixotic whim had persuaded him to undertake an inevitably fruitless mission. If a minister was needed he could be of no conceivable use. The chill dampness cleared his head in no time and he nearly turned back. Only the sight of Herbert, patiently plodding through the mud and looking at him beseechingly as if he read his mind, made him continue. He pulled down his hat and hunched his shoulders against the persistent rain.

They were skirting a coppice when a shot rang out. Startled, Rusty reared. Under normal circumstances, Lord Dominic would have had no difficulty controlling him, but his weak leg betrayed him. As a second shot cracked, he slid backwards over the horse's rump and landed flat on his back in the mud in the most undignified posture.

Sitting up, he saw Herbert running hell for leather back the way they had come. There was a crashing among the trees that sounded like a horse galloping through brush, and then Osa came and licked his face. By the time he had fended her off, the departing drum of hooves was the only evidence that he had not been alone.

He picked up his hat. There was a neatly drilled hole in each side of the crown.

No one in Spain had ever impugned Lieutenant Marshall's coolness under fire, though more than one had called it foolhardiness. This was different. It looked very much as if someone had deliberately set out to put a bullet through his head, and it was all too possible that if he had not dismounted in that abrupt and inelegant fashion the second try would have succeeded.

Cold with foreboding, he went to catch Rusty, who was grazing placidly nearby. As far as he knew, no one hated him enough to put a period to his existence. That left only one motive for murder. And the only man who would profit by his demise was Sir Gregory Markham.

Often as he had inveighed against his cousin, accused him of coveting lands and title, he had never dreamed that the big man would see him as a removable obstacle. Even now he found it hard to believe. He remembered a time, he must have been eight or nine, when he had worshipped Cousin Gregory, had thought the sixteen-year-old schoolboy a buck of the first cut. In his heart he recognised that the dislike in which he had since held him had been a reaction against that excessive admiration. He had hoped that meeting him man to man, on a new footing of equality, he would be able to make him a friend.

Instead, he had been caught in an irresponsible prank, forced into a defensive position. He had quarrelled bitterly with Sir Gregory, had said, as Linnet guessed, unforgivable things. But murder?

There was no one else.

Gerald was incredulous. They talked of nothing else all evening, and though he could think of no other possible suspects, he still did not believe Dominic's theory.

''It was a farmer after some bird of prey,'' he insisted, ''or a poacher looking for a rabbit for his pot.''

''It was a rifle.'' His friend was adamant. ''Just look at these holes. That was a bullet, not shot.''

For the umpteenth time they studied the hat.

The evidence was produced again in the morning, when Miss Sutton, Miss Brand, and Lady Elizabeth arrived. Lord Dominic was displaying it before the vicar could warn him not to alarm the ladies. Beth refused even to consider the possibility that Sir Gregory was responsible. She retired to a corner of the drawing room with Gerald, and if they spoke of the incident it was only to each other.

Angel, on the other hand, had had a minor tiff with the baronet the previous day and was no longer in charity with him.

''It is monstrous exciting!'' she exclaimed. ''Only do be careful, Dom. Suppose he tried again to kill you? I never guessed he was half so wicked!''

'' 'Why, he's a devil, a devil, a very fiend,' '' quoted Catherine ironically.

"Do you think so?" asked Angel. "I quite thought you liked him, for you never agreed when I said he was odiously starchy."

"Lord Dominic, surely you cannot believe your cousin would descend to such a level of depravity!"

"I wish I could deny it, but try as I might, I can think of no one else who has any motive. While I live he can expect only a few farms and a comparatively small amount of money, for the rest is entailed and cannot be left away from me, though I get nothing from it at present. If I were dead, he'd inherit the title and the entire estate. It is enough to tempt any man."

"Not Sir Gregory, not to murder! He is an honourable gentleman." But he had taken advantage of her, kissed her against her will. Fighting doubt, Catherine went to discuss with Mr Leigh the parish business her father had been persuaded to concoct.

"Tell me exactly how it happened," coaxed Angel. "You were riding through the fields?"

"Yes. There was a call for Gerald and as he was away I went in his stead, though I've no notion what I hoped to accomplish. I never completed the errand, but I suppose it cannot have been excessively urgent or they would have sent again. The half-wit must have exaggerated."

"I should not be at all surprised. It would make him feel important, I expect."

"I daresay. He came with me to lead the way, for I am not absolutely certain of the Upthwaite farms. We were passing a spinney, elms and a lot of undergrowth, when I heard a shot. I thought nothing of it—poachers, perhaps, but it is not my land. Rusty was startled into rearing, and poor Herbert took to his heels in a panic and will not go near the place again, I'll wager."

"And then you realised he was shooting at you?"

"Oh, no. Then I descended from the horse in the most ludicrous manner, which I will not describe, and on the way down a second shot rang out. When I picked up my hat from the mud I discovered the bullet holes, and I could hear someone galloping off. Doubtless when I fell he thought he had finished me off.

"But why would Sir Gregory have been over here?"

"I was not far from the boundaries of Grisedale. If he was inspecting the estate he might have ridden on, on the off chance. Did he know that Gerald was not at home yesterday?"

"Yes," said Angel slowly. "Beth told him when we were talking about Helvellyn. So he knew you were alone, and it was not likely you would stay indoors all day. He was at the Hall in the morning, but in the afternoon he went out, for several hours. I was with Beth most of the day."

"If only I had some proof!"

"You did not even see him? Just heard the horse? Then I suppose there is nothing we can do about it."

"Is he intending to climb Helvellyn with you?"

"Yes. I'll make sure he does not leave us halfway and go back to murder you, if I have to cling to him like a leech. But Dom, *promise* me you will not go riding alone in the hills?"

"I promise, Linnet. Meet me tomorrow by the lake?"

Angel was thoughtful on the way home, and that afternoon she cornered an apprehensive Catherine.

"It has stopped raining," she announced. "John Applejohn says it will certainly be sunny tomorrow."

"Yes, I really think it might. Shall we plan on climbing tomorrow? We had better send notes to the Hall and to Upthwaite."

"Will you write them? Listen, Catherine. Lord Dominic will not be able to come all the way and I don't want Sir Gregory to go back and kill him. So you must keep him occupied."

"I thought there was something brewing. Must I?"

"Yes, for I shall have to make sure Lord Welch does not bother Beth and Mr Leigh, and I shall be too busy to keep an eye on him too."

"But Angel, do you really think it necessary? After all, if he absented himself from our party and then Lord Dominic were found dead, suspicion must inevitably fall on him."

"If Dom was dead it would be too late, and I daresay he would

152

make it look like an accident so we could not prove anything. I could not bear it if anything happened to Dom.''

"I was afraid that that was the way of it.''

"Why afraid?''

"Have you any reason to suppose that he thinks of you seriously?''

"N-no. He does like me.''

"It is difficult not to, Angel dear.''

"Sir Gregory does not. Which just goes to show. Well, even if I never see Dom again after I go home, we cannot let him be murdered in cold blood. Will you help, Catherine, please?''

"Very well,'' said Catherine resignedly. "I will not let the wicked baronet out of my sight.''

=15=

SIR GREGORY TOOK on the unenviable task of persuading Mrs Daventry to allow Beth to climb Helvellyn, a proposal she described as "shockingly unladylike." Since she went on to stigmatise Angel as an "an encroaching, underbred hussy" and complained that her charge was never seen without her, the baronet decided she was jealous.

A spot of shameless flattery brought her round in the end, and he thought he had forestalled the possibility of her complaining to Lord Grisedale. That accomplished, Sir Gregory remained as short a time in the lady's company as was consonant with the barest minimum of civility. He went to announce his success to Beth.

He found her conferring with Cook on the proper ingredients of a picnic for seven hungry climbers and a guide. She was pleased but not surprised, having every faith in his ability to get his way in any situation.

Abel, the groom, had volunteered to be their guide.

"I were up t'mounting wi' t'sheep every summer when I were a lad," he had announced on hearing of the project. "Know it loike t'back o' my hand. 'Sides, ye'll not want summun as might tell tales on Master Dom."

The three from the Hall arrived at the Barrows End vicarage at an unconscionably early hour. Shivering in the chill of the misty morning, Catherine and Angel joined them, and they took the track over Dowen Crag.

Angel was far from certain how she should behave towards Sir Gregory, convinced as she was of his perfidious attack on Lord

Dominic. To ignore him or accuse him were equally out of the question. Fortunately he was not in a talkative mood, having resumed the air of cynical boredom which he had for the most part abandoned in their company. She hoped his conscience was pricking him.

Catherine was also unsure how to go on. Though nearly convinced the shooting had been an accident, she had her own reasons for constraint. Since the night he had kissed her she had only seen the baronet twice, in company, and had scarce exchanged a word with him.

Having promised Angel to "keep him occupied," she made an effort to converse as they set out. Her openings sank without trace in his abstracted silence, and she was greatly relieved when the narrowness of the path forced them to ride single file.

Her next concern was how Dom would treat his cousin. Their quarrel would account for a certain coolness between them, and she hoped he was not anxious for a confrontation. If only Mr Leigh had represented to him the impropriety of an open accusation based on mere guesswork! She was pleased with Angel's restraint; perhaps his lordship would be equally amenable to reason.

She need not have worried. When they arrived at Upthwaite Park, Dominic was already there and managed to include all five, even Abel, in his careless greeting. As he immediately monopolised Angel, the fact that he never directly addressed Sir Gregory went unnoticed. Osa, bestowing lavish salutations on each and every person, made up for her master's neglect.

Angel had decided to begin as she meant to go on, that is to devote herself to distracting Lord Welch so that he would not plague Beth and Gerald. However, her good intentions went for naught. Lord Dominic claimed her attention, and she could not bring herself to abandon their delightful intimacy for the dubious joys of a meaningless flirtation. Besides, the viscount was being positively genial, even towards his rival. He had provided a substantial breakfast and seemed to revel in his rôle as host.

When they had all eaten their fill, Lord Welch was much inclined to give them a tour of the splendours of his house and gardens, with which only Dominic was familiar.

"Lady Elizabeth has not been here since we were children," he pointed out. "There are many improvements I should wish to show her, and all of you, of course. I do not pretend to equal the luxury of Grisedale Hall, but I can claim a degree of elegance and comfort to be found in few homes in this neighbourhood."

Mr Leigh nobly ignored this scarcely veiled taunt, and left to the others the task of persuading his lordship to postpone the inspection till another day. This done, Abel was called from the kitchens and they set off once more.

As soon as they left the shelter of Upthwaite's valley, they found themselves on steep, rugged moorland. Abel, in the lead, was closely followed by Lord Welch, who kept up a running dispute as to the correct path. It was a one-sided dispute, as Abel uttered not a word and at every point where trail and opinion diverged took his own way with unswerving determination.

Whenever there was room to spread out, the party divided itself instinctively into pairs. The viscount continued his unheeded argument with their guide. Behind them rode Lord Dominic and Angel, both of whom appeared to be deriving immense amusement from some private joke. Then came Beth and Gerald, their horses so close it was amazing they did not trip over each other's heels. Bringing up the rear were Catherine and Sir Gregory.

"I do not wish you to think that I am not grateful for the loan, sir," said Catherine, "but you must admit that this nag is excessively sluggish. I do not believe I shall reach the summit until after dark!"

"He considers our present course fit only for a mountain goat, Miss Sutton. I have never seen such a disgruntled expression on a horse's face. Fortunately you will be able to abandon him shortly and carry yourself the rest of the way."

"Fortunate indeed! I must hope I shall not reveal myself to be equally sluggish."

The track narrowed again, rising steeply between gorse and heather. They were forced to ride single file until they emerged on a gently sloping pasture dotted with sheep. Abel awaited them by a rough stone shepherd's hut. With him was the old man who had been in church their first day in Barrows End.

The shepherd was delighted to have company, and his black and tan dogs were persuaded to reach an accommodation with Osa. She and Lord Dominic would have to stay here, as the way grew too steep for horses. The others left their mounts in the drystone-walled sheep pens behind the hut.

At the top of the next slope Angel, hot and panting in spite of a refreshing breeze, looked back to see Dom and Osa gazing wistfully after them. She waved, half minded to go back to them. Then Lord Welch said something to her and the moment was lost. She went on, though conscious that the day had lost some of its brightness.

The path was interrupted here and there by rocky steps. The group began to straggle, Catherine and Sir Gregory once more in last place. They had no breath to spare for talking now.

As Sir Gregory helped her over a particularly awkward rock, Catherine realised with misgiving that she had all too easily returned to the informality she had sworn to abjure. If he had not yet addressed her as Kate, that was doubtless because he had been unable to call up an apposite quotation. Useless to attempt now to return to strict etiquette, but she must make an effort to catch up with the others. Trying to ignore the amusement in his eyes, she hurried on until she was so out of breath she simply had to sit down on a convenient boulder to recover.

Though there was plenty of room on the rock, Sir Gregory did not at once join her. He shaded his eyes and gazed after the rest of the party, then, apparently satisfied that they were sufficiently distant, turned to her with a perfectly serious face.

"Miss Sutton," he began, "I have not until now had an opportunity to apologise to you for my disgraceful behaviour last week. I hope I have at last been forgiven, but I am aware that your good nature has had a long struggle to overcome your natural aversion for my company."

Crimson, eyes fixed firmly on his boots, Catherine mumbled an incoherent mixture of affirmation and denial, hardly sure herself which was which. He made a motion to take her hand, then drew back deliberately.

"The only excuse I have," he revealed, and now the laughter was back in his voice, "is that you were irresistible. But I will be good, Miss Sutton, I promise. Only do not again tempt me by moonlight!"

"Such was hardly my intention!" she retorted.

"No, I was to blame. Say you are not angry with me, and then if you are rested we had best resume our upward struggle before someone thinks an accident has befallen us."

Catherine sighed. "I am not still angry with you, Sir Gregory, though I have a lowering feeling that I ought to be. I fear I am sadly lacking in sensibility, a mortifying reflection." She rose. "Oh, dear, how much farther have we to go?"

It was not far. The ground levelled off, then suddenly fell away before them, leaping and bounding precipitously in a jumble of rocks towards the narrow valley invisible below. The valleys were mere creases in the wrinkled face of the world. Range after range of rounded mountaintops spread to the horizon, and above them in the cloudless sky, eagles wheeled and soared effortlessly.

Even Lord Welch was bereft of speech. Several minutes of silence ensued, which were ended by Abel.

"Ye'll be ready to go down?" he suggested.

There was a general cry of outrage and he looked abashed.

"Soulless yokel," murmured the viscount to Angel. Rather uncertainly he pointed out the summits of Sca Fell, Great Gable, and Skiddaw. "Dash it, Miss Brand, I don't know! They all look much the same to me."

Angel had to agree. The overwhelming effect of the sudden

distances was wearing off and she was beginning to be sharp set by pangs of hunger. To admit this, she felt, would be to classify herself as another "soulless yokel," but she did go so far as to sit down on a rocky outcrop, where his lordship joined her.

A few admiring remarks were exchanged upon the clarity of the air, the warmth of the sun, the desirability of being able to float with the eagles. Then Angel noticed that her companion was regarding Beth and Gerald, hand in hand at the edge of the precipice, with an air of smug complacency.

"Do you not mind them being so happy together?" she asked with her usual lack of ceremony. "Are you being noble or do you not wish to marry Beth any longer?"

"I have every expectation and intention of marrying her," he said smoothly. "That being so, there can be no harm in allowing her to sow a few wild oats first. She will behave differently when she is my wife."

Angel thought it highly unlikely that Beth would change her mind, the glories of Upthwaite Park notwithstanding, but she hesitated to disillusion the viscount. As long as he was sure that she would turn to him in the end, he would not harass her and, it seemed, was even prepared to be pleasant to Mr Leigh. Angel did wonder how he would react when he realised that he had no hope of winning her. She hoped he would continue to be noble, though rather suspecting that he might cut up stiff.

She changed the subject to one of more immediate interest.

"I'm hungry," she announced loudly.

Walking down the steep paths turned out to be almost as exhausting as climbing up had been, but considerably quicker. They were soon slipping and sliding down the slope to the shepherd's hut, to be welcomed rapturously by Osa and the shepherd, and with relief by Lord Dominic.

They drank from the tumbling beck, and then saddlebags were opened to reveal a veritable feast, while the old man produced a battered tin kettle of tea as his contribution.

After eating, Angel and Dominic wandered off in search of wild flowers. Beth and Gerald soon followed suit, in the opposite direction, and after a few minutes Lord Welch went after them.

"I hope he is not going to make a nuisance of himself," said Catherine lazily, settling herself in a more comfortable position on the rug-covered grass. "He has been amazingly agreeable today."

"He has indeed," said Sir Gregory with a frown. "As if butter would not melt in his mouth. Now what does he have up his sleeve, I wonder?"

"Must he have something up his sleeve?"

"I'll wager he's not given up hope of Beth's dowry so easily. Did you notice the state of his fields as we passed?"

"Thistles and ragweed. Can you think of no pleasanter topic than neglected farmland for such a perfect day?"

"I'm sorry. But there is another unpleasant subject I must introduce, I fear. What do you know of Dom being involved in a shooting accident?"

"Did Beth tell you about that?" Catherine was suddenly wary. If, as she was more and more certain, he was innocent, she did not want to hurt him by letting him know he was under suspicion. And if by some horrid chance he had contrived the incident, then that knowledge might drive him to make another and perhaps more successful attempt.

"She mentioned it in passing," said the baronet. "If you can supply the details, I shall be very grateful."

Did he want to know where his plan had gone wrong, or was he concerned for his cousin's safety? Either case pointed to a real danger for Lord Dominic, and she was suddenly afraid for him. It seemed all too likely, now she considered, that such a careless young man might have made enemies he was unaware of.

She could see no harm in telling the full story just as Angel had insisted on recounting it to her. Sir Gregory listened carefully, asked a few questions, and thanked her.

"Why do you want to know?" she enquired at last. "Do you think it was not an accident?"

"I'm sorry, Miss Sutton, I cannot tell you at present." He was frowning again, and thoughtful, and she was glad to see Angel and Dom returning.

"Look, Catherine!" cried Angel, displaying a handful of flowers. "I brought you the prettiest ones. This is lady's slipper, and this with the tiny face is heartsease, and this one is toadflax. If you press the sides it opens its mouth!"

"Just like a snapdragon," said Catherine. "Dom, can you see Mr Leigh and the others? I think we should be starting down. There is a haze over the sun and I should dislike excessively to be caught in a fog or a rainstorm on the mountain."

They managed to avoid that fate, though by the time they reached their various homes the sky was threatening.

"I refuse to believe it is going to rain again!" groaned Angel.

=16=

IT RAINED DURING the night, but the next morning was merely grey and damp. Angel walked up to the Hall, and as she entered the park, by the gate, a watery gleam of sunshine split the overcast. By the time she reached the house the sky was a patchwork of blue and white, and the breeze which was breaking up the clouds brought a delicious green odour of growing things. With her new-found interest in flowers, she decided to suggest to Beth a walk about the gardens.

The butler, who opened the door to her, looked worried. As he took her wrap he seemed to be carrying on an internal debate. Then he apparently made up his mind.

"Mrs Daventry is in the drawing room, miss," he informed her. "I fear madam is not—ah—in a happy mood. Lady Elizabeth is above stairs."

"Can I see her, Venables?"

"Certainly, miss. That is, I believe so. I, ah, rather think her ladyship would prefer not to come down. If you will be so good as to wait a moment, I shall ask her ladyship's abigail to conduct you to her chamber."

Rather puzzled, Angel wandered about the hallway examining the portraits of a number of gloomy-looking ancestors. The atmosphere in the house seemed even more oppressive than usual, and she imagined Lord Grisedale hunched in his cavernous room, spinning a web of tyranny over the household.

She became aware of a whispered altercation in the passage leading to the servants' quarters.

"I'll not take it on my head, Mr Venables, to disturb the poor dear," hissed a female voice.

"Then upon my head be it, Miss Ordway. If anyone can cheer her up, it'll be Miss Brand, you'll see. Quite a changed person is her ladyship since miss came to the vicarage. It's a great pity Sir Gregory went off so early to Penrith, or this 'd never have happened, but being as it has, we must do our best for her."

The butler reappeared with the abigail in tow, and Angel, by now alarmed, followed her up the grand marble staircase.

She found Beth lying on her bed, sobbing her heart out.

"Beth dear, what is it?" she cried, running to her and embracing her. "Has Sir Gregory done something to distress you?"

"N-no, it's Papa."

"He's found out about Dom and Gerald!"

"No, only about us climbing Helvellyn, and he doesn't know they were there. Oh, Lyn, Mrs Daventry told him we went and he was so angry, and then I had a horrid quarrel with her, and I can't see Gerald today and Papa will never let me marry him, I know. What am I going to do?"

"If he won't, then you shall come and live with me until you are of age and he cannot prevent it. You make me feel very lucky that my own papa is such a darling, and even Uncle Clement is a dear." A martial light entered Angel's eye. "And in the meantime, I'm going to give *your* papa a piece of my mind!"

"But Lyn—"

"No, don't try to stop me. I am quite determined. Wait here, Beth, and don't be afraid. He cannot eat me, after all!" She marched to the door, leaving Beth wide-eyed and caught between horror and admiration.

Fortunately, Angel remembered the way to Lord Grisedale's room, so she did not have to stop and ask, which might have sufficed both to impair her resolution and to give him warning. She flung the double doors open, and a footman who was bending over his lordship looked up aghast. As she stalked in, he scuttled forward expostulating.

"You may leave us," she declared in the grand manner, and turning her back on him went to stand arms akimbo before the thunderous earl. "What do you mean by upsetting Beth so?" she attacked immediately.

"It is none of your demmed affair, hussy! I happen to believe in keeping a short rein on my womenfolk. If your father did likewise he'd have less cause to blush for your conduct!" The old man was snarling but there was a lively gleam in his eye as if he enjoyed a good battle.

"He has not half so much cause as Beth has to blush for yours!" Angel shot back. "You are an odious tyrant and an ill-mannered churl and—"

"And you are a pert saucebox who ought to be—"

"Don't interrupt me! And don't threaten me either! You have no authority over *me*. I was going to say that just because you are miserable yourself there is no excuse to make the rest of the world miserable. I do believe Aunt Maria is right. Everyone panders to your every whim and dares not cross you and it only makes you sourer. I daresay you even bullied your doctor into recommending this ridiculous set-up!"

Gibbering with rage, Lord Grisedale pulled himself to his feet as Angel rushed about the room opening curtains and the windows behind them. The damp freshness blew into the fusty murk and the heat of the blazing fire at once became less overwhelming.

"Why, you have a French window onto the terrace," said Angel in a pleased voice, "and the sun has come out. Will you take a turn with me, my lord?"

Taken aback by her sudden change of tone, the earl muttered something indistinguishable as she handed him his handsome, ivory-knobbed cane and offered her arm. She clearly heard the word "hussy," but he laid his crabbed claw on her steadying arm and hobbled to the window with her. They stepped out. Behind them, the footman had returned with the butler, and they both stood and gaped. Angel concentrated on supporting the old man's steps as far as the stone balustrade. He seemed to grow stronger as they went.

Leaning against the wall, he gazed out over the luxuriant greeness of gardens, park, and woodland, and up to the mountains.

"What exactly did your aunt say?" he asked thoughtfully.

It was Angel's turn to be taken aback. "Well, not precisely what I told you. She did say that modern medicine would prescribe light and air and exercise, not shutting yourself away in a hot, stuffy lair. The rest was me."

"Minx," he said, but not with any malice.

Greatly heartened, Angel ventured a question. "Why were you so angry that Beth climbed the mountain?"

"Why, I can't say. Perhaps because she did not tell me about it."

"That is entirely your own fault!"

"Or perhaps because I myself am confined to the house."

"You need not be, I'm sure. Besides, Uncle Clement says that happiness is desiring the accessible."

"Do you subscribe to that doctrine, Miss Brand?"

"Well, it makes sense. And I hope by the time I am your age I shall have sufficient self-control to abide by it," she said severely. "Do you wish to return to your room now?"

"With your permission, ma'am! If I am to turn over a new leaf, we must take things gradually. You must not expect miracles of me."

"I do not," she assured him, helping him back towards the house. "I expect you will still be irritable at times. Even the best-tempered people fall into the megrims now and then."

During their absence, Venables and the footman had hurried to close windows and curtains, leaving only the door open. As they stepped through it, they saw the footman making up the fire.

"Dolt!" roared the earl, throwing his stick. "Put that fire out, it is the middle of August! And take down those devilish red curtains. This place is like Hades! Why am I served by none but nincompoops and boobies?"

Angel sped back to Beth's chamber and reported on the astounding success of her mission. Beth, who had expected her to return emotionally if not physically mangled, was incredulous.

"You mean you just read him a lecture and his disposition miraculously changed?"

"Oh, no! You should have heard him denouncing the servants when I left! And he was not at all polite to begin with. I think it gave him such a shock when, instead of withering, I drew the curtains and invited him to go out, that he could not think of anything else to do. And once we were outside, we went on famously. It is most fortunate that it happens to be a beautiful day."

"Lyn, you are not hoaxing me? You know, Dom always said Papa was not nearly such a dragon if one squared up to him. Only Mama never did, and she said it was unladylike to brangle and brawl, so I never got in the way of it."

"Look where defiance took Dom! But I shall not land in the suds like that because I am not given to making wild pronouncements and then insisting on carrying them through. It is a very lucky thing that females are expected to change their minds. I have frequently thought so."

"You don't suppose you could persuade Papa to be reconciled with Dom? And to let me marry Gerald?"

"Anything is possible and I am perfectly willing to try, but as your papa said, we must take things gradually. After all, all he has done is open the windows and admit that he was unreasonably angry this morning. It is an excellent start, but I confess I shall be excessively surprised if he should go so far as to apologise to you."

"I do not expect it. Oh dear, I suppose I must apologise to Mrs Daventry."

"Well, I do think *she* owes *you* an apology for bearing tales, but it will be much more comfortable in the end if you make the first move. Let us go and get it over with at once."

Mrs Daventry was very ready to be conciliated. She even ventured to hint delicately at the mildest possible criticism of Lord Grisedale.

"*Dear* Lady Elizabeth," she gushed, "I never *dreamed* for a *moment* that your papa could have any *objection* to your expedition and *indeed* I am *still* quite unable to guess at the *reason* for his disapproval but *you* are too good-natured to suppose that I should have breathed a *word* had I been able to foresee his reaction for I am sure . . .''

She rattled on, every word making Angel the more certain that she had acted out of spite. Presumably she had genuinely not foreseen Beth's anger, and her present anxiety could be put down to the fear of losing all influence over her charge.

Growing impatient, Angel interrupted to ask Beth to walk with her in the garden. Mrs Daventry soon grew bored and left them, and the rest of the morning passed more pleasantly than seemed possible considering the earlier upsets. A footman came to call them to luncheon, and they went in reluctantly.

The earl joined them for the repast. He was astonishingly genial towards the two young ladies, and ignored Mrs Daventry completely, perhaps having decided to blame her for the entire fracas. The poor woman dared open her mouth only to fill it, and Angel almost found herself pitying her.

That afternoon, Angel and Beth rode down to Ullswater to meet Lord Dominic. He had been out on the lake in Gerald's boat, rowing Osa up and down the shallows.

"Take us out, oh, please take us out!" cried Angel.

"There is not room for both of you as well as Osa, and if I leave her behind she howls. I'll take you one day, Linnet."

"Does rowing not hurt you?" asked Beth.

"No, scarcely at all. It does not seem to strain my leg. In fact I can almost feel it growing stronger."

Angel extracted a promise that he would take her boating next week without fail, as well as go with them on the trip to see Mrs Leigh. Then she told him about her encounter with his father. He congratulated her but was not unduly surprised at her success.

"I can see that you have been truckling to his every capricious freak," he said severely to Beth. "You know that is not the way to go on with him."

"I'm very sorry, Dom," apologised Beth meekly.

"She is doing the very same thing with you!" accused Angel. "I am glad that Mr Leigh is not of a similar tyrannical disposition!"

"Do you think me tyrannical then?"

"Not to me. I have never learned to truckle, and it is impossible to be a tyrant if your victim will not submit."

"I fear it is too late for me to reform," said Beth.

"Never mind," consoled Angel. "When you are married to kind, gentle Gerald, it will not matter in the least. By the way, Dom, are you and Mr Leigh invited to dine at Upthwaite? Lord Welch has invited me and the Suttons and Beth and Sir Gregory."

"Yes, he asked both of us. Knowing, I am sure, that Gerald has a parish meeting every Friday evening. I shall be there though."

"Good. Then there will not be an excess of females, which is a thing I abhor."

Lord Welch's dinner party started off badly. Mr and Mrs Sutton scarcely knew him, had not been favourably impressed at their few meetings, and had only been persuaded to accept by considerations of politeness. The viscount's effusive welcome did nothing to banish their reserve. He seemed unaware of it, possibly considering it a manifestation of the deference due to his exalted rank.

Lord Dominic was next to arrive. He laughingly apologised to the vicar and his wife for having previously been introduced to them under an alias. They were rather shocked to hear both Catherine and Angel address him simply as "Dom," even when it was explained to them as a precaution against accidental disclosure of his identity. Nor were they best pleased to find the young man on such intimate terms with their niece.

Mrs Sutton was about to turn to Catherine for reassurance on this point, when Sir Gregory arrived, alone.

"Where is Beth?" demanded Angel.

"Lady Elizabeth is, ah, indisposed, and begs you to excuse her," said the baronet blandly, directing his words at his host.

A look of fury crossed Lord Welch's face. It was plain as a pikestaff to most of those present that he considered her absence a direct snub. He recovered his countenance immediately and hoped politely that her ladyship was not seriously unwell, a possibility which Sir Gregory denied with unnecessary vigour.

"Not at all," he assured. "A slight headache, I believe she mentioned, or some such thing."

The viscount was an abstracted host. Lord Dominic and Angel spoke to Sir Gregory as little as common courtesy permitted. All in all it was not a convivial evening, and the party broke up early.

Sir Gregory rode beside the vicarage gig, homeward bound, and Angel abandoned mistrust and dislike long enough to enquire whether Beth was truly in good frame.

"Certainly, Miss Brand. I believe she is playing a game of draughts with my uncle. I have to thank you for an extraordinary transformation on that score. Had I dreamed so simple a cure was possible I'd have tried it months ago."

"Lyn told us she had reformed Lord Grisedale," said Mrs Sutton. "The improvement is lasting then? She used precisely the methods I had advocated."

"I told him it was all your idea, Aunt Maria. Or at least that you said he should not lurk in that gloomy cave. I think I shall go and see him tomorrow morning, to make sure he has not relapsed."

Aunt Maria was by no means equally approving of Angel's relationship with Lord Grisdedale's son. When they reached the vicarage and Sir Gregory had gone on his way, she tackled the subject.

"Angel dear, I did not like to see you so much in Lord Dominic's pocket this evening. I am sure you are not aware how particular it looks, but you know your intimacy with his sister cannot excuse familiarity with his lordship."

"I am afraid I am at fault, Mother," put in Catherine apologetically. "I have been too preoccupied with my own affairs to be a proper companion to Angel. I had not realised she was seeing so much of Dom."

"Yet you too call him Dom. I cannot think it proper!"

"There is no impropriety, I promise. I believe he looks on me as a sort of aunt."

"He does not look on *me* as an aunt!" exclaimed Angel. "You do not understand how desperate it is. I have only two more weeks!"

"Then it is not merely a flirtation," said Mrs Sutton slowly. "Oh, dear! Have you any reason to suppose that he thinks of you seriously?"

"That is just what Catherine asked, and the answer is still no. He likes me, I know he does, though we often argue, but he has never tried to kiss me or . . . or anything."

"I should hope not!" Catherine was scandalised. "He is an honourable gentleman!"

"A great many gentlemen have tried to kiss me, I assure you, and some of them succeeded. It is quite commonplace when one is a reigning Beauty."

"But it is no guide to serious intentions, I think," pointed out Aunt Maria gently. "Well, I am exceedingly sorry to learn that things are at such a pass, but in the circumstances I will only beg you not to allow your feelings to betray you into any ruinous indiscretion, Angel. I hope and believe I may trust in your commonsense and your duty to yourself and your family. Good night, my loves."

Both Catherine and Angel prepared for bed in thoughtful silence.

"I thought Aunt Maria would lock me up," said Angel as they climbed into bed.

"That is not her way, nor Papa's. They think only freedom can teach responsibility. I have always done my best to deserve their trust."

"I shall too."

Catherine blew out the candle.

"Angel, have you truly been kissed by a number of gentlemen?"

"Yes. But Aunt Maria is right, it is no sign of serious intentions."

"Oh."

There was another silence.

"It is perfectly horrid to be in love and not to know," Angel uttered presently in a despairing voice.

"Isn't it?" agreed Catherine.

=17=

BETH HAD NOT seen Mrs Leigh in over three years and was decidedly nervous at the prospect.

"Suppose she takes me in dislike!" she wailed to Angel when the landau picked up the vicarage ladies on Monday morning. Mr Sutton and Sir Gregory were riding ahead down the narrow lane towards Patterdale, where they were to meet Gerald.

"Why should she do that?" asked Angel in surprise. "I thought you were already acquainted."

"Yes, but I was a child then, and now I want to marry her son."

"She can have no reason to object to that, surely! You are above him in both rank and fortune."

"There are other considerations, Lyn," suggested Aunt Maria. "Mrs Leigh might for instance doubt whether Lady Elizabeth will be of assistance to her son in his profession. I shall endeavour to convince her to the contrary, for Clement often speaks of how conscientious she is about visiting dependents and the poor and the sick."

"Thank you, ma'am, you are very kind. I daresay I am being stupidly gooseish to worry so. Only what if she takes exception to Papa being so horrid to Gerald?"

Mrs Sutton, Catherine, and Angel hastened to reassure her on that and every other head, and by the time they arrived at the appointed meeting place she was able to greet her beloved cheerfully.

Mr Sutton, boasting of having been a famous oarsman in his youth, took one pair of oars in the hired boat. Sir Gregory and Mr

Leigh took up the others, while the ladies arranged themselves on well-cushioned seats, parasols held aloft. Angel took charge of steering, which was accomplished with a pair of ropes ingeniously attached to the rudder and leading thence to the rear seat. Before they had rowed a hundred feet she had them going round in circles. Gerald clambered precariously past the voyagers and removed the rudder from its slot.

"We will steer with the oars," he said severely.

Since the gentlemen were, of course, all facing backwards, this involved a great deal of clamour from the ladies.

"Left a bit!"

"A bit more."

"That is too far, go back!"

"Why can you not row in a straight line?"

"Now right!"

"No, Lyn, that's left!"

Their zigzag course seriously discommoded a pair of ducks, which fled squawking into the rushes. Then it was discovered that neither Mr Sutton nor Sir Gregory, though pulling away with a will, was precisely sure which oar to pull on to turn in a given direction. Mr Sutton, already slightly winded, was retired to the replaced rudder, which he promised he could manage. A few minutes of intensive coaching sorted out the baronet's ideas, and at last they proceeded at a reasonable speed towards the spot where they were to pick up Lord Dominic.

Dom was waiting, for once without Osa. Gerald had succeeded in persuading him that to add a large and lively dog to a cargo of novice boaters was to invite disaster. He waved and called from the shore, and then was very soon helpless with laughter as two flustered gentlemen with oars, one with a rudder, a young lady with a paddle, and another wielding a boathook attempted to bring the rocking skiff close enough for him to step in. Mrs Sutton saved the day by tossing a rope to him.

Under Angel's anxious eye, Lord Dominic took up the third pair of oars. She pushed off with the boathook, and once they had struggled away from the bank and the shallows, it became plain that rowing in deep water was altogether an easier matter. Mr Sutton was even permitted to take another turn at the oars when Sir Gregory complained of developing blisters. Angel found it excessively difficult to keep a straight face as the tall, lanky vicar and the taller, broad-shouldered baronet cautiously changed places, creeping past each other like a pair of beetles on a narrow grass blade.

Lord Dominic seemed to be rowing easily and without strain. Noticing Angel's watchful regard, he smiled at her.

"I am allowing the others to do most of the work, Miss Brand," he told her, "but I assure you there is no cause for concern. I have been out in Gerald's boat as often as possible for the last couple of weeks, you know. My only problem is that my shoulders are developing so that my coats begin to be too tight!"

"Then you will soon be in the first stare of fashion," she answered, "and without using buckram or wadding."

"But, like me, Dominic prefers comfort to alamodality," put in Mr Leigh.

All too soon the boat ride came to an end, and they pulled up to a small jetty where a manservant waited to help them disembark. Beth was once more in a quake.

"Am I quite tidy?" she asked anxiously, brushing down her skirts and patting and poking at her hair.

"Perfectly," reassured Mrs Sutton.

"Delightfully," said Mr Sutton.

"Charming," said Sir Gregory.

"Enchanting," was Mr Leigh's verdict, accompanied by a squeeze of the hand and a loving smile.

As they walked up the long lawn towards the manor, a pleasant-looking though unpretentious building, Angel glanced down with a sigh at her own plain grey muslin, contrasting it with Beth's lace-trimmed walking dress of primrose jaconet. She was growing very tired of being so dowdy. Even Lord Dominic had murmured approvingly at his sister's appearance. It was time, she decided, to have a pretty gown made up. She would wear it only as a last resort, keep it as her final card. And to back it up she would write to Papa and ask him to send her a letter of introduction to Lord Grisedale. If it became necessary to reveal her true identity, that would serve as proof. It was all very well hoping that *someone* would wish to marry her in her lowly disguise, but to lose him because of it was a horse of a different colour!

Mrs Leigh welcomed her guests with delight and very soon made them feel at home. Mrs Sutton took it upon herself to smooth the meeting between Beth and her prospective mother-in-law, and they were soon wholly occupied in sharing their mutual admiration of Gerald.

The embarrassed object of their commendations invited the rest of the party to take a turn about the gardens. When they returned to the house, they found an elegant luncheon set out for their refreshment. The gentlemen were particularly grateful after the morning's exertions, though Angel's always healthy appetite had in no wise suffered from having merely sat with her fingers trailing in the water.

Mrs Leigh and Beth were like mother and daughter, and while he had expected no less, Gerald Leigh was obviously gratified. He was an attentive and sociable host, and when Angel compared this party with the dinner at Upthwaite Park, she at last admitted to herself wholeheartedly that her friend had made the right choice. Beth blossomed in the loving atmosphere and became actually gay, glowing with happiness. Lord Grisedale must be won over, Angel vowed, if she had to hit him on the head to accomplish it.

The return trip across Ullswater was effected with more expertise, but no faster than that morning, all the oarsmen being somewhat somnolent. As they dropped off Lord Dominic, well away from the village, he pointed out Gerald's small boat, pulled well up on the grassy bank and covered with a tarpaulin.

"I shall probably go rowing tomorrow afternoon," he said, looking pointedly at Angel. She gave him the tiniest nod.

"My poor old boat is working for its living these days!" declared the young vicar.

They returned the rented boat to its owner, and Mr Leigh, having been duly thanked for a delightful visit, rode off to Upthwaite. Angel announced that she had an errand or two in Patterdale, and the rest of the ladies at once remembered odds and ends they simply could not do without any longer. Mr Sutton and Sir Gregory exchanged glances, and the former suggested they should ride on, while the latter advised the coachman to look after the ladies. They departed towards Grisedale.

When they reached the shops, Angel drew Catherine aside and disclosed her decision to provide herself with an attractive gown.

"Just in case," she said vaguely. "Only I do not want Beth or Aunt Maria to know. So, *dearest* Catherine, could you draw them off for me, while I go to Doan's?"

"I'll try, Angel, if you will be quick. I've never known you take less than an hour or two to make up your mind."

"They do not have much choice of materials, so I will not be long."

"Very well. Let me think. Ah, I know. Mother, I believe I saw Miss Weir waving to us. Do you not think we ought to go and pass the time of day?"

"Oh, yes!" said Beth. "I know her only to bow to, but I should like to thank her for the novels I borrowed through Lyn."

As they walked up the street, Angel mysteriously vanished. In accordance with Catherine's expectation on this sunny afternoon, Miss Weir was found in her flower garden, where she might well have waved to the Suttons. She was thrilled to be properly introduced to Lady Elizabeth and insisted on calling "dear Tabitha" to share the treat. It was a good twenty minutes before they managed to tear themselves away.

Walking back towards the draper's, they met Angel looking angelic.

"Where have you been?" she demanded. "I went into Doan's

and nobody followed! I quite thought you had gone off home without me."

Catherine gathered from her smug face that her search had been successful, and so it proved. When they reached the vicarage and went up to their chamber to change, Angel produced a scrap of forget-me-not blue sarsnet.

"With blond lace," she explained, "and knots of deep blue ribbon. They are to deliver it direct to the dressmaker here in Barrows End. Will you come with me in the morning to choose a pattern?"

"Of course, dear. You will look quite ravishing in that colour. Fit to break a thousand hearts."

"One will do," said Angel softly.

Catherine thought it best not to delve too deeply into the meaning of that remark.

The following afternoon, Angel slipped out of the house alone. If she was missed, everyone would suppose her at Grisedale Hall, or at least out with Beth. She hurried towards Patterdale. Dom had not been able to name a time for their tryst, and she did not want to keep him waiting. It took her over an hour to reach the place where the boat was kept, and by the time she got there she fervently hoped that she would be offered a homeward ride on Thunder.

The boat, its cover removed, was already afloat, but there was no sign of Lord Dominic. In a very few minutes she heard the thud of approaching hooves, and Osa bounced up to her.

"Down, girl!" called Dom, swinging down from Thunder's back. "I hope you have not been waiting long, Linnet. I came down half an hour ago and launched the boat, but Osa kept trying to reach it so I took her for a run. I thought you'd not appreciate a wet dog for a fellow passenger."

He pulled on the painter and brought the small vessel to where they could step in. Osa took a flying leap as he steadied it. Angel was surprised that she did not go straight over the other side. She herself stepped in more decorously, with a helping hand from Dom. The dog was sniffing about the boat suspiciously, and Angel noticed that some letters had been carved in one of the seats.

"Look!" she exclaimed. "Herbert has made his mark on Mr Leigh's boat. 'HER' here, and over there too."

"Yes," said Dom with a frown. "I've not known him to do such a thing before. I saw it at once when I pulled the tarpaulin off. I don't suppose Gerald will be pleased. He has had the boat since we were boys and has always taken good care of it."

"Perhaps it can be smoothed away," suggested Angel. "It is not deeply cut. But don't let it spoil our afternoon. Let's go."

They pushed off, and were soon floating some twenty feet from the bank. Dom sculled gently, just enough to keep them moving. Osa sat in the bow, peering over the side, presumably at fish below the surface. Moorhens and coots paddled out of their way, a family of swans regarded them with supercilious curiosity, and a water rat emerged from a hole in the bank to watch their passage with bright brown eyes. The air was balmy, and the only sounds were the gurgle of water about the oars, Osa's panting, and an occasional quack.

"This is heavenly," said Angel, "but I don't think you are getting much exercise."

"I shall row harder on the way back," Dom replied lazily. "If you go at it overenthusiastically to start with, the return voyage is too long."

"I should like to try rowing. I thought yesterday that it looked too difficult, but it seems easier when people are not getting in each other's way."

"I'd rather not attempt to switch seats out here, especially with Osa in the boat. We could pull in to the shore if you wish."

"Not today, perhaps. I had to walk all the way here, and shall have to walk back again afterwards."

"Don't worry about that. I'll take you on Thunder. I'll even go all the way to Barrows End. I cannot skulk about in the undergrowth forever, expecially since you have Father eating out of the palm of your hand. Beth says he is a different person.''

"I cannot guarantee that he will welcome you with open arms, Dom. It might be best to wait a while, until he is so used to being cheerful that he is less likely to nab the rust.''

"Well, I shall take you home on Thunder, so let us have a rowing lesson.''

Angel found that one oar was as much as she could cope with, so they sat beside each other on the narrow bench. The footboard had to be moved forward so that she could reach it, which meant that Lord Dominic had his knees under his chin and had the greatest difficulty in making a stroke at all. Angel had no less difficulty, but they struggled on with a great deal of laughter, until she caught a crab. There was a huge splash, the boat rocked, to Osa's vociferous indignation, and she just saved herself from going over backwards into the bilge.

"I'm soaked!'' she cried. "You are wet too. We had best go home, lest you catch a chill. The water is shockingly cold for midsummer.''

"Most of it hit you,'' he pointed out with a grin. "I only caught a few drops. But I think it is growing late. We'd best be on our way.''

Angel managed to wriggle back to her original seat, and Dom turned the boat expertly. He began to row vigorously back along the shoreline. The water parted in ripples before them and streamed back on either side. Ducks fled in dismay, and their wake lapped noisily at the bulrushes as they passed.

They were no more than fifty feet from their destination when the rhythmic creak of the oars in the rowlocks became an ominous cracking noise. Before Angel's horrified eyes, the boat's sides splintered at each end of the rower's bench, then fractured cleanly. As the icy water flooded in, an oar rose abruptly and hit Lord Dominic on the chin. His eyes lost their focus, and he crumpled.

The boat sank, and Angel found herself shoulder-deep in the lake and ankle-deep in mud.

There was no sign of Dom. Her skirts dragged at her legs as she stepped forward and felt frantically in the murky water. Something heavy knocked against her and a patch of white cloth broke the surface: his shirt. She found his head, pushed it above the water, and with it balanced on her shoulder she struggled towards the shore, an endless distance away. A dozen times she nearly fell, then miraculously a strong arm was about her waist, the precious burden no longer weighed her down.

"Come on, Miss Brand," urged a vaguely familiar voice. "Just a few more steps."

She collapsed, half in half out of the water, her face buried in soft, sweet-smelling grass. For a few moments she was conscious of nothing else, then Osa nuzzled her cheek and a sense of desperate urgency forced her to her feet, up onto the low bank.

Dick Burchett had Dominic draped over his horse's back. With one hand he held the bridle, with the other pounded on the unconscious man's back. Seeing Angel moving, he called her to come and hold the horse, which was growing decidedly restless at this unusual treatment, especially as Osa apparently considered it responsible for her master's plight. The dog was alternating volleys of deep barks with despairing howls.

"That's what brought me," said young Mr Burchett, hooking a thumb at Osa as Angel staggered over to take the reins. "Deuced lucky, too. Making enough racket to wake the dead."

He went to work on Dominic with both hands, and soon a stream of water gushed from his patient's mouth and nose. Angel noted with horror that it had a pinkish tinge.

"He has a lung injury," she whispered. "Please be careful!"

"Breathing now," said Dick cheerfully, lifting him down. As he laid him on the grass, Dominic's eyes opened.

"Linnet," he croaked, and was seized with a spasm of retching and coughing.

Angel abandoned the horse.

"Dom, I'm here, I'm all right. Oh, Dom, don't try to talk. Just rest and we will take you home as soon as we can." She cradled his head in her lap, then realised she was soaking wet and looked around helplessly.

"Cold," he muttered, and closed his eyes again.

She was beginning to shiver herself. Dick Burchett, who was wet from the thighs down, was leading Thunder over.

"Don't see quite how we're going to do this," he said in puzzlement. "Maybe best ride for a carriage."

"No, we must get him warm and dry quickly! You get up on Thunder and I'll lift him up to you somehow. Or I will hold him, but I don't know if I am strong enough to support him all the way."

"I c'n stand," Lord Dominic said thickly. "Get up there, Dick."

"Yes, my lord!" The farmer's son swung up onto Thunder's back.

With Angel's help, Dom stood, swaying. A single uncertain step brought him within reach of Mr Burchett, who leaned down to grasp him beneath the arms. Angel pushed from beneath, and an undignified moment later he was slumped astride the horse in front of his rescuer.

"Master Dom'll do," he mumbled with a crooked smile, and then appeared to lose consciousness once more.

With her wet, heavy skirts clinging clammily to her legs, Angel did not find it easy to mount the other horse, but driven by desperation she managed it.

"Go on home, ma'am," said Dick. "I'll walk over later to fetch my Brownie."

"No." Angel rejected the proposal adamantly. "I'm coming to Upthwaite."

They set off across the lane and up the hill.

=== 18 ===

Gerald Leigh was writing a letter when his gardener, a lad of some sixteen summers, burst unannounced into his study.

"Come quick, sir," he cried. " 'Tis Mr Marshall!"

"What has happened?" asked the vicar in alarm, jumping to his feet. "Where?"

"Out t'front. He'm hurt!"

Mr Leigh ran, but Forrester and Mrs McTavish were there before him. His maid was hovering in the front doorway, wielding a feather duster. The housekeeper had her arm about the waist of a soaked, exhausted, and shivering Miss Brand and was helping her towards the house. Dick Burchett, mounted on Thunder, was passing the limp body of Lord Dominic to Forrester, who took him in his arms like a baby and turned to follow Mrs McTavish. He saw his master.

"Master Dom's hurt," he called. "Best send t'lad for the apothecary, sir."

"Yes, go at once, Billy. Tell Mr Leaven it's urgent. Miss Brand, are you all right?"

"Just wet. Mrs McTavish will take care of me." Angel summoned up a wavering smile. "Look after Dom, *please*. I'm afraid he is very ill."

"Forrester, take him above stairs and get him dry and warm quickly."

"Aye, sir. Mabel! Stop gawking and go light a fire in Mr Marshall's chamber, girl!"

The vicar turned at last to Mr Burchett, who had dismounted.

"Dick, what happened? Man, you are almost as wet as they are! Come in and dry yourself."

"Think I'd best hurry over to Barrows End, sir, and tell Mrs Sutton what's to do."

"It might be as well, if you are not going to take ill yourself. But at least tell me the story first."

"Was riding along the lane down by the lake, heard a dog barking and howling. Deep voice, Master Dom's dog; recognised it at once."

"So much for secrecy!"

"Rode down to the water and there was the dog jumping up and down on the bank, carrying on deuced peculiar. Saw Miss Brand trying to carry Master Dom out of the lake, so I pulled 'em out. One end of your boat's sticking up, if you want to salvage it."

Mr Leigh frowned thoughtfully. This was the second accident involving his friend in scarcely a week.

"I think I will," he decided. "In fact, I rather think the sooner the better. I hate to leave Dom but . . . Dick, will you help me? Wait just a minute while I give the servants instructions. I shan't stop to change and I'll ride Thunder since he is saddled already. If you're quite sure you'll survive in wet breeches a while longer?"

"Right you are." Mr Burchett was puzzled but ready for anything.

A few minutes later they were cantering back down the hill, and before long they stood on Ullswater's bank.

"I'm afraid we are going to be soaked," Mr Leigh realised as he saw the stern of his skiff rising a foot or two above the water, some distance from shore. "Perhaps I can manage by myself."

"Already wet," pointed out Dick philosophically. "Little damp never hurt a Westmorland farmer. Come on."

They waded out, shivering, and grasped the protruding stern. Their feet had stirred up the muddy bottom so that they could see nothing in the usually limpid water, and the same mud made it difficult to brace their feet. Nor was it easy to work in four feet of icy water. At first they were unable to move the boat at all, then a hefty wrench released some obstruction and it came loose.

Or rather, half of it did. They found they were hauling the stern half only towards dry land.

It was easily emptied of water and they dragged it onto the grass. The broken end was curiously straight edged.

"Been sawed half through!" exclaimed Dick in horror.

Mr Leigh looked at it grimly, hands on hips.

"Don't spread this around," he warned. "I was afraid it might have been something like this. We don't want half the world discussing it."

"Not a gossip!" Mr Burchett was intrigued but discreetly suppressed his questions. "Look, some sort of carving back there. 'HER.' "

They looked at each other in sudden comprehension. The half-wit was known to be a skilled carpenter. Dick could not imagine why he should have sabotaged the boat. Mr Leigh was all too afraid he could guess: only yesterday Dom had announced in Sir Gregory's presence that he intended to go rowing today.

"Go home and get dry," he said abruptly. "I'll send the boy over to Barrows End. Thanks for your help, Dick. I must get back." He swung up into the saddle, turned Thunder, and without another word was gone.

Dick Burchett looked after him, shaking his head. A chilly breeze had arisen, and he decided to go to his aunt in Patterdale rather than riding all the way home in his dripping clothes.

Busy concocting a story to account for his soaking, he rode into the village. He had nearly reached his aunt's cottage when he saw Sir Gregory Markham riding up the street ahead of him. Surely the baronet should know what had happened to his cousin, he thought. That was not telling half the world. He hallooed.

Sir Gregory turned back.

"What the devil have you been up to, young Dick?" he asked.

Mr Burchett succinctly described the afternoon's adventures.

"Only damme if I can see why old Herbert should do such a thing," he confessed. "Deuced odd, if you ask me. Well, just thought you ought to know. Going to dry off."

"Thank you, Dick." Sir Gregory's eye had a coldly distant look. As he turned Atlas's head towards Upthwaite, the farmer shivered suddenly and hurried for his aunt's warm kitchen.

Gerald Leigh reached the vicarage at the same time as Mr Leaven, the apothecary from Patterdale. He sent him straight upstairs to Lord Dominic and went to find Miss Brand.

Angel was in the kitchen with Mrs McTavish. She was huddled in a chair by the stove, wrapped in Gerald's second-best silk dressing gown, with Osa hunched watchfully on the floor at her side. The dog did not move as he entered, but Angel jumped up, her face white and strained.

"Please, sir, may I go to him? Mrs McTavish says I must not but I can, can't I? Please?"

"Not now, my dear," he replied gently. "The apothecary is with him. Will you write a note to your aunt explaining the situation? I would do it, but I must change and go to Dom. Billy will take it at once."

"Come set ye doun tae the table, lass," said the housekeeper. "Mabel? Mabel! Fetch pen and paper tae the young lady. Awa' wi' ye."

Angel managed to write only that Lord Dominic was ill and that her clothes were wet. She sat staring blankly at the paper.

"Hae ye nae mair tae write, missie? Pit thy name then." Mrs McTavish folded the sheet and went to the kitchen door. "Gang quickly noo, Billy, tae Barrows End, an' gie this tae Mrs Sutton."

Some two hours later, Mrs Sutton arrived in the gig. Gerald went out to meet her.

"Miss Brand is with Lord Dominic, ma'am. I could not stop her."

"What happened?"

"They had a boating accident."

"Is she unharmed? Thank heaven! And he?"

"Mr Leaven is not sanguine. You know about Dom's wounded lung? He is coughing blood and in great pain, and his leg is also painful, I think. He is only half conscious so it is hard to know just what he is saying. He complains of feeling cold."

"I shall stay and nurse him if you will have me, Mr Leigh. Catherine is perfectly able to take care of Clement and Lyn. I have brought dry clothes for Lyn, and she can return with John Applejohn."

"If you can persuade her, ma'am. You know how she feels about Dominic?"

"I have some inkling, but I am sorry to hear it is so evident as to draw *your* attention. Now, tell me exactly what the apothecary had to say, if you please."

They had reached the front door. Gerald heard the sound of hooves in the lane and glanced back, to see Sir Gerald riding down the lane on Atlas. Behind him, clinging to his belt as he bounced up and down on the horse's broad crupper, was Herbert, the idiot.

Gerald was no longer able to dismiss the probability of the baronet's guilt. He stared after him until Mrs Sutton repeated her request, then relayed Mr Leaven's words with half his mind while in the other half revolved the question of what to do. All the evidence was circumstantial. It seemed useless to go to a magistrate even if he ignored the resultant scandal. Surely Dominic would be safe as long as he was confined to his bed, if, indeed, he ever rose from it again. It seemed horribly possible that the second attempt at murder might prove to have succeeded.

The appearance of Mrs McTavish interrupted his speech and his thoughts. He told her to prepare a room for Mrs Sutton, and her relief on hearing that the vicar's wife meant to stay was obvious. They went upstairs, and Gerald opened the door of Dominic's chamber.

"Miss Brand," he said softly, "your aunt is here. I will sit with him."

Angel came out, looking wan and tired.

"I am glad you are come, Aunt Maria," she said simply.

"My poor child!" Mrs Sutton embraced her. "John is bringing in some dry clothing for you and then he will take you home and—"

"No! Don't make me leave him, oh please don't!"

"I will stay and nurse him, Angel, and when he is better you may visit—"

"I'll help you! I'll do anything you say, only please, please let me stay! I promise I won't be a nuisance. I won't . . . I won't even go in his room if you think I ought not, only I could not bear to be so far away!"

Mrs Sutton had never seen her usually equable niece so distraught. She was far from sure of the wisdom of letting her remain, but at present it was clear that forcing her to depart would distress her far more than anything which might occur here.

"Very well," she acquiesced. "If Mr Leigh has no objection you may stay, at least for tonight. But Angel, you must promise me that if I decide it is better for you, or for Lord Dominic, that you go home, you will do so without enacting me a Cheltenham tragedy."

"I will, Aunt. Thank you. Tell me what I must do."

"First we must speak to Mr Leigh. And then, child, you will drink a bowl of soup and go straight to bed. You will be of no use to his lordship nor to anyone else in the state you are in."

"Yes, ma'am. But you will wake me if . . . if anything happens?"

"I will," promised Aunt Maria.

With the aid of the apothecary's drugs and a soothing syrup from Mrs McTavish's stillroom, Lord Dominic's cough was brought under control that night. When Angel was allowed to see him in the morning, he was sleeping, breathing laboriously, his thin face hollowed out and so white his scar was virtually invisible.

"I believe the worst is past," her aunt told her in a whisper, "as long as he does not take a fever. But we must take very good care of him, and his recovery is certain to be slow."

"May I stay beside him?" Angel was calm and collected, a little pale but perfectly composed. "You look fagged to death, Aunt Maria."

"Well, someone must watch him," she said dubiously. "Mrs McTavish was up with me most of the night, and I don't believe Mr Leigh or Forrester had much sleep. There is always the maid, but I am not sure I should trust her. Yes, you may stay. If his breathing changes, if he coughs more than once or twice, or seems feverish, you must call me immediately."

"Of course. Now you go and have some breakfast and lie down. I shall manage very well."

Angel sat down in a chair beside the bed and studied Dom's face. Translucent lids hid his usually sparkling eyes, the mobile mouth was slack, lips half parted in the struggle to breathe. His suffering hurt her.

She had never realised that love could hurt so much.

He opened pain-filled eyes and reached for her hand. "Linnet." His lips formed the word; no sound came to her.

"Don't talk, Dom. It might make you cough. If you want a drink, nod your head just a tiny bit."

He shook his head. His eyes closed again and his brow furrowed, but he kept his clasp on her hand. She sat there, silently willing her strength into him through their joined palms.

Later in the morning, Catherine came. Angel reluctantly left Forrester guarding her patient and went to talk to her cousin.

"Beth wanted to come with me," Catherine said. "She came to the vicarage to see you and was shocked to hear what had happened. At least, she knew of the accident from Sir Gregory, but he had not realised Dom was seriously ill."

"You did not let her come?"

"I thought it best not to. I will take her news, and to see her brother can only add to her distress. He is not in danger, is he?"

"Aunt Maria thinks not now, though he was. Catherine, it was quite the most awful experience of my life!"

"Tell me what happened. I only know that you were out on the lake."

Angel complied. "And never again shall I sneak off without telling someone where I am going!" she ended with a shudder. "If Dick Burchett had not come along . . ." A sudden thought struck her. "I did not tell you," she said slowly, "that when we first got into the boat we saw that Herbert had been carving his name inside it. And he was there the last time, when Dom was nearly shot. You don't suppose he made a hole in the boat or something?"

"Why on earth should he do such a thing?"

"I'll wager Sir Gregory paid him! How else should he know about the accident? And he was there when Dom said he was going rowing yesterday."

"Angel, I am sure you are mistaken. Sir Gregory is not trying to kill Lord Dominic; you cannot believe it."

"I've a very good mind to ask him outright."

"He is not here. Beth said he left for Derbyshire unexpectedly yesterday evening."

"In the evening? That just proves it! He is afraid of being suspected."

"It is not true! You don't know him, Angel. You must not say such things!"

"Even if I do not say it, I think it. At least Dom is safe while he is gone. I'm sorry, Catherine, but you cannot make me change my mind. It is not as if *you* know him very well."

Catherine was silenced. She gave Angel a message for Mrs Sutton, and went to find Mr Leigh to present another from Beth. He agreed with her that she should not come to Upthwaite.

"I cannot say when I shall be able to see her," he said sadly. "If I can get away for an hour or two I will send her a note to ask her to meet me on Dowen Crag."

"I'll tell her. And you will let her know at once if Lord Dominic's condition deteriorates? It would not be fair to keep her from him if it comes to the worst."

"Of course. Comfort her for me, Miss Sutton."

Catherine promised to do so, but the next few days were so busy she saw Lady Elizabeth only twice, and that briefly. She was unused to having the whole charge of the household upon her shoulders, and there was no one to share the chores.

Gerald, meanwhile, on top of his parish duties, lent a hand from time to time with the nursing, and tried to make sure his hard-working guests took a stroll in the garden every day and relaxed in the evening. On Friday he managed to meet Beth and was able to reassure her. Dom had not developed a fever, the apothecary was satisfied with his progress, and he had eaten a whole egg for breakfast.

"And Osa ate today for the first time since Tuesday," he told her. "I believe Miss Brand was almost as relieved at the one as at the other."

"I suppose I understand why it is," said Beth, sighing, "but it is very hard that Lyn can be with him and I cannot."

"You shall visit next week without fail," he promised.

"How long will he be confined to his bed?"

"Several weeks at least, before he can expect to be up and about. And he needs constant attention for a few more days, lest he should start coughing again. I expect Mrs Sutton and Miss Brand will return home at the beginning of next week."

"At least I shall have Lyn then. With Cousin Gregory gone too, it is very lonely, even though Papa is so much pleasanter now. Francis has been visiting a great deal. I have never known him to be so obliging and sympathetic. Indeed I told him that if he always behaved so and if I were not in love with you, I might consider accepting his offer!"

"How very glad I am that you are in love with me, my darling!" responded Mr Leigh, and the rest of their conversation was of interest to no one but themselves.

"Dom is really getting better?" Beth asked as they parted.

"Yes, beloved, he is."

It was apparent even to Angel's anxious eye that Lord Dominic was considerably improved. His breathing had eased and he ate docilely what was put before him. He had a couple of alarming coughing spells, but the second produced scarcely any blood. However, his leg ached fiercely, keeping him awake at night, and any slight exertion that made him breathe deeply brought stabbing pains in his chest. He was docile because he was listless and uninterested.

His face always brightened when Angel entered his room, but he never again took her hand, seeming rather to avoid touching her. As she sat by his window with her hateful mending in her lap, she would feel his eyes upon her, but always when she looked up his gaze had withdrawn. Talking was both too much effort and one of the things which made his breathing painful, so they were usually silent. She longed to make him laugh, but that was of all things absolutely forbidden, as certain to bring on a fit of coughing. When they spoke it was of the weather, of the next meal, of Osa; never of her rapidly approaching departure.

"You are growing thin, Angel," said Aunt Maria severely on Saturday. "I believe you have lost ten pounds in half as many days. You must eat properly, child. You are not worrying about Lord Dominic still, are you?"

"I know he is not at death's door. Only he was used to be so alive, more alive than anyone I've ever met. Now he is so weak and languid, and it hurts me here." She placed her hand between her breasts. "And then I cannot eat."

"Perhaps I ought to send you home."

"Oh, no, Aunt!"

"Catherine is coming on Monday. If you are not eating better by then, I shall send you back with her. We will be leaving Tuesday or Wednesday in any case, I believe. There will be nothing by then that Mr Leigh and the servants cannot manage."

For the sake of a few extra hours, Angel forced herself to eat.

=19=

SIR GREGORY RETURNED to Grisedale Hall late on Sunday evening. Beth had no chance to speak to him privately that night, but the next morning they went riding in the park and she told him how ill Dom had been.

"I'd not have left had I realised how serious it was," he said. "I thought he merely received a ducking. He is out of danger now?"

"Gerald said so on Friday. Mrs Sutton and Lyn have been nursing him, but Catherine thought I ought not even to visit. She is going over to Upthwaite today. Do you not think I might go too?"

"I cannot think it wise, my dear, especially since your father is no longer confined to his room. And did you not promise him a game of chess this afternoon?"

"Yes. I suppose you are right. If only I could at least see Gerald!"

"This situation will not last much longer, Beth. Oh, here come Welch, devil take the man!"

"He has been very comforting this past week. I have come almost to like him. Good morning, Francis."

"Morning, Beth. You back, are you, Markham?"

"As you see."

Sir Gregory's air of cynical boredom had an edge of contempt, and it was plain that Lord Welch was none too pleased at his return. As they rode back towards the house Beth struggled to carry the conversation, with indifferent success.

They had nearly reached the stables when Abel came riding towards them with a note for Beth. She read it quickly.

"I cannot go!" she cried. "Gerald wants to see me just at the time I am to play chess with Papa. Abel, you will have to take a message to Upthwaite vicarage."

"I have to be getting back now," interrupted Lord Welch. "I'll take a message, Beth. You are supposed to be meeting Leigh?"

"Yes, on the Crag at two. If only he had made it later, but I daresay he is busy as usual. Will you tell him I cannot come, Francis?"

"Willingly." His lordship had a glitter in his eye. It was not to be supposed that the relaying of such a message to his rival could give him anything but pleasure. He took his leave in a hurry and rode off at a canter.

Sir Gregory looked after him thoughtfully.

"An excessively short visit," he commented.

"I was going to ask him to tell Gerald I must see him to-morrow," said Beth with a sigh. "Then I decided it was hardly fair. I will write later."

"Two o'clock on the Crag?" asked her cousin. "I believe I shall ride that way."

"Do you think he might not deliver the message? He might hope that Gerald would be angry when I did not come."

"He might indeed."

"Well, I shall be prodigious annoyed with Francis if he does not warn him."

"The more I consider the matter, my dear, the more I'd be prepared to wager that warning your sweetheart is the last thing his lordship has in mind."

"Then he is odious after all. I shall give you a letter for Gerald. Or come to think of it, I could send Abel over, then you need not go."

"No, no, do not do that! Suppose we have misjudged Welch and he should see Abel on the same errand? No, Beth, leave things as they are. I do believe that this may turn out to be precisely the occasion I have been hoping for.''

Beth would have liked to ask for an explanation of that cryptic utterance, but they had entered the house by now and Mrs Daventry was at hand.

''I *quite* thought I saw Lord Welch riding with you,'' she said, ''and so I told your papa, Lady Elizabeth, and *he* remarked that you have an *excessively* persistent suitor though he did not say 'excessively' only I cannot repeat *that* word, and I had thought he *favoured* Lord Welch but he sounded quite *vexed* so I am sure I cannot—''

''Perhaps, having seen so much of Welch this week,'' interrupted Sir Gregory, ''he has discovered that he is not after all the ideal husband for Beth.''

Mrs Daventry expressed her disagreement at length, until luncheon and Lord Grisedale's presence silenced her.

Meanwhile, Catherine was lunching at Upthwaite vicarage. She was shocked to see how thin Angel had grown, in spite of her noble efforts to dispose of a substantial plateful of her favorite foods. They seemed no longer to hold any attraction.

Mrs Sutton had consulted Catherine on the wisdom of sending Angel home a day early.

''Let her stay, Mother,'' was the response. ''One day can have no lasting effect on her health. We must hope that the knowledge that she is to leave will nudge Dom into speaking.''

''He is still very unwell, dearest. I think it excessively unlikely that he will have anything to say to Angel at present, even if he should wish to. And I have seen no sign that her affection is reciprocated, I am afraid.''

''Poor Angel!''

Gerald Leigh was soon another object of sympathy. Half an hour before he had intended to leave for Dowen Crag and his meeting with Beth, he received an urgent call from an outlying farm.

"Forrester and young Billy have gone down to Patterdale," he despaired. "There is no one I can send to explain why I cannot be there. She will think I have abandoned her."

"I will go and meet her," proposed Catherine. "I have had scarcely any exercise this past week, it is a beautiful day, and it is not so far from here as from Grisedale."

"Will you really go? I fear I cannot even offer you a horse as we have no sidesaddle."

"No matter. I feel guilty that I have not seen more of Beth while everyone else has been otherwise occupied, and this will appease my conscience. I had better leave at once, I expect. I was going to leave soon anyway, Mother, so I will walk home with Beth. Good-bye, Lyn dear. I shall see you both when you come home tomorrow."

It was pleasant in the green shade of the woods, but the last part of the climb was exhausting. Catherine was not wearing her stout walking shoes and the stony track bruised her feet. Reaching the top hot and tired, she found she had arrived first and went out on the overhang to look down towards Grisedale.

As she stepped onto the huge rock, she thought she felt it quiver. Nonsense, she told herself, don't be a goosecap! It had always made her slightly nervous, and this was the first time she had been here alone. Pure imagination! She moved forward to obtain a better view of the path.

"Miss Sutton, come back!" called Lord Welch's voice urgently.

She turned to see where he was. He came running down the steep grass slope beyond the track, with such a strange, wild look on his face that she stepped back in alarm.

With a terrifying rumble, the boulder beneath her tilted. She fell to her knees, scrabbled for a fingerhold, as an avalanche of earth, pebbles, and uprooted bushes slid towards her, engulfed her, swept her over the edge.

"Catherine!" came a despairing cry, the last thing she was aware of before blackness closed in.

How long she was unconscious she could not tell. Awareness

came back gradually. The first thing she knew was that she ached all over, then that someone was bathing her face with cool water. Sound resolved itself into birdsong, the sough of wind in leafy branches, and a gentle but insistent voice.

"Kate, Kate, my little love, you're safe now. Catherine, dear heart, speak to me."

She would have liked to lie there forever, listening, but behind the gentleness was a note of anguish. She opened her eyes.

"Gregory," she murmured.

A huge relief lit his face and he bent and kissed her lips. Softly, tenderly as before, but not briefly this time, until she raised one scratched, bruised arm to his shoulder and pulled away.

"I feel a little dizzy."

"From your injuries, my own, or from . . . ?"

"Must it be one or the other?"

"Oh, Kate, Kate!" he groaned, burying his face in her hair, which had come loose from its pinnings and spread in tangled disarray, spilling off the folded coat that pillowed her head and coiling across the grass. "Kate, I thought you were dead. I nearly killed him on the spot but I could not believe it, could not abandon hope!"

"Lord Welch?" She frowned painfully. "What happened? I remember seeing him just before . . ."

"He has been trying to kill Leigh. Dominic was riding his sorrel, remember? And everyone knows that he rows across the lake every Thursday. Had the boat collapsed halfway across Ullswater instead of in the shallows, the result might have been very different. He forced poor Herbert into helping by threatening to leave him homeless for the winter. Though it is doubtful whether the half-wit realised what he was doing. In any case, I removed him from the scene, so the viscount had to do his own dirty work this time."

"I don't understand."

"Having, he thought, made certain that Leigh would be here and Beth would not, he took a pickaxe and shovel to the underpinnings of the great rock. And dirty work it was! It is possible he might have explained away his presence in hiding behind a bush, and even his shouted warning to you. But he will find it difficult to persuade me that there is an innocent reason for the filthy state of his clothing, and I'll wager there are blisters on his hands.''

"Gregory, what are you going to do?" Catherine asked in alarm.

"Merely confront him with the fact that I have Herbert's 'signed' and witnessed confession, plus a great deal of circumstantial evidence. I shall suggest that he might find it healthy to remove to another part of the country.''

"No! He will try to kill you, too!''

"I don't think so, my love. He has always been rather afraid of me, whereas he despises Leigh. I shall take precautions, however, if you care what becomes of me?''

"I do, you know I do. Gregory, be careful! I am black and blue all over!''

"And for that,'' he said savagely, "I shall ignore the fact that he is not up to my weight and knock him down as many times as he will get up!''

"I had not thought myself bloodthirsty, but I find I should almost wish to watch you do it. It was quite the horridest experience I have ever been through. And I cannot imagine how you succeeded in rescuing me from the bottom of that cliff.''

"It is not the least use asking me, for I have no idea. If I had stopped to consider I should have been certain it was impossible. And if the rock had fallen rather than tilted, there'd not have been anything to rescue. I shall knock Welch down at least three times, even if I have to pick him up in between.''

"It is hard to believe that he is a murderer. He very nearly managed to kill Lord Dominic by mistake. It was touch and go for a day or two, according to Mother, and he is still very ill.''

"He is? Beth gave me the impression that he was well on the

way to recovery. This charade has gone on long enough! My uncle must at least be given the opportunity of taking the lost sheep back into the fold.''

''Do you think he will?''

''Two weeks ago I'd not have laid my money on it at any odds. Now, I believe there is hope. Your little cousin is something of a miracle-worker, you know. But if he does not come around, he will have to run his own estate henceforth. A married man cannot be forever abandoning home and family to see after his uncle's bailiff.''

Catherine absorbed this in silence for a moment. Then she raised eyes at once amused and shy to his face.

''Are you going to propose to me?''

''Not until I have your father's permission.''

''Well! For once I must agree with Angel's opinion of you: you are shockingly old-fashioned in your notions of propriety. Besides, I am of age and have no need of Papa's permission.''

''Very well, then,'' agreed Sir Gregory amiably. ''Madam, will you do me the honour of becoming my wife?''

Catherine dimpled. ''Thank you, sir, I should like it above all things.''

''Are you not supposed to hum and haw a little to make me anxious?''

''Do you wish me to?''

''No, love. 'Never make denial; I must and will have Katherine to my wife.' ''

''And do you want 'a Kate conformable as other household Kates'?''

''Not I. I want a tall, teasing bluestocking who makes up her mind for herself and quietly does as she thinks best. Kate . . . Catherine, do you, do you think you might come to love me?''

''Do you think I would marry you if I did not?''

''Come, give me a plain answer!'' he said roughly.

''It is very forward in me, I know, but I am afraid I love you already, Gregory. Gregory, gently! Beloved, remember how recently I fell off that cliff!''

"And I have kept you here talking when you should be at home in bed! Sweetheart, I will have to leave you while I fetch Atlas. He is not far off.''

Sitting with her back against the broad trunk of an oak, she watched him stride up the slope. He turned to wave and blow a kiss, then disappeared among the trees. But for her aching body, it might all have been a dream. And for her filthy, torn dress, she amended wryly, for the first time noticing her appearance. She was not precisely in the state in which one might expect to receive an offer. She rather thought that made the moment yet more precious.

The ride back to Barrows End was painful. Even cradled in Sir Gregory's arms, Catherine felt jolted at every step, though Atlas never moved above a walk. When they reached the vicarage, her betrothed carried her unceremoniously into the house and straight up the stairs to her chamber.

"Go to bed and do not stir before the morning," he ordered.

"I can see that your approval of independent females is a chancy thing!" she exclaimed with a shaky laugh. "However, this time I'll obey.''

" 'Why, there's a wench! Come on, and kiss me, Kate.' But hurry, for I hear footsteps on the stair.''

Mr Sutton appeared in the doorway.

"I suppose there is a good reason for this," he remarked with a resigned sigh. "Since Angel has been with us I have grown quite accustomed to a certain disregard for propriety, but I do not remember that she has as yet entertained a gentleman in her bed-chamber.''

"I can explain, sir," said Sir Gregory, firmly ushering the vicar out of the room. "I shall send Beth to look after you," he tossed over his shoulder to Catherine, and closed the door before she could protest. "I think we had best retire to your study, sir, if you do not object. I have a great deal to discuss with you, and a great deal to accomplish this afternoon.''

Half an hour later, the two gentlemen emerged from the study well pleased with each other. The baronet had Mr Sutton's blessing on his betrothal, his approval for his proposed confrontation with Lord Welch, and his promise of support in the coming interview with Lord Grisedale.

The vicar went to speak to his daughter, while Sir Gregory headed for the kitchen to beg a glass of ale from Mrs Applejohn. Then they rode up the lane together to tackle the earl.

Lord Grisedale had thoroughly beaten his daughter at chess, had taken a refreshing nap, and was sitting on his terrace gazing over his domain with a benevolent eye. Having sent Beth off to Barrows End, happy to have a practical occupation, Sir Gregory and Mr Sutton joined him.

"Ah, Vicar!" he boomed in the outsize voice that accorded so ill with his meagre stature. "Glad to see you, sir. And how is your family?"

Before Mr Sutton had to confess that he had not seen his wife in several days and that his daughter had retired to bed bruised from head to toe, Sir Gregory took over.

"It is about Miss Sutton that we wished to speak to you, Uncle. She has done me the honour of accepting my hand in marriage."

"Splendid, my boy, splendid! Liven up the place a bit, what, and good company for little Beth."

"I'm afraid I have every intention of installing my bride in Derbyshire, sir. As a married man I shall be unable to continue to oversee your affairs."

A wary look entered his lordship's eyes and he produced the expected outburst in a perfunctory way, as if realising that this news was only an introduction to the battle proper.

"What the devil do you mean by it, sir!" he roared. "If ever a man was so plagued by an undutiful family!"

"Sir Gregory is merely your nephew, my lord," reminded Mr

Sutton mildly. "There are other claims upon him. I believe he has exceeded his duty to you for the past few years."

"I can't deny he's made himself useful," grumbled the earl. "Unlike that harebrained niece of yours, Vicar. Where is the chit? I've not seen her in a week."

"She is staying with my wife at Upthwaite Vicarage. They have been nursing someone who may, I believe, be able to take Sir Gregory's place in supervising your estates. In time he—"

"Nursing?" the old man croaked, suddenly grey-faced. "I had thought the boy, not seriously hurt!"

The sight of their astonishment revived him a little, and he explained that rumour of his son's return to Westmorland had reached him some two weeks earlier. Then Sir Gregory told him about Dominic's "accident," concealing the fact that it had been an attempt on Mr Leigh's life. Time enough to deal with Beth's complications when his lordship had recovered from the present predicament.

"I am not certain of his present condition," he finished, "though he is out of danger at least, is he not, Mr Sutton?"

"So I hear. My lord, as your spiritual counsellor I must ask your intentions. Lord Dominic is your son and heir. He is a brave young man who has been wounded fighting for his country. Can you find it in your heart to forgive his disobedience? Or can you find it in your conscience not to?"

"Gregory, bring the lad home. As soon as it is safe to move him. Devil take it, he is just like his mother! Takes every word a man says literally! Now go away, I want to talk to the vicar."

Sir Gregory found himself once more on Atlas's back, heading for Upthwaite. And if he made a detour via Barrows End vicarage neither Beth nor close-mouthed Mrs Applejohn ever gave him away.

=== 20 ===

WHEN SIR GREGORY rode up to Upthwaite vicarage, Angel was astounded at his effrontery. He asked first to speak to Mrs Sutton, who emerged from the interview looking, Angel thought, like the cat who stole the cream. She went straight to Dominic's chamber, and Mr Leigh took her place with the baronet.

The gentlemen were closeted for a considerable length of time, and Angel was dying of curiosity by the time they reappeared.

"Do you want to see Dominic now?" enquired Gerald.

"No, I think not. Mrs Sutton is breaking the news to him, and I must be off to Upthwaite Park."

"You are quite certain you do not wish me to accompany you?"

"I need no assistance," Sir Gregory said grimly, "nor encouragement. Whatever his intent, as things have turned out my motives for retaliation are greater than yours."

"If you are not back within the hour, I shall follow you."

"If you insist. I shall see you shortly then. Your servant, Miss Brand."

No sooner had the door closed behind him than Angel turned to her host.

"I do not know why I am always the last to be told everything," she said with injured dignity. "It is excessively unfair. What in the world is going on now?"

"Good news first," proposed Mr Leigh. "Lord Grisedale is willing, anxious even, to take Dominic back."

When Angel had recovered from this announcement and been persuaded not to run upstairs immediately to congratulate Dom, he told her the full story of Lord Welch's nefarious plots, as recounted to him by Sir Gregory.

"Oh, dear," she said guiltily, "I was quite convinced that *he* was trying to kill Dom."

"I'm afraid that I was too," admitted the vicar, "at least after the business with the boat."

"I suppose I shall have to apologise to him. How very lowering!"

"Does he know you suspected him?"

"I don't think so. I never told him as much."

"Then I believe you should let the matter drop. Confession and apology might serve to relieve your feelings, but what of his?"

"You mean it would hurt him? I daresay you are right," said Angel thoughtfully. "Only it would be much easier to tell him and forget about it."

"It is not easy to keep silent, but I hope you will try. Dominic will have a more difficult time of it."

"Yes, for he has known Sir Gregory all his life, and now has to thank him for interceding with Lord Grisedale!"

"I hope guilt will spur him to make an effort to win his cousin's friendship. The estrangement was largely on his side in any case. He is going to have a great deal on his mind in the next few days."

Before Angel could consider whether this might be taken as a friendly warning, her aunt joined them.

"He wants to go home," she reported. "I think that if it is done carefully, tomorrow we may restore the Prodigal Son to Grisedale Hall!"

An hour later Sir Gregory returned, with a grin on his face and bloody knuckles. A penitent Angel demanded a description of his encounter while she bound them up.

"The best part is not fit for a lady's ears," he told her, "but while I was there Lord Welch took a sudden, unaccountable desire to remove from the county. I understand Upthwaite Park will shortly be put up for sale."

"How very clever of you!" Angel applauded.

"Unfortunately, his lordship will remain our neighbour for at least a week. It will be that long before he is able to appear in public.''

"I think perhaps I will call on him one day, just to say good-bye.''

"You will do nothing of the kind!'' forbade Aunt Maria. "Sir Gregory, your cousin will be able to travel to Grisedale tomorrow, if you think it advisable. He is not as fit as one might wish, but he longs to be at home. His spirits have been as much depressed as his health, and I think it wise to accede to his wishes. It is unlikely to do any lasting harm, though it may set back his recovery some-what.''

"Very well, ma'am. With your permission, I shall call at Barrows End vicarage this evening to say that the Grisedale carriage will bring you home tomorrow morning.''

"Pray do so. You are sure that Catherine does not need me tonight?''

"Unless her condition has materially altered, in which case I shall send someone to fetch you. It is extraordinarily fortunate for a certain person that she was not seriously injured. Beth was plan-ning to spend the night with her, so do not worry.''

"Perhaps I shall ride over beside the carriage after all,'' mused Mr Leigh. "I daresay Lady Elizabeth will not leave before Mrs Sutton arrives?''

"You may certainly do so,'' agreed Sir Gregory, "but I assure you that you will be welcome to visit at the Hall after tomorrow. Dominic will want to see you, and my uncle can scarcely throw you out when you have been nurturing his lost lamb.''

"Dom is not a lamb!'' said Angel indignantly. Everyone laughed.

"No,'' admitted the baronet, "it was an ill-chosen metaphor, Miss Brand. I must take my leave now. It has been a busy day.''

To Angel's surprise, her aunt stood on tiptoe and kissed Sir Gregory's cheek when she said good night. She nearly asked in her forthright way for an explanation, but she was overcome by a sud-den lowness of spirits and it did not seem worth the effort.

The Grisedale carriage arrived at nine the next morning. Lord

Dominic was obviously eager to return to his family, yet his mood was more subdued than his illness could account for, seeming closer to melancholy than to content. Whatever blue devils assailed him, he had no thought for them as Forrester carried him down the stair. It took all his concentration not to faint from the pain, and he could not suppress a moan as he was laid on the well-cushioned seat of the coach.

Angel and Mrs Sutton fussed over him, tucking in rugs, re-arranging pillows.

"I hope I was right to permit this," muttered Mrs Sutton, looking at his white face and closed eyes.

He opened them at once. "I am not about to stick my spoon in the wall, ma'am," he assured her, summoning up a grin. "My pride was hurt more than anything else. It is highly undignified to be carried like an infant!"

The ladies settled themselves opposite him.

"Ye'll do, Master Dom," said the coachman, who had been peering at him anxiously, with the typical taciturnity of the mountain folk.

"Home, Jason!" ordered Lord Dominic.

They went very slowly to avoid jolting and swaying, but all too soon for Angel they reached the vicarage. Beth ran out, followed by Catherine with a purple bruise visible on one cheek, and Mr Sutton. In the midst of a hubbub of questions and answers, Lord Dominic hurriedly thanked Mrs Sutton for her care. She stepped down from the carriage, and as Angel followed he took her hand, gripping it so tightly that it hurt. He looked up at her with despair in his eyes, then closed them.

"Good-bye, Linnet," he murmured, and let her go.

Beth was speaking to her. Her uncle was offering his arm to help her down. She reached towards Dom, but his eyes were still shut, his face rigid. Swallowing hard and blinking, she descended.

Without a word, Catherine put her arms about her and led her into the house. She managed to hold back the tears until they reached the little chamber, then flung herself on her bed and sobbed helplessly. Catherine stroked her back for a few minutes, until the worst was over, and then held her hand comfortingly.

"He just said good-bye," gasped Angel at last. "He didn't even ask me to go and see him."

"He has a great deal on his mind, Angel, returning home after all this time when he left in such a fashion. Think how he must feel to see his father again, and *not* to see his mother. And then, he is an invalid—"

"Don't say that!" she cried sharply. "He is ill at present but he is not an invalid, nor a cripple as he keeps calling himself! But if they treat him as one he will become one. He'll do something bacon-brained to try to prove he is perfectly healthy, and it will make his injuries worse. Then he'll retire to a dark room and sit there feeling sorry for himself and making everyone else miserable, just like his father!"

"You changed Lord Grisedale," reminded Catherine. "Don't give up hope yet. We have another five days here, and if nothing else your friendship with Beth will allow you to call at the Hall."

"Ah, no, things are different now. I cannot go without an invitation."

"Well, Beth will certainly invite you, my dear, so cheer up."

But no invitation arrived. Between her father, her sick brother, and her now openly avowed suitor, Lady Elizabeth had her hands full, as Sir Gregory reported. It seemed to Angel that he called with unconscionable frequency, and somehow Catherine always found the leisure to entertain him, to walk or ride with him. They always asked her to join them, but she did not want to go far from the house lest a message should arrive in her absence.

She spent long hours sitting on the bank of Grisedale Beck, where a shout from the vicarage would reach her. For the most part she gazed listlessly at the stream. Now and then, in a burst of energy, she would seek out flat pebbles and spin them at the water; in the rocky, rippling shallows, they never skipped.

Catherine worried about her, and spoke to her betrothed about her worry.

"It is not like her to give up like this. If you had not offered for me, I'd have gone home meekly and turned into a sour old maid, but that is not Angel's style. She is a fighter, and I cannot understand why she is tamely submitting to this situation."

"Have faith in her, Kate. For all we know, she is plotting deep, dark plots."

"I wish I could think so, but I do not believe it. She'd have told me, for she is the soul of candour and has no notion of reticence. And every night she cries herself to sleep. Angel never cries!"

"If you told her about us it might give her hope, because of the family connection. She would know at least that there was always a chance, a probability even, of future meetings."

"Perhaps I should, only I cannot bear to flaunt my happiness when she is so unhappy."

"Are you happy, love?"

"Yes, I am, in spite of poor Angel."

"To the devil with Angel! Tell her you are all invited to a farewell dinner on Saturday, and stop worrying."

"*Are* we invited to dine on Saturday?"

"Yes, sweetheart. I keep forgetting to convey the message because when I see you all other thoughts flee my head."

"Oh, Gregory."

At first Angel brightened when she heard about the dinner party, which by that time was due on the morrow. Then she considered. It seemed unlikely that Lord Dominic would be well enough to dine in company. Even if he did, or joined them afterwards, such an occasion would be the worst possible setting for solving the puzzle of his behaviour.

Jolted out of her despairing misery, she realised for the first time that it *was* a puzzle. He had not, as she had been thinking, rejected her out of hand. She remembered the look in his eyes when he had pronounced that awful good-bye: it had been as painful for him as it had for her!

Dom, she said fiercely, though silently, if you do not want me you are going to have to tell me so!

She ran upstairs to try on her blue sarsnet morning gown. There were matching forget-me-nots down by the stream, she thought exultantly.

The gown, with its lace trim, was as pretty as ever, but now much too large about the waist. Angel was shocked to discover how much thinner she had become. Catherine was called in and the two of them, neither good needlewomen, managed to make it fit acceptably.

"Let me brush out your hair," Catherine offered. "A few hours without pins and your ringlets will be as good as new, you lucky creature."

"Do you think I should sleep in curl papers? I have not the least notion how to put them in."

"Nor I. You will have to do without. There, that is better. Your face is thinner too, but still pretty as a picture. I shall walk up to the Hall with you in the morning, if you like, to keep your courage up."

"I'd like you to come, only there is nothing wrong with my courage now that I have decided what to do. I must see him alone, though."

"Of course, my dear. Now, where did you put your father's letter?"

"Here, I have it out already. Is it nearly dinnertime? I am ravenous!"

A substantial dinner, a good night's rest, and a hearty breakfast did a great deal to restore the roses to Angel's cheeks. A brisk walk up the track and across the park completed the transformation. On the way, they stopped to pick a posy of forget-me-nots, which Catherine pinned to the bodice of the blue gown, where they nestled in a bed of lace.

"Tell Lord Grisedale that I wish to speak to him, if you please, Venables," requested Angel when the butler admitted them.

"Sir Gregory?" enquired Catherine softly.

"In the library, madam," Venables informed her. "I'll tell his lordship at once, miss." He bowed and left.

"He makes me feel like a dowager, calling me madam," sighed Catherine. "I'll see you later, Angel. Good luck, my dear."

Venables reappeared and ushered Angel to Lord Grisedale's room. It had been transformed by cream brocade curtains and open windows, and in the fireplace glowed a huge bouquet of chrysanthemums. Bronze, white, and yellow, they filled the air with their spicy scent.

"Well, young lady, what can I do for you today?" growled his lordship. "Take a seat, take a seat."

"Thank you, my lord. It is not precisely that I want you to do something for me. I have to tell you something."

"A confession, hey?"

"Sort of. Will you read this letter, sir? It explains part of what I want to say."

The earl took the paper she held out to him and studied the seal.

"Tesborough, is it? I seem to remember that dratted companion of Beth's rattling on about your aunt being sister to Lady Tesborough." He cocked an enquiring eye, but Angel was silent, so he unfolded the letter and read aloud. " 'To whom it may concern: I hereby declare that the young lady calling herself Miss Evelyn Brand is my daughter, Lady Evangelina Brenthaven, and that she has been living under this alias with my permission, for reasons that seem to her good and sufficient.' Signed, 'Frederick Brenthaven, Marquis of Tesborough.' "

There was a pregnant pause.

"You see . . ." Angel began.

"I suppose," Lord Grisedale said drily at the same moment, "that you can twist your papa around your little finger, you naughty puss! So, Lady Evangelina, are you going to disclose your good and sufficient reasons?"

"That is not at all necessary," Angel told him with dignity.

"Then why, may I ask, have you chosen to divulge your secret at this time, when you are about to return to the bosom of your indulgent family?"

"I thought you ought to know, sir, because I hope to make Lord Dominic propose to me."

"Ha! You do, do you? Well, you are candid, at all events!" The earl pondered for a minute, then said unexpectedly, "I'll wager that is why the lad has been pining since he came home. I hope you will succeed, young lady, and you have my blessing, but let me warn you that my son is every whit as pigheaded as his sire. Run along now, child. He is in the small drawing room with his sister, I believe. You may tell Lady Elizabeth that I wish to see her immediately."

"Thank you, my lord!" Angel curtsied, then impulsively leaned down to kiss his wrinkled cheek. "I am prodigious glad that I was bold enough to beard the lion in his den!"

"Provoking wench!" snorted Lord Grisedale, beaming.

Walking towards the small drawing room, Angel found her steps slowing, her courage faltering. The hurdle she had crossed was as nothing to the coming confrontation. It was heartening to have the earl's blessing, but she had been fairly certain of it. No false modesty suggested that she could ever be unwelcome as a daughter-in-law, and she knew very well that open defiance and hen-hearted submission were the two things that set his back up. It was not only her own papa she could bring around her little finger with a modicum of coaxing!

Yet that minor victory would go for nothing if Dom did not want to marry her. Taking a deep breath, she knocked on the door, braced her shoulders, and went in.

Lord Dominic had his back to the entrance. Beth looked up, jumped up, ran to embrace her.

"Lyn! I am so happy to see you! I was afraid—"

"I'm glad to see you too, Beth," interrupted Angel, "but your papa asked me to send you to him at once."

"How odd! Never mind, we will talk later. Pray keep Dom amused for me." She hurried out.

Lord Dominic was reclining on a sofa. His head was turned away, and Angel could see that his neck and back were rigid. With tentative steps she approached and stood at the end of the sofa, so that he could not help but see her.

"Good morning, my lord."

"Good morning, Miss Brand." His voice was very low, and

though he turned towards her at last, he did not raise his eyes. His face had more colour than the last time she had seen him, and the scar was clearly defined, a white line from eyebrow to jaw. She felt a sudden urge to kiss it, sternly suppressed. Silence stretched between them.

"We are going home on Monday," she said at last in desperation.

"I . . . I hope you have a pleasant journey."

Angel's voice stuck in her throat. She fought the obstruction, won the fight, abandoned caution.

"Is that all? Do you not care for me at all?"

"I am happy to think that we are friends, Miss Brand."

"Friends! I love you, Dominic!"

Startled, he looked up at last, to be startled again by a totally unexpected vision of enchanting elegance. His reaction was no less unexpected.

"So," he sneered, "you have dressed up in all your finery and are come to set your cap at the heir to Grisedale! Believe me, it did not escape my notice that you did not cast out your lures until you found out that my father is an earl!"

"How dare you, you toplofty, conceited wretch! Until I knew who you were, I thought you were in love with Beth! And your father may be an earl, but mine is a marquis, and excessively rich besides!"

"Doing it rather too brown, *Miss* Brand."

"That is not my real name."

"Why should I believe that?"

"I just proved it to your papa, so you can ask him. I am Lady Evangelina Brenthaven."

"Lady . . . Angel? No! Why, half the officers in Spain used to dream about you! Lady Evangelina, I apologise for doubting—"

"Don't call me that!"

"Angel?"

"No," she said, suddenly shy, "call me Linnet. It is the nicest name I ever had."

"Oh, Linnet, Linnet, I cannot marry you," groaned Lord Dominic. "This only makes it worse. When you were plain Miss Brand I could sometimes persuade myself that you'd be better off as my wife than living a life of genteel poverty. But the daughter of the Marquis of Tesborough cannot be allowed to throw herself away on a cripple."

"Don't call yourself that!"

"It is the truth. You have no notion what it would be like to be tied to a man who is liable to fall ill at any moment and who cannot walk farther than a quarter mile, cannot dance with you—"

"Dancing! Pfui! Besides, it is shockingly unfashionable to dance with one's husband."

"Be serious. I cannot let you throw your life away caring for an invalid. If you realised what it would be like, you'd not want to be my wife."

Angel moved to stand over him, looking down in exasperation.

"Dom, do you know how many gentlemen have offered for my hand? Eighteen. And here I am wanting nothing else in the world but to marry a man who not only refuses to propose, but is doing his best to persuade me that I don't wish to do it!"

"Linnet—"

"I know: I'll kneel down. Then at least one of us will be in the correct position. There, is that better? Now you do not have to look up at me."

"Linnet . . ." His lips trembled and he wet them. "Linnet, will you be my wife in, in spite of—?"

"Of course I will, Dom. And when we are married I shall take care you do not fall into any more horrid cold lakes, and in a year or two you will be as fit as ever."

"I'll always limp."

"Do you know, the very first time I saw you I thought how romantic that was. Just like Lord Byron!"

"All the ladies find Byron romantic?" Dom's voice still wobbled, but he was smiling.

"Not I. He is odiously vain. Oh, Dom, I do love you!"

"Linnet, I never really believed that you cared only for my title It was less painful to be angry with you than sorry for myself. Can you forgive me?"

"I'd forgotten all about it. There is nothing to forgive."

"Then kiss me!"

As they embraced at last, the sofa began to shake. With enormous difficulty Osa emerged from underneath it, having apparently decided that the tension in the air had dissipated. With impartial adoration, she lavished dog kisses on the faces of her master and her future mistress.

Angel and Dominic fell apart, laughing, as a knock on the door heralded the arrival of Beth, Catherine, and Sir Gregory.

"Papa sent me to find out if you two had browbeaten each other into making a match of it," explained Beth, relieved to see their laughing faces and clasped hands.

"My Linnet did all the browbeating," Dom assured her. "I am happy to announce that I am about to become a henpecked husband."

"Dom, Papa said that if you are to marry, he will at least consider an offer from Gerald!"

"Beth, that is wonderful!" cried Angel, then turned remorsefully to her cousin. "And I really did mean to find a husband for you too, Catherine. I am sorry I did not succeed, but I shall keep trying."

"Pray do not, Angel dear. I have somehow managed to find one for myself." She looked up at Sir Gregory. "Do you think he is tall enough for me?"

"More than tall enough," he said firmly, putting an arm around her shoulders possessively. "Come, we must end my uncle's suspense."

"Take Osa with you," requested Lord Dominic. "We have unfinished business that she interrupted."

The promise of a walk enticed the dog to leave with them.

"Catherine and Sir Gregory!" exclaimed Angel as the door closed and she finally found her voice. "I never—"

"Don't talk," ordered Lord Dominic. "Now, where were we?"

It was some time later that Angel removed her head from his shoulder and uncurled her stiff legs. Dropping a last kiss on his forehead, she stood up and stretched.

"Dom?"

"Linnet?"

"Do you suppose Beth and Gerald would like Upthwaite Park for a wedding present?"

"The very thing! Why did I not think of it?"

"I'm serious!"

"Naturally. I daresay you will purchase it with your pin money?"

"Of course not. I expect Papa will buy it for them. I told you he is excessively rich."

"You did, pet. That is why I am going to marry you."

"It is a very fortunate thing," said Angel severely, "that I do not believe you!"